CW00821607

Praise for *Ocean*

'A ferociously intense portrait of a mind, marriage and family in extreme turbulence. Startling and dramatic, it made me very glad to be on *terra firma*'
Amanda Craig

'Such a powerful novel, with moments of real tenderness and outright terror, but all firmly in the realm of real feelings and emotions. Assured, human and compelling'
Gerard Woodward

'Polly Clark is one of the most gifted writers working in Britain today. *Ocean* is both lyrical and page-turning, a thrilling novel that takes the reader on an epic journey, not only on the high seas but also in a marriage and within the mind of its fiercely intelligent and witty heroine'
Jane Harris

'Visceral, lyrical…speaks to any woman who has ever loved and feared to lose'
Jane Campbell

'Such a thriller – I was gasping at the end of each chapter'
Clare Pollard

Praise for *Tiger*

'Combining the propulsiveness of a thriller with the raw yet meditative tone of a memoir, Clark writes with a poet's ear and a naturalist's eye'
Liz Jensen, *The Guardian*

'Fierce, elegant and compelling as the tiger itself, this is less a novel than the very force of nature caught in fiction'
Laline Paull

'A real and memorable achievement'
Allan Massie, *The Scotsman*

'A captivating walk on the wild side'
Heat

'Visceral ... exotic ... an impassioned celebration of second chances'
Daily Mail

Praise for *Larchfield*

'That rare first novel that utterly achieves its great ambition'
Richard Ford

'A beautiful novel: passionate, lyrical and surprising'
John Boyne, *Irish Times*

'Clark has a wonderful eye for detail and a light comic touch...
Funny, poised and affecting'
The Times

'A beautiful debut about a woman's struggle with isolation and
sanity woven with the story of poet W.H. Auden, which signals
Polly Clark as an author to watch'
The i Paper

'An imaginative novel, written with poetic force... Moving and
wonderful'
Daily Express

'A measured and graceful novel'
The Observer

'Mysterious, wondrous, captivating'
Louis de Bernières

OCEAN

Polly Clark

Published in 2025 by Lightning
Imprint of Eye Books Ltd
29A Barrow Street
Much Wenlock
Shropshire
TF13 6EN

www.eye-books.com

ISBN: 9781785634468

Copyright © Polly Clark 2025
Cover design by Ifan Bates
Typeset in Adobe Caslon Pro, Zona Pro and Brandon Grotesque

The moral right of the author has been asserted. All rights reserved. No part of this publication may be reproduced, stored in a retrieval system, or transmitted, in any form or by any means without the prior written permission of the publisher, nor be otherwise circulated in any form of binding or cover other than that in which it is published and without a similar condition being imposed on the subsequent purchaser.

British Library Cataloguing in Publication Data.
A catalogue record for this book is available from the British Library.

MIX
Paper | Supporting
responsible forestry
FSC® C013604

Our authorised representative in the EU for product safety is:
Logos Europe, 9 rue Nicolas Poussin, 17000, La Rochelle, France
contact@logoseurope.eu

The imagination is not a state:
it is the human existence itself
William Blake

If you don't become the ocean,
you'll be seasick every day
Leonard Cohen

For Lucy

PROLOGUE

BEAUTY IN A WIFE is so essential that if it does not exist, it must be invented. I became quite a bit better looking as a direct result of being Frank's wife. I was his prize, and my body remodelled itself to fit the pedestal. My accent improved. My hair thickened. Can you imagine? To be prized when you have never even really been noticed before? Who'd have thought that clunky old heteronormative marriage could have such transforming power? There is no woman its inferno cannot fire from plain Jane clay into porcelain Venus. And no woman it cannot contain, no matter how ship-launchingly lovely she may be, for marriage is a gallery of possessions; a display case, with the wife at the centre. Other men will look, and covet, and plot, but they will factor into their considerations that the wife belongs to another man. Of course I could not be Frank's prize without being his possession, but I loved that too. Beauty in the wife reinforces the marriage.

But beauty in the husband is a catastrophe. It's a bomb rolling unexploded in the hull. The beautiful husband draws assaults on the marriage, and the assaults will not relent until either the marriage is extinguished or the beauty fades. Women, as Frank and I found, recognise no possessions of another woman, respect no marriage. The beautiful husband remains free and at large.

Frank's catastrophic beauty came upon us so gradually, like a kind of weathering, or even a despoiling of the Frank I once knew, that I did not spot the moment of definitive change. But then, one day, he accompanied me to nursery to pick up our son Nicholas, and one of the other mothers stared at the baby, then at Frank, then sidled up to me to whisper, '*That's* your husband?' and I realised something momentous had taken place. I was confused because my husband was still in my mind shy dreamer Frank of the *Innisfree*. That night I observed him critically as he undressed to come to bed.

He had definitely filled out; he had hardened round the eyes and jaw; confidence inhabited his movements. If I squinted, he was still benign, still sweet to someone who had known the young man, but to someone who had not... I could see it now, the accumulation of masculinity, like a patina upon him. Instead of devotion, equality, fun – he radiated sex.

In that moment, as he casually threw his trousers over the chair, my husband Frank transcended us both, for now he held a monopoly over all the resources of the marriage. He occupied more space and seemed to have more weight than both of us put together. The beautiful husband recasts the physics of the marriage. He alters gravity.

Perhaps a different woman would be delighted to see her partner of many years in a new and ravishing light. But Frank's beauty did not ignite desire in me. It struck me dumb with fear.

Love does not alter when it alteration finds...

The words turned in my head.

But what does it do when faced with a premonition?

The day Frank's beauty announced itself was an anniversary more profound than the one we marked with cards and varying levels of ardour every year on 29th April. It was as if a countdown to a devastating event had begun, from which no amount of cultivated cynicism about marriage, trust in Frank, nor love for my child could save me. Sometimes I lay awake at night beside my beautiful husband and wondered if the devastating event had actually already happened, I had missed it, and I was wandering deluded in its aftermath.

For the truth of it was that I loved my husband, with all my heart. My love for Frank embarrassed me with its cheerfulness and its hope. When we married, back then on the deck of the *Innisfree*, I cried with happiness, and not because I was young and stupid.

I believed our marriage to be the most beautiful thing either of us had made, outshining even the child it contained. Even as it would come to splinter inside us and smash around us, still I could not fully imagine myself without it. And this was surely why I could not breathe a word to Frank about what I had glimpsed in our future. The survival of our relationship felt basic to my own survival, as vital a mechanism as thirst. My faith in what we had created made any journey comprehensible, every fire possible to withstand; without it there was only wreckage strewn all the way to the lonely horizon, and the slow collapse to the deep sea bed.

1

THE DAY EVERYTHING changed was a day suffused with quiet excitement. I waved Nicholas off to primary school with a packed lunch that pleased me, with its neat crustless sandwiches, hand-cut cucumber batons, and its little illicit surprise, a Kinder Egg that I knew he loved, tucked in. Frank gave me a lift to work, as he did every morning now. At the grand age of forty-three I was unexpectedly pregnant for the second time, and felt like I was carrying my own ocean, the person formerly me bobbing about on its surface like a shipwreck. At the school gates Frank helped me out of the passenger side and hugged me tenderly.

'Call me if you need anything, and I'll zoom round here and bring it to you,' he said.

'Even pickles?' I said, remembering my craving when pregnant with Nicholas.

'Even pickles. I'll feed them to you in the staffroom.'

'That will be entertaining for them all.'

He threw me a full-wattage smile as he reversed the car. Despite my bulk I felt myself floating towards my day. Things were falling right, this time around.

Between me and my science classroom loomed the technical block, a brutalist concrete box on stilts. In this dank cavern the loners, losers, graffiti artists and skateboarders collected to smoke, grope and fight. I peered in as I shuffled by, looking for familiar faces. It was early, and cold, so it wasn't too busy. Just a few students getting in their first smoke of the day against the backdrop of graffiti.

Sindi gave me a nod over her shoulder as she contemplated a tiny patch of undefaced wall, spray can in one hand, cigarette in the other. Her bare thighs beneath the tucked-up skirt gleamed like stalagmites. Dwayne roared so close to me on his skateboard I almost overbalanced. 'Sorry, Miss!' He swept between the pillars, then hopped off and flipped the board up into his arms before vanishing into a corner with his mates.

I waved, and shuffled on.

Horizon Heights was not for everyone, but I'd unexpectedly found my niche. These kids were survivors, mavericks and weirdos, and I felt drawn to them. I had trained as a biology teacher long ago in Preston, near Fleetwood, where I grew up, having a nerdy interest in the natural world that I longed to share with others. But after my father died, my mother wanted me to stay nearby, and I could see my life shrinking before it had even begun. I'd run away as far as I could, taking a sailing course in Lanzarote in order to escape further, and the idea of teaching fell away. I met and fell in love with Frank, so deeply that even when eventually a life with him meant coming back to land, a baby, adult responsibilities, it still felt like freedom. We had, after all, come to London, one of the biggest cities in the world.

When Nicholas was no longer a baby and staying at home all day became unbearable, I returned to the idea of teaching, and was grateful that Horizon Heights liked the look of me. It was a rough school, like the one I had attended myself. We might be in the capital, but I recognised these kids. They seemed to recognise me too. We gave each other the benefit of the doubt.

Breathing heavily, I paused at the bins. I had to pace myself today. A full day of classes, followed by an intervention, which I had been planning for ages. I was a little apprehensive about it, as I simply got so tired these days, and an Intervention was not something to be undertaken lightly. Frank kept urging me to take my maternity leave early, and I was starting to see his point. I was tired of lugging myself around. Looking down, I realised how much I missed my feet. I used to love shoes, and I had small, pretty feet that looked wonderful in anything, or naked. Now my belly charged ahead of me like some kind of ill-designed hull pounding through the waves of life. I was only twenty-three weeks gone, but my body had gone into overdrive at the sheer impossibility of this pregnancy. It was throwing everything at it. As if expressing its own astonishment at being here again, it was creating the most marvellous grotesque out of my base material. I sallied on to the front door, and all my weariness was swept away by the joy I felt as I entered my own domain.

Sprayed in purple on the door of the classroom, new words:

FUCK U MISS AND
THE HORSE U RODE IN ON

The smell of paint was overwhelming. I covered my nose and mouth and observed the tag, the uneven lettering. A snort at the inclusion of 'Miss' leaked out from behind my fingers. This was Sindi's work. I imagined her sneaking out early, breakfastless, yelled at by Clint, her foster father, the can stashed in her rucksack. And then, lifting off after 'Fuck U', where so many would have stopped in triumph, her tongue fat in her cheek.

The thing was, she was proud of her vandalism, and lately the incidents had been escalating. I believed they showed spirit, rather than personal attack. Nevertheless, it couldn't go on – her rude talents would never be appreciated by wider society. I braced myself to inform Sindi and the whole class that any more defacements of the classroom would have consequences. In addition, the fumes were bad for me now. Coughing, I opened the door and went in. A moderate quiet fell across my science class.

I consider myself a practical person; in no sense a dreamer. No schmalzy Hollywood film would be made about my inspirational teaching. No children would stand on their desks in unified protest at my sacking. But I had found my niche. I did what I could. Day to day, I dealt in scientific facts. Simplified for lower streams and younger children, but facts all the same. And every now and then, when I could see a child was falling too far into hopelessness, I dealt in transformation. Today was one such day.

I shuffled to the desk, as if we were not all suffocating in the stink of paint, and paused to gather myself. My biggest and gentlest loner, Chalmers, appeared before me and laid, solemnly on my desk, a tiny pottery fawn, curled up, the size of my palm. No box, just a square of toilet paper neatly folded for it to sit on.

'Congratulations, Miss,' he said, nodding at the bulge of my belly, with the shy smile that is the preserve of some boys in the presence of women who could be their mothers. I didn't know why I was to be congratulated now, as everyone had known about the pregnancy for some time. I wasn't prepared, and stood frozen, a teenage-intensity blush detonating slowly up my neck.

Chalmers had a marvellous squall of black greasy hair and was eternally reviled for having wet himself repeatedly in class between the ages of thirteen and fifteen. He'd sit on the high stools around the benches to the side, and suddenly the ransacked silence, the warm stench. He survived it, in part because of his sheer pale mass. He seemed to be made of an indestructible yet benign substance, like a cow. And also, he said, the intervention had saved him. It was the first time I had attempted such a thing – realising that, without action, he would be bullied to a place from which he would never be retrieved.

I held the fawn up to examine it. It wasn't expensive, but these were kids who had no money. Without its box, and with this odd timing, I knew they had stolen it – but I didn't care. I turned away and wrote on the board behind me:

17

Intervention, Technical Block, 5.00 pm — Sindi Jackson.

Then I had to exit to the staff toilets to collect myself. Chalmers gave me a thumbs-up which I saw in the gloss of the door as I fled. I was so proud of him, as he was proud himself, of surviving and of becoming the natural orchestrator of a class activity, the theft of the fawn.

From time to time, throughout the day, I reached into my pocket and clutched the fawn in my hand. I felt its rough underside, the hole in its belly for firing. It was my lucky charm, from kids who loved me, and I would be so sorry when it was gone.

2

Rush hour found me leaning against the map on the wall of the Underground, eyes closing in exhaustion. Frank had texted to tell me he had a client meeting and couldn't drive me home, so I had hauled myself along to the Tube. I willed the train to arrive; all I wanted was to sink into a warm, comfortable place, drift on the soar of hormones like a pleasure boat on a holiday sea, feel the turn of the baby like a porpoise in the waves. Nicholas was with his friend Louis; Frank ended his text with a promise to cook something delicious tonight to compensate for not picking me up. On the surface, all was well. But as the day played back over my half-closed eyelids, I worried that perhaps I had gone too far.

The train arrived, and gratefully I crumpled into a vacant seat.

How marvellous it would be never to disembark from this

train, I thought; instead, simply pound drowsily back and forth along the Northern Line forever. In that way I could remain the timeless orb of possibility I was now. I was full of love for this baby. It was a love more direct and simple than that for my son, conceived and experienced in a very different time. I could say this to myself, because I had not always been suffused with love for the baby. I was *grateful* for the baby, because I had come to feel our lives were no longer enough for Frank and me, and we desperately needed a fresh start. That's how it began. But love can begin in all kinds of ways, can't it, and evolve into something else? It can begin incomprehensibly, wrongly, and yet become something that defines an entire life.

As the various risk points of pregnancy passed, and scan after scan showed a perfect foetus gazing kindly back at me, my love for the baby grew. It grew as we told people and imagined our family having this new person in it. And it grew as we talked about the baby to Nicholas, whose eyes lit up as he realised he would no longer be alone.

I love my baby. I smiled to myself, leaning back in the seat, imagining the day this new life would be out in the world and safe in my arms.

But my pleasure was interrupted by unease about Sindi's Intervention. Though I am a scientist by training, life is painful and I believed that sometimes the only defence against it was radical metaphor. And I'd found it was a strong defence, as strong as anything science or society could throw up. But not everyone is strong enough to be reminded of their broken heart. I unpicked Sindi's intervention, trying to find where I might have slipped up.

These rituals took the form I had developed over several years. It took place in a corner of the block completely out of view, which I had decorated with candles and lights. Dwayne produced an oil drum and wood to burn, as it was a December evening. No matter the cold, there was always an excellent turnout for Interventions. No truancy for such theatre. Chalmers was master of ceremonies, stooped and half-smiling with the photocopied schedule in his hand. Over time the interventions had become quite elaborate, though never exceeding the hour of a detention. I encouraged this sense of occasion. I grew excited myself as the day approached.

In the centre of the space, supported on some bricks, stood an open coffin. This was lovingly made from plywood by Dwayne and Carol, whose woodwork skills were enthusiastic, and painted black with gorgeous silver curlicues by Petra, who was on track for an A at GCSE in art, but clinging by her fingernails in science. The space inside was lined with sheets in different colours. They had been lifted from different homes – including mine – then carefully pleated and upholstered with scraps of material pilfered from the Home Technology classroom. Dwayne and Carol had cleverly installed hinges, so that the whole ensemble could be folded away and stored. It was really very beautiful. I laid flowers inside.

With twenty or so students gathered round, Sindi hopped into the casket with a kind of alacrity that I remembered in my own little boy, leaping into bed with me with not a tweak of shame at his need. Eagerly, she got into position, her uniform pulled modestly to the correct length, woolly tights on, her eyes closed, her hands crossed over her chest. I laid the lid over her, sending an obelisk of shadow over her pale skin, a wisp of frosty breath escaping from her lips. A barely discernible ripple of fear faded from her cheek as the lid closed.

Now, it was sealed shut, with a little vent for air. I leaned over the vent and said, 'You okay in there, Sindi?'

A tiny *yes Miss*.

Sindi was fifteen, and I had been thinking about her Intervention for weeks. I could not see that anything less radical could save her. An orphan, she strolled around inside in my conscience as if auditioning to be my daughter. She had the kind of charisma that was about force, not beauty; like certain men possessed. She was not vain in any way, wore no makeup, but if anything her lack of mask over her strong features only increased her magnetism.

Every day, when Sindi got off the bus, she would hitch up her skirt to micro length and tie her blouse up, exposing as much midriff and leg as possible. Having done this, however, all she'd go on to do, the same every day, was to spray her tags beneath the Technical Block, or sit barelegged alone in a corner of the playing field and smoke her Embassy Regals. She wore no jewellery and her long hay-coloured hair hung around her in matted vines, less a deliberate attempt to cultivate dreadlocks than indifference.

No one, not the boys, not the male teachers, let alone the world outside, was going to let Sindi smoke peacefully, half-naked, alone. It had started already, lads making that journey across the scrub to loiter beside her. Teachers lifted their heads as she made her sensational way down the drive.

She was an inspiration to the younger girls, who tried to copy her. Classroom windows would fly open: 'Sindi, pull your skirt down!' And she would, absently, until out of range, when up it would go. I brought in wool tights because she looked so cold. It was a sign of the trust between us that she did, later, wear them if it was freezing in the class. Off they'd come for the technical block or the playing fields though. She resented covering herself, but had no coherent reason for why. She didn't see any provocation in her actions, nor danger. She expressed no interest in her future.

Watching her in the hallucinogenic swirl of my hormones in the early days of pregnancy made me want to cry. In the end I could stand it no longer. I waddled over the playing fields to sit with her, putting my arms around her and resting my swollen cheek on her cold shoulder. She turned that strong face to me, nose too big, eyes too close together, gap in the front teeth, the whole effect enough to make me give her everything to save her from all the things I didn't understand, and all those I understood too well. She breathed Embassy Regal smoke into my face and said, good-naturedly, 'Miss, if you're going to do that, budge your chin.' We sat there like that for the rest of the lunch hour, mostly in silence, with occasional flurries of chat about things that interested her. She was interested in money, how it worked, what it meant, how bits of paper or numbers on a screen could mean anything. She asked me to explain the stock exchange, which I couldn't, but I promised we'd look it up together. My back hurt and my legs went to sleep and I inhaled at least three cigarettes' worth of second-hand smoke, but I loved that hour. I had deterred the hyena approaches of the lads. But it wasn't enough. Only transformation would be enough.

With a wave of his hand, Chalmers indicated that the ceremony was about to begin. The lid was lifted to reveal Sindi, eyes closed, wearing the Funeral Tie, velvet black, awarded to the corpse. The ceremony would stop if the corpse showed any sign of life. This was serious.

All the pupils were in full uniform, or as full as they could manage on their meagre household budgets. The uniform was black and *gold*. Not yellow, although the school did turn a blind eye to yellow items, instantly marking out those who could not afford to go to Farrah and Sons on the high street next to the school for the correct colours. There was a lot of yellow in my lower-stream classes. I kept an eye on the second-hand sales of uniform, occasionally slipping a pupil a gold item. I believed in uniform; it was probably the only thing that prevented many of the girls from coming in a glittery boob tube. But gold? This was a battle I had decided against taking up with the Head. I was doing what I could. I had found my niche. And in return I knew the Head ignored my theatrical activities.

Chalmers, with his shy smile from under the black mop, said, 'We are here today to celebrate the short life of Sindi Jackson, who was *hung for murder.*' His voice echoed round the shadowy pillars. Corpses were allowed to choose the manner of their untimely deaths. The only proviso was that they should be believable.

'*Hanged,*' I corrected. 'Sindi deserves good grammar.'

This scenario was truly excellent. I could see Sindi snapping after yet another worthless man abused her, whacking him in his sleep with one of his own spanners or stabbing him in the heart with a screwdriver. I could also see her as misunderstood in a time of witches, where she could never be sexy and unpunished. Anyway, a hush fell over the group.

Chalmers went on, 'Although Sindi's neck was snapped so violently her head actually came off, miraculously her face was untouched.'

There was a pause as everyone digested this vivid scene.

Sindi remained as stony as if she was smoking out on the playing fields.

'So,' Chalmers continued, 'I turn to her classmate Petra for what she would like to say about what she remembers of Sindi.'

'Remember Sindi nicked that microphone thing from music? On my birthday?' said Petra. Nods and soft laughter went round the coffin. 'And we had that party down here and took turns singing. And she got out this red wig and sang "Dancing Queen"?'

Sindi remained like alabaster. It was very impressive.

'Remember she got you to play it on your phone, Dwayne, – the music? But I'd told her a bit before about how… depressed I was since my dad left and how I…had been cutting myself and I don't know, it was just so funny.' Petra stopped and bit her lip. Then she added, 'Also she had a really nice voice.'

'Thank you, Petra. Who's next?' Chalmers said.

And so the ceremony went on, with each student coming forward to praise Sindi's good nature, her sexy voice from the smoking… (This one was borderline as I insisted all praise had to be about what she had done, or had potential to do, or her character. Thinking of herself as sexy was the mess I was trying to save her from.) One lad surprised us all by mumbling, 'Sindi could always tell you how many cigs you'll get for your money. In a flash. She could tell you how many twenties, or tens, or even singles.' There was nodding round the group.

'Had she lived,' I asked them, 'what might she have done with her life?'

Fortunately interventions were planned. Everyone had two days to think up their answers. Without that time we would all have gawped, mesmerised, at Sindi in her casket, unable to visualise anything else.

Carol said, 'I think Sindi would have made a great nurse, because she was so caring.'

We all stared fervently into the coffin.

I said, 'I think she'd have been a good artist. Her graffiti was brilliant! Any more from the boys?'

Dwayne raised his hand. He spoke off the cuff, having clearly only just thought of it. 'I think she could have been anything she wanted to be,' he said, and there was a silence while we pondered this blessing that so many luckier children had bestowed upon them from infancy. I had said it often to my own little boy.

Uttered over Sindi, it sounded like a curse. Her perfectly composed face suddenly crumpled, and a tear slid out of the corner of her eye swiftly down into her hair. Her nail bitten hands covered her face and she began to sob inconsolably. I had never seen Sindi cry and I was horrified. The other children looked to me for guidance.

Dwayne said, 'Did I say something wrong?'

'No, Dwayne. That was a great thing to say.'

'Put the lid down!' Sindi cried.

'But Sindi—'

'Now!'

Reluctantly I lowered the lid and directed the other kids' attention to the cake. There was always cake after the ceremony, which the kids usually guzzled with the solemn intensity of five-year-olds.

'Sindi will be fine – eat up!' I said cheerily.

Sindi's muffled sobbing drifted out in pauses across the hovering students. Chalmers got the music going, drowning out the sound, and slowly everyone began to relax. I stood beside the casket in the gloom, hand on the lid, a smile stuck on my face, frightened to open it. Had it been too much? I tapped gently and asked though the vent. 'Won't you come out Sindi? Have some cake?'

To my enormous relief, the lid slowly raised and Sindi clambered out. Her eyes were red, her face pale. She submitted to an embrace and accepted a cigarette from Dwayne. 'That was intense Miss,' she said.

'Did you hear them?' I asked. 'All the wonderful things about you?' There was a daisy crumpled in her hair. I picked it out and she stared at me.

'I wish you were my mum,' she said.

With that, she wandered off into the group.

3

THE SQUEAL OF THE TRAIN as it arrived into into London Bridge jolted me from my thoughts of Sindi. The doors heaved open and I pushed myself towards the exit to cross to the Jubilee Line. But my way was blocked by people pouring into the carriage. *How rude*, I thought, wishing for once I had one of those Baby on Board badges so that I might receive some small consideration. Why did no one remind these people that you're supposed to let passengers get off first?

Then I realised the people were screaming. And by *pouring*, I mean they were an undifferentiated slam of torsos and smoking hair. There was no room for any more people, but still they came. Smoke filled the carriage and someone pushed me so roughly I hit my head on the central pole. My arms swept around myself, because that's a primal action. Protect the baby. I was falling, though in the crush it seemed impossible to fall, bodies were pressed against every inch of me. Light shrivelled, like that final moment of birth, when you know you're going to die and you accept it.

For a second I fell back to my childhood; the times my trawlerman father let me come on the boat with him, with the crew he knew far better than he knew us. I loved to be among them, their oilskins drenched in scales, as they hauled the creatures from the sea. Numberless shoals creaked in the net, and crashed like treasure upon the deck. Now my own cheek slammed, unwanted, on the floor, and a body, a woman, was squashing me, the buckle of her coat digging into my cheek – how? And a heel, a spike, like a needle in a microscope against the edge of a cell. That cell being my belly, her heel digging in.

The baby fluttered in my belly, like the first time I felt it. Quickening, they call this, but now it felt like a struggle. Coughing, I pushed vainly against the hot floor, against the woman slumped upon me, as if we were in a Flanders trench and she was a dead comrade toppled onto me. I knew she was dead; she had the weight of the dead. She was a mess of broken parts all in the wrong orientation. Her ribs were crushing the last of the oxygen out of my throat; her heel was puncturing me; her metal belt was branding my cheek. Maybe she was in fact many people; I could not be sure, but outrage gripped me, that *my baby* was kicking and turning, that *my baby* was wriggling to reach me, and I was doing nothing, pinioned like a dissected frog.

In the stories I would hear from other survivors, many were certain they were going to die, and their only regret in that moment was that they would be so badly burned they

29

would not be recognisable to their families. I was prevented from that kind of equanimity by the fact of my baby, which was fiercely alive in the tiny crushed space of my body. The smoke was affecting the foetus; it thrashed like a panicky heart; like a fish hauled over the gunnels. All I could see, writhing on the screen of my eyelids, were my baby's eyes, similarly closed, sealed for the ta-da moment of birth when the world would be revealed. The two of us, blind and gasping for oxygen. The grimy floor of the carriage was our slab, and a body our lid.

I screamed, but there was no sound. The heel poked into my abdomen and the air turned to ash.

Something hooked my arm. Yanked. Again. I was hauled inch by inch through smoke and flesh to the open door. Blindly I kicked, giving everything to return to my element. Fingers clutched at my body, like sinners in a crater of hell.

Mind the gap! – an almost-laugh gnashed through my jaws because air, a tiny trickle of air, like water, was whistling down the tracks alongside the train. It was bulky with diesel, brittle with the abandoned atoms of old electrics, but it was not smoke and I drank it, I sucked it like an infant. Then I was pulled slithering onto the platform. No no no, I cried, because the smoke came down like a burning cannonball onto my face. Somehow I got onto my knees. The hand turned into an arm around my waist, a man's voice in my ear. *Hold on to me.*

The arm I was clutching was hot and torn. I did not know then if I was clinging to fabric or burned-off skin. The air was a furnace: I dared not open my eyes, fearing my eyeballs would melt, or perhaps they had already melted and this was afterwards – the world of blindness. Everything hurt, especially my belly, where my baby lay still. This must be because – and this I *knew*, I knew *for certain* – I had taken up the load. I was saving us, fortified with my life-giving gulp of track air, and so my baby could rest, while I dragged us to safety.

At the end of the platform, the arms lifted me down onto the track. The chaos of shouting and screaming faded as we stumbled away from the scene, leaving a wall of heat and smoke behind us. Gravel prickled the soles of my bare feet as I felt along the sooty warmth of the tunnel wall. We walked for a long time.

'Here, step into my hands,' said the voice, at last, and I found myself being pushed up into a space in the wall. It was damp and lightless. I crawled into the space, dark as a grave.

A cigarette lighter smacked alight. A face glimmered into view. A man, soot-faced, glasses broken, blinked behind the flame.

I shouted, 'I'm pregnant. Help me!'

Please let the baby move again. My arms cradled my belly.

'You're safe now,' he said. 'What's your name?'

'Helen,' I whispered.

'I'm James. I saw you falling inside the train. I was on the platform. There's been an explosion.' He erupted into spluttering.

'I don't understand,' I said.

'A bomb went off on the other platform as you were pulling in. Everyone rushed onto your train. But I guess all the electrics are gone, so it stopped dead. Ow!' He dropped the lighter which had burned his fingertip, and we were in darkness again. He felt around on the floor and clicked it into life again. 'I just went back to cigarettes from the vape last week,' he said. 'Stroke of luck. Lost my cigarettes though.'

'Where am I?' I said, sure then that I was going to die here, in this crack deep in the earth, my last human contact this person whose face I could not make out. I would never see Nicholas again, never see Frank, never hold my baby. The walls flickered, giving echoes to James's every movement.

He held the lighter up to examine the space we were now in. It was a stone chamber, built quite deep into the tunnel wall, but just wide and high enough for the two of us to crouch inside. At the end of the chamber was an opening to a shaft, wide enough to crawl into. Cold air wafted thinly down it, and, I thought I heard tinny voices and sirens.

'We're in a vent,' he said. 'Lucky this station has one. I studied them, years ago. I never thought it would come in handy. You know there are vents from the Underground all over London? They look like little buildings on the surface.' He smiled at me in the shadows.

'What are you talking about?' I gasped. The thought flashed across my brain that I was in some kind of intervention of my own. I blinked hard, in case he wasn't real. But there he remained, curiously examining the walls.

'Sorry, I'm just amazed at the coincidence. I went down quite a nerdy rabbit hole of this stuff years ago. Anything broken? I had to pull you really hard. I thought your arm might come out of its socket.'

I lifted each arm to show him, and myself. Pain seared through every movement: it was the pain of joints crushed, panels of muscle compressed like chipboard into unnatural alliances with other materials. The shouts and screams from the platform sharpened and then faded, like reflections in a pool. I wondered if this little chamber – James himself – were a vision, like people reportedly get before they die, and really I was crushed on that carriage floor, the woman on top of me. But the floor was cold, and I was in pain, and there was no white light of bliss; just the tiny orange segment that wavered as he breathed.

James went on, 'I was just going into King's Cross to see something. Last minute. About to get on your train and then – and I saw you. Where were you going?'

'Home. After work. I live in Rotherhithe... So I was getting off to go onto the Jubilee Line.'

'I...couldn't help anyone else. There wasn't time.' He rubbed his eyes behind the glasses.

My...my baby.' I whispered. Pain was beginning to focus on my belly. I had to look. I had to know.

The flame in James's hand soared on its tiny mooring towards the oxygen from above. I ran my hands over my belly, wincing where the heel had pressed into me. My dress had the cracked shine of dried blood.

'Do you think my baby is still alive?' I asked James, urgently. My voice died to a whisper. 'I mean it must be, right?'

James put his glasses in his pocket, so broken they were useless. His eyes were bright in the darkness, like an animal's. 'Helen, try to focus on what we do now, okay? Imagine we're in an aircraft. You have to fit your own mask first so that you can help the baby. So, we know you have no broken bones. You're not bleeding too badly. You're awake. We are doing well. Here. Have a drink of this. You need to steady yourself.' He placed an object in my hands. There was a lid: as I unscrewed it, alcohol wafted over me.

'What's this?' I asked.

'Talisker! It's malt…'

'I don't know if I should,' I said.

'I think we're beyond government guidelines, don't you?' he said. 'It's medicine at this point. You need to feel calm, and warm.'

Eagerly I gulped, and warmth enveloped the cold void inside me.

'Good. Right. My phone's gone. Don't suppose you have yours? We could use the torch on it. There's not much left in this lighter.' But I had nothing, no bag, no phone, no coat. My bare feet were cut and sore.

'I'm sorry…' I mumbled.

'Don't worry.' He shuffled to the vent entrance, his movements exaggerated by the shadows. 'It's steep but doable. We just need to wait till you're strong enough to crawl up there. No problem!' He beamed in the gloom.

There was absolutely no chance of me getting up that shaft. Pain was spreading from the wound in my belly. I slumped against the wall. James shuffled back and peered at me. There was a desperate edge to his voice as he said, 'Take a look at it. That flask in your hand.'

'What is it?' I murmured, squinting.

'You can't see in this light, but it's silver; really beautiful. Engraved. It belonged to my father.'

I ran my fingertips over the engraving. It was an intricately detailed sailing boat with a single tall mast and elegant lines. He said, 'There's an inscription along the bottom: *I place my hope in the sea.'*

'I sailed on a boat like that! When I was young. She was called the *Innisfree.*' I felt air closing round me as if I was falling asleep.

The lighter flame sputtered out. The darkness enveloped us as cold and final as a vault.

James's voice echoed close to me. I felt the vibration on my lips.

He said, 'Helen, tell me about that, the *Innisfree,* when you were young. Don't stop. Tell me it all.'

'I can't remember... I...' Leaning now against him, the memory drained from my mind. I rested my head on his chest, and through the charred fabric caught the faint scent of lemons. It transported me for a moment to a garden Frank and I had once visited in Lanzarote, and there was a lemon tree in it, and the lemons were massive and ripe, filling the palm of Frank's hand. Dreams were coming for me, I knew this. Tears poured down my face. I knew what was going to happen, what had already happened.

'James, I can't live without my baby,' I whispered.

In the darkness, I felt James's hand upon my head. He said nothing, just stroked my hair while I wept.

4

FRANK'S VOICE: 'There are cordons everywhere. I ran all the way from the intersection.'

A woman's voice: 'You're James?'

'No, I'm her husband, Frank. You rang me!'

'Oh! It's just that she called out James and woke up very distressed. We gave her some sedatives.'

My dry eyes opened a crack. A bag of saline dripping light. A harsh smell of antiseptic. *Frank.* My swollen tongue tried and failed to form his name. I was so happy to see him. He would sort out this mess. But my face remained immobile, my arms trapped beneath the sheet.

Frank said, 'She's pregnant. You know that, don't you? And I meant to drive her home, and I couldn't. I had a client meeting and I couldn't, I didn't…' His eyes were red and wide, like a man stumbling into a smoking carriage. 'Is she going to be all right?' he asked.

The nurse adjusted my drip, right at the edge of my field of vision. Even though I could barely see her, I knew she was staring at my husband. It is perfectly possible to be half-conscious in hospital and simultaneously fully cognisant of the effect of Frank. She was very young and had dyed black hair volumised and arranged into a generous bun at the back of her head, like an air hostess or Jackie Kennedy. 'Your wife lost a lot of blood when we operated. She has torn muscles in her shoulder and, we think, a concussion. She will be all right. But James – *Frank* – she may be very shocked when she comes round. You should prepare yourself.'

The nurse laid a hand on my husband's arm. It is entirely possible to receive good news about your survival, and yet to want to smack your nurse in the face. Frank didn't react to her hand on his arm, nor her standing close to him. He seemed not even to notice. The sedatives were like quicksand, dragging me down and away.

'Do you want to know?' she asked.

Of course he doesn't want to know! He's nodding because… because…

'A little girl. We couldn't save her. I'm so sorry.'

My husband put his head in his hands and wept. I watched him sorrowfully through the bars of my eyelashes. Sleep clawed me down again.

*

Frank said, laying some very expensive chocolates on the nurses' station, 'Thank you for all you've done.'

37

It was a week later, I'd been cleaned and tidied, and I was being discharged. They'd have preferred to keep me in, for psych evaluations. But I was a walking burial mound now and would permit no further exhumation.

Breezily, I'd agreed to some outpatient counselling so that doctors' brows would stop furrowing and I would be allowed to go. But I knew that what awaited me could not be exorcised by words or tamed with medication. Already I was a stranger to myself, as if I had been raised by wolves and stumbled back into society. Everything carries on, the world keeps turning, running on dismay.

The three nurses at the station cooed thanks as one for the chocolates. They were, I was sure, given every brand and type of chocolate in existence multiple times a day, and I hoped our unoriginality didn't make us seem ungrateful. For I was not ungrateful. I was indeed alive. It was just that this fact was irrelevant now.

The nurses were incarcerated in identical uniforms. Despite this they had an individuality that mesmerised me – one had a paperback of *Game Of Thrones* splayed to the side, and her hand kept creeping towards it and resting on it, as if it was a tiny hand-pillow; another brought me out in a sweat with her resemblance to my mother; the third, my Jackie O, my ghastly flirt-nurse, was smiling fretfully at Frank as she sashayed out from behind the station and handed me an office file box. It had the clothes I'd been found in, and an ultrasound. I slammed the lid back shut.

She placed a sympathetic hand on my arm. 'I know it doesn't seem that way right now, but you have been really lucky. Seventy dead! That's many more than the July 2005 attacks.'

'My baby wasn't lucky,' I said.

'Of course. I'm so sorry. I wasn't thinking…' she said.

Frank smiled amiably, said, 'Thanks again,' and gently turned us away.

We walked in silence down the stairs, as I could not face the lift. Our shoes squeaked on the floor. I remembered a long time ago when I had taken a three-year-old Nicholas on his only visit to my mother. The house had a chilly, sad feel. Nicholas had climbed down from my knee and gone to the front door and waited there like a dog. When I went to bring him back to the sitting room, he whispered, 'I want to go home.' Sometimes the world you know explodes, depositing you in another. You can't talk about your baby, because no one speaks that language here. The person who brought you here has gone.

At the exit I pressed the box with its ultrasound into the bin. The automatic doors were iridescent in the winter sun. I took a deep breath and touched them and they sailed open, bathing us in freezing air.

Frank squeezed my hand. 'Now I should warn you,' he said. 'Nicholas is extremely excited and he has supervised a whole welcoming party. Balloons. A cake. Can you cope with it?'

'Does he understand about the baby?'

'I told him, and he only cares about you.'

'Okay,' I said.

Frank kept his hand over mine in the car, only moving it to change gear. As we sat for a while in traffic, he said, 'I'm sorry I wasn't there, Helen. I'm so sorry.'

'It's all right,' I said. 'It's not your fault.'

When at last we pulled up outside the house, with its clutch of balloons on the door, I did not, at first, recognise it as my home.

5

ROMY, THE BEREAVEMENT counsellor, was straight-backed and clear and her clothes crackled like a newly kindled fire. She had a strict parting in her luscious white hair, but a libidinous crown, where the hair bobbed up and would not be contained.

I did want to talk – I was overflowing with everything that was inside me – but what I wanted was to talk about my classroom kids. I was worried about them, especially Sindi. How would they survive until I could get back there? And also Frank and Nicholas, my *unit*, that remained, as if the walls of a house had evaporated, leaving the furniture standing untouched. I didn't want to talk about anything else; nothing that would disturb the burial mound. I hoped I radiated sanity so one session would be enough.

But after a few pleasantries, Romy got down to business.

'Did you give the baby a name?'

She was clearly on a mission and was not going to indulge any flim-flam. That's not how you get results. I was bereaved and we were going to talk about it. My file lay on a desk behind her. It was very skimpy for one so clearly ambitious. Her question hung between us.

My will softened, becoming gelatinous as an ocean-bottom dweller.

'Cariad,' I mumbled.

'Ah! *Beloved* in Welsh,' she smiled. 'I'm half Welsh myself,'

Loathing gnawed through me. (She demands the name, then she appropriates it.)

'I am not going to cry over the baby,' I said, summoning up my strength. Then, wanting to shock her with my finality: 'The baby is dead as a doornail.'

'Cariad,' she said.

'What?'

'*Cariad* is dead as a doornail.'

The only thing that stopped me slapping her elegant face was the catastrophic weight of my limbs. I felt like I was mid-somersault underwater. Curling over, as if catching myself, a groan squeezed out of me. I burned for Frank; a sudden, visceral desire. If he'd walked through the door I'd have fallen to my knees in front of him, starving, urgent, not caring who saw us. Or was it Nicholas I burned for? My little boy, pale as a fish. I couldn't remember what he felt like against me any more. His kicks inside me, always so vivid in my memory, were lost, taken away by the one who came after.

Hard concern rode the plains of Romy's face. I writhed on my horrible chair several miles beyond the tissue box.

'Let's talk about it,' she said.

'Talk about *what*?'

'Your fury.'

'I'm not furious.' But spittle did sail from my lips and, I believe, landed upon her watch-face. She didn't blink. Instead, she pointed with a palely manicured finger at my coat, which I had not taken off. The breathing world was arctic at all times now, no matter the actual temperature, presence of sun or not. The physical universe didn't follow the old rules any more. *You* try surviving a bomb blast and see if *you* start experiencing reality differently, and wearing inappropriate clothing, I wanted to say, but did not.

I looked down. A slip of paper was dangling from my pocket. As we both watched, it slid out onto the table. As if a breast had escaped my bra, I froze.

I glanced at my bag on the floor. It was exploding with more papers.

'May I?' Romy reached over and, hesitating minutely, picked the one from the table. It was a letter. Of sorts. I tried to grab it from her, but my arms were lead. She put on a pair of stylish half-moon reading glasses and read it aloud:

Dear James

I text myself as if it was you, hundreds of times a day. I've exceeded my text allowance, I've had to upgrade. And yet it's not enough. Millions of you are in my brain. You're the shrapnel of my exploded life right here all over me, inside and out. I am drowning, incinerating in my thoughts of you.

43

She looked over the glasses at me, laid the letter down and picked up another:

Dear James
It's because I met death, and carried death, and permitted death, and failed to prevent death, and saw death and touched death and I know what it is, it's a blunt blade of desire. It's a stake through me. I'm made undead by what I have seen. I can't live without you.

'Are all of these letters to James?' she said. Her eyes, magnified to bovine dimensions behind the lenses, were mapped by meandering capillaries. She had a skin tag on her eyelid. I didn't know why, but I was afraid.

In answer I snatched the letter out of her hands, cradled it to me. I began to cry. I felt sure Romy wanted this, but these were not the tears she would approve of. They were not for the baby. I wasn't sure what they were for, or perhaps they just *were*, like the crests of waves, or the dark torso of the wave itself, rising, solidifying, transcending its element to become the striding, ocean-sucking mountain.

Romy said, as I wept, 'Sometimes people's desires are unleashed by disaster, as if destruction of the self reveals the primal creature within.'

I leant towards her, humiliation animating me like electricity in a corpse.

'I'm a *teacher*. I'm a *mother*. I'm a *married woman*. These letters are for processing my thoughts. Like a diary. You weren't meant to see them.'

She buried words, like mines in the no man's land between

us. 'Helen, everything you're demonstrating, the anger, the need, the…writing… These are part of the stages of loss. You will pass through them all. You will survive.'

'I *have* survived.' I knew I was frightening her a bit. I was frightening myself too. 'The baby…the woman who lost the baby…she is just *sloughed-off skin.*'

She indicated the letters splayed before us. 'You're keeping that sloughed-off skin very close, aren't you?'

I'd read my share of self-help and psychology books. You don't leave the traumatised person with nothing to cling to; no privacy or secrets at all. You don't do that. Romy was irresponsible. She should be struck off. Unbelievable. The vision flashed in my mind of the tribunal where this would happen. I would be called forward – dignified Mrs Bell, who survived a bomb blast – and I would say, full of regret but truth: she left me with nothing to cling to. If I hadn't had a loving husband and son, I would have, I would have—

I sat back, wonderingly.

She spoke softly, as if to an animal. 'It's wonderful that your husband and son are so strong for you.'

'It *is*. They *are.*'

'But I think it will help you to talk about James. And ultimately, about Cariad.'

A scene from my childhood swam into my mind. A man we all knew who wandered the streets of Fleetwood; a 'character' as we put it then. In his arms he carried armfuls of letters. I realised I was telling Romy this. 'There were dozens of them, all in their envelopes. He had dirty hair and a stringy beard and stained trousers and no socks, and funny blue shoes with tassels on them that were rubbing his heels raw. I remember those funny shoes, treading carefully, because he couldn't see his feet, because of all the letters. In the post office one time he queued patiently with them all and he laid them at the window in wobbly towers while he argued with the teller about his Giro. And then…when it was all over he gathered them up and went out again. The point is, he went to the post office with all his letters and the letters were *nothing to do with it.*'

There was a silence.

'We should talk about that next week,' she said. 'We need to finish there.'

'I thought as much,' I snarled, gathering up the letters, stuffing them into my bag, stumbling out like a tramp.

*

I had written too many letters to James to hide them and they poked up around the sheets and on the floor around the bed. Sometimes a text to myself was not enough; I needed to feel the glide of the ink on paper, though the notes were so hurried that sometimes I simply stabbed through the paper and the whole thing was an illegible mess. Between the two – the texts, which I punched into my bright new phone until my eyes ached, and the notes – I must have churned out a whole book's worth of words.

To give me space, and probably to escape the fetid bed and the frantic catatonia of his wife, Frank was sleeping on the sofa. But he could not avoid the letters. They crackled beneath his feet when he came into the bedroom. He read one while I burned under the covers. I said, from underneath,

'They don't mean anything. It's like a diary.'

It didn't wash with him any more than with Romy. He sat on the edge of the bed. 'Are you in love with this guy?'

'No! It's a diary. I'm *bereaved*.'

'It doesn't get you off the hook for absolutely everything, Helen.'

'I know,' I said. I owed him more than this. I poked my head out. 'Look,' I said. 'If you take the "Dear James" off, they could be to anyone. They're philosophical musings… I'm sorry, I…can't help it.' I couldn't look at him when I said it. The letters included panting sexual references. Some of them were tear-stained.

My husband's mouth hardened into a dissatisfied line. He reached out and stroked my arm. 'Maybe…put them away. I don't think Nicholas should see them, do you?'

I heard him leave, through the fiery burn of my embarrassment. Was I in love with James? How could I be? What kind of terrible person falls in love instead of grieving? Frank's steps were the thoughtful plod of a husband knocked from his orbit.

Some days after this wake-up call, this time-up on my outpourings (not that I stopped at all), I was dressed and invigorated beside Frank, ready to witness our eleven-year-old son compete in the school swimming gala. I was shivering. Frank had requested I take off my anorak indoors, and also leave all the letters behind. He was right, of course. I liked that my life now was becoming the opposite of the life Romy was pressing me for. Frank didn't want to talk about my letter-writing, about James, about the baby. He was one hundred percent with me on the lucky-to-be-alive aspect of things, and the fortification of the unit.

No matter my disarray, no matter my failure to order the words in my mouth, never mind to place them in some kind of normal social bandwidth, I would not have missed being here, at this municipal swimming pool. Had I been in a coma, I believe Frank would have unplugged me, wheeled me in and propped me up with a flag in my hand.

As I shivered on the hard bench, chlorine flagellating my corneas and gums, something came over me. The urge to pull off my rings – the wedding and engagement rings that I had not taken off in over a decade – took hold. It was a kind of vertigo. Excitedly, almost as if it belonged to someone else, a lover, a rescuer, *James*, my right hand crept to my left and touched the metal.

The wedding ring, a thin white gold band, still gleamed, as will all metal in the light, even a thread in a boulder, even a chassis consumed by rust. It was in no way dazzling, but I liked the is-what-it-is quality of the unpolished shine. Next to it was the pearl. It had been Frank's maternal grandmother's engagement ring. She had caused quite a sensation in the family by having a pearl instead of a diamond, and Frank liked the oceanic connotations of a pearl, as well as the notion of a marriage being like one, created by labour and friction. I adored this ring. It made me want to run my tongue over the pearl, and this I actually did in nervous moments. It was indestructible and impenetrable, and as hard against my tongue as a piercing.

I realised I was doing it now, anxiously, on my bench, as Nicholas stood at the pool's edge with his toes curled around the rim. I was dry-mouthed from whatever medication they were filling me with, and my saliva was sour and thick, drying almost instantly on my finger like a slug trail. I gazed at our son. Oh, Nicky.

Around him, other boys were scrawny as pencils, or with the shadows of muscles beginning. They shuffled and stared, a pubescent line of shyness and ego. Nicky's solemn face, behind the neon goggles, was turned to us. His lips were pressed together in a determined line. Frank gave him a thumbs-up.

My tongue continued its patient fellatio of my finger, which had no effect on the rings whatsoever. *Dear James* I began another letter in my head. I wanted to tell him about my son, the kind of love that was.

The snap of the starting gun, and Nicholas launched from the side. Frank ricocheted up from the bench. It was hard to see what was happening as the water boiled around the boys. A great bang! as he belly-flopped the water and immediately began to swim. My eyes streamed; parental cheers battered round the tiles, none of it fading or drifting away, until it was a savannah-sized gallop around my brain.

I chewed and licked and despaired. I had swollen while pregnant and bloated again with all the medication. The calming pleasure of running the pearl over my tongue had turned to a terrible need to be free, as if I was a creature chewing its paw from a trap. I didn't even understand how getting the rings off would make me free, I had simply been taken over by desire, which I could not suppress nor hide.

'What are you *doing*?' Frank asked.

To tear him from the sight of our son arcing out of the water with a perfectly executed butterfly stroke, I must have looked amazing. My finger stilled between my lips, like a terrible adult baby.

It struck me then, heavily. *This* was what I had to be free from. My catastrophic failure to be properly human, and being required to answer for it.

I hated my husband then, with a passion as visceral as my desire for him had been.

'I...' My finger slipped from my mouth, dragging a string of spit with it.

'For fuck's *sake*,' Frank pressed his forehead to his hand, and my hate twirled on its terrible cloven hooves into sadness. The collapse of his neck, the tired flop of his hair, the fingers supporting his head without conviction, like an unwanted trophy.

The room erupted into a roar that made me clap my hands to my ears and whimper. Everywhere was a tunnel now, sucking the air from me. My body was a dark space in which I cowered. I grabbed my husband's arm, and hauled myself upright beside him. Frank was clapping and shouting and so I did the same, though it felt like I was crying out for rescue.

Nicholas was closing in on another boy. He was churning through the water like a mill wheel. The other boy was in the next lane.

And I saw it, clear as a revelation. Nicholas grabbed the boy's ankle. He did it seamlessly, without pausing in his own stroke. It was a yank of unexpected force, disguised in white water. The boy jerked underwater, lost his rhythm, and Nicholas pulled ahead.

I flushed with horror and pride. Oh, the shy criminality of all the children I loved: the kids with their stolen fawn, Sindi with her graffiti and lawless flaunting, and now my son, the swimming cheat. All of these children preparing themselves for a world that pretends to follow rules but doesn't really.

The boy Nicholas jerked came second, his hand raised in protest the moment he touched the side. He stared at Nicholas, who was grinning around him in innocent delight. Oh, the torments of evidence! *My boy*.

Then the tannoy, shearing though me like electricity. 'And in first place… Nicholas Bell!'

Frank whooped, and punched the air. I slipped down into my seat, clapping until my hands hurt. Nicholas's eyes met mine. His beautiful, dark, uncertain eyes.

Events were moving smoothly on. Boys were being ushered onto the podium. Boys I once knew as toddlers. Boys who had grown in the time I had been working, and latterly, locked in my bereavement. I had barely stepped out of the house in weeks, except for my ill-fated journeys to Romy. I imagined going into school all the time. I imagined all my kids floundering in their unsuitability for living. It chewed at me.

There he was, our boy, on the highest of the blocks. He was grinning. As the Head put the medal round his neck, our son stared right at me, a soft, serious look. I clapped harder, wanting to send approval across the heads of parents, across the shaky water, to him. Then it was over. Nicholas, like some kind of strange-skinned sea creature, clambered from the blocks and disappeared into the changing rooms.

He was quiet in the car, turning over the medal in his hands. He looked small again, younger than his years.

'Are you proud of me, Mummy?' he asked.

'Nicky, *so* proud. You were…amazing.'

'Yes, son, that was just brilliant. We should celebrate,' said Frank, excited at the wheel.

I seemed to have lost all muscle tone. I slumped inside my anorak like a lonely mound of ice cream.

'What do you think? Takeaway? You choose. And you–' Frank looked at me tenderly. He mouthed, 'Well done.'

My finger throbbed inside its metal hoop. I reached behind myself and offered my hand, and Nicholas's crept into it. I closed my eyes, trying to feel his hand properly, my *son*, my *living son*. It was as if I was leading him through a tunnel in the blackness, going forward, though I did not know then into what.

6

NICHOLAS USED TO SLEEPWALK as a toddler. He would turn up at the bedside in the early hours, narrating urgently, his little hand reaching out to me. On each cheek a feverish spot, his fringe stuck to his brow with sweat. Was he traumatised by something? A premonition? Was he crazy? I hated it; my baby tugging at me to go somewhere I did not want to go. I feared to wake him, instead gently taking his clammy hand and guiding him into bed with us, where, at last, he would fall into a normal sleep. For several years it went on, until abruptly it stopped. And now it had spread to me, hefting me out of bed through the torpor of my medication.

My eyes opened onto the nursery we had half-completed for Cariad. It was late afternoon, and shadows cut across the curtains. My hands were tight around the monitor, still in its box. We'd have heard her cry from anywhere in the house. I snuffled round the room. I continued to bleed from the stillbirth, my breasts weeping milk. During pregnancy, oestrogen levels rocket by some 7,000 percent. After birth, even stillbirth, they plummet immediately. Was it any wonder I was half out of my mind? I must tell Romy, or the GP, or Frank or *someone* that it wasn't anti-depressants and anti-anxiety medication I needed. I needed my oestrogen back. *Dear James, If I can't have my baby, I want my oestrogen.* But my brain possessed a fully formed panel of voices which responded kindly before I could formulate the language that would communicate my need. *Your suffering is in your mind. It is not located in your body, nor in the world.*

Neatly draped over the bassinet was the cute babygro with a rabbit on it that my mother sent. The prospect of a new baby had touched my mother. She kept in contact for the first time in years. The baby got me more approval than anything else I had done. There was, however, no condolence card. She didn't know what to say, and so went back to saying nothing.

Frank's cheerful ringtone vibrated from the sitting room below and through my socks. Journalists were still calling. He answered every time, not wanting to miss a client.

'She's not available,' he snapped. 'When will you do some actual investigating? Stop parading that murdering bastard's family!' His voice rose. 'There's not a shred of remorse from them! So you can take your forgiveness and moving-on shit– And if I see anything about me or my family *anywhere*, you will hear from my lawyers. You heard me. Fuck off.'

My poor son, hearing this fury. Should I go and be with him? But I had to arrange the babygro inside the bassinet.

Dear James. Dear James.

My lack of anger about the bomb infuriated Frank. Yesterday he'd found me in the sitting room doorway staring at the news. The bomber's mother was talking about him again. She had my haunted look, her tone, expression and words were confused and out of synch, just like mine. He was called William. He was twenty years old. She ended by gazing brokenly at the camera, repeating, 'I had no idea…'

The bomber had uploaded a video, which I didn't watch, before setting off on his mission, explaining that he was making the ultimate sacrifice alongside his victims. Frank had followed me from to room, pressing me for an appropriate reaction. 'Don't you see how evil this is? Our child died for… Nothing at all! Some kid!' He grew furious when I simply wept, pushing past him to get back into bed.

Now, the front door slammed and Frank strode down the path, heading for his secret fags in the car. How fiercely he moved! He moved of his *own volition*. That no longer applied to me. I'd been blown from one world to another. Now I only moved if a force greater than inertia was applied to my mind or my body.

A man with a camera stood on the other side of the street. A couple walking down the road paused; one of them pointed to our house. There'd be a blue plaque one day, I'd joked with Frank. The youngest casualty of the worst underground bomb attack in London almost lived here. The dead were bathed in morbid celebrity. There was still interest in me because the most shocking victim had a spokesperson, almost as if Cariad could speak from beyond the grave. People were looking for *insight*. Cariad was a symbol of innocence lost; public before she even existed. There had been no trace at all of James in the press. His face, as I remembered it anyway, did not appear in the gallery of photos of the dead. The published accounts of survivors did not feature his name. I wondered how this could be. I gave no interviews and avoided photographs; nevertheless, since I had been in hospital, my name had been recorded and my baby was in the death toll. I thought he might see and get in touch, but he had not.

Frank towered over the man with the camera, his shirt hanging out. The low winter sun bestowed long shadows. Frank's shadow gesticulated. His words ricocheted off the concrete path, rendered unintelligible.

(Dogs yawn when they are scared. Did you know that, Nicholas? That's why your mother is yawning, as she watches your dad yelling at a man in the street. I'm frightened. I'm trying to hide it.)

Inside the jewellery box on the windowsill before me was the pregnancy test with the first positive line. Not an expensive one with a handle from Boots but one of the cheap ones I bought in bulk over the internet because I was so amazed to be pregnant that I tested myself obsessively. Five, six times a day. And this one – I held it up to the light – was the very first positive. The lines, control and result, were sharp as the stripes on a wasp.

What now? After all, she was gone. Our family had been reinvented by the fact of Cariad. And now... Why should Frank stay with me? He could start all over again, with someone not broken-hearted.

Could I argue a technicality? Could I show him the test stick and say, But she is still here, *in this line*? The test stick was a relic, like Jesus's finger. I shut it back in the velvet-lined box and began to throw things into a pile in the corner, to tear them from the walls, tossing them onto the growing pile. Why did people get so much stuff for their babies, when this could happen? Because it could. It happened to me.

Then, from under a patchwork blanket, a framed picture clattered to the floor. The glass was smeared and dusty. I wiped it vigorously with the bottom of my T-shirt and almost dropped it again in shock.

There we were, Frank and me, in our mid-twenties, on the deck of the *Innisfree*. The sky was a dizzy blue. There was a line of sea, turquoise. In Frank's arms, a dorado.

I sank to my knees. In that moment, I could smell the waves, hear the laughter of our friends. Beneath my feet the solid, warm planks of the *Innisfree*'s deck. Time stretching out its warm hands forever. Frank's grin was genuine, not yet his salesman's smile. How we battled to catch this fish! After this shot was taken we barbecued it on the beach and partied. In my hand was the lure that Frank had carved with our names, and which had caught this handsome creature. I ran my finger round the outline of our young bodies.

Look at him, the young man, my husband, the father of my future child.

Look at her, the young woman, smiling, completely in love.

And the *Innisfree*, the warm palm in which this couple was created.

I paced the room, excited. This was more than just a picture. Why had we never put this up on the wall? I held it to me. *Dear James, this is what I wanted to describe and could not. This was my beautiful life. I wish I could show it to you. Where did you go? Where did the* Innisfree *go?*

Stumbling back to the bedroom, I fished out my laptop from under the bed. A search did not bring up the *Innisfree*. On impulse I tapped in the name of our old skipper, Corin, and swiftly brought up the news that he had died five years ago of cancer. No! It seemed impossible that anyone from that time could die. The *Innisfree* herself had seemed indestructible. What could have happened to her?

There was a hesitant tap on the door and Nicholas stepped shyly into the room. In his hand, as always these days, was his phone.

'Hey Nicky,' I said, closing the laptop and running a hand through my greasy nest of hair.

'Dad's flipping out again.'

'It's just the journalists. They're very intrusive. He's just trying to protect us.'

'What are you doing?' he asked, sitting on the edge of the bed.

'Oh just looking up something from the past,' I said. 'But how about I find a movie? Something we could watch together.'

'I can't,' he said. 'I've got an interview for the mod job in Roblox.'

'Oh,' I said, eager to participate. 'Congratulations!' I was very much in favour of Nicky's gaming. Frank was not. In fact Nicholas's disappearance into the internet scared him. 'Can't you see how dangerous it is? Lonely kids, radicalised!' he protested, when I just couldn't get worked up about Nicky's hours in front of a screen. It was true, our son had become rather pale and had developed a slouch, but his obsession produced a kind of glow around his spindly frame which I understood. It was the shine of a vibrant, emotionally dynamic, conceptually satisfying, secret life. This was something I understood, for what had James become, but the same to me?

Lately Frank had taken to unplugging the router as this was the only thing that could bring the gaming to a halt. I knew when this attempt at discipline had occurred because a wail rose from Nicky's room and the door tore open: 'Plug it back in! They will give my place to someone else!' Then, 'Muuuuum! Tell Dad!'

I wished Frank would leave Nicholas alone, because the existential rage that now overflowed the house disrupted my James time. I needed to write my notes and texts. I needed to abandon myself to James-reverie. It was my *only peace*.

And, truthfully, Nicholas's anger was frightening to behold. His body vibrated with it, he was torn from himself as surely as a crack addict whose pipe had been snatched away. He was in terrible pain. I would turn off the light and cover my head with my pillow, their voices thudding in its fibres. Sometimes Frank would give in. Sometimes he would storm out to the car for his secret fags. Sometimes he would simply sit in the kitchen, the router hidden, and wait for Nicholas to storm himself to sleep.

Early on, Nicky would barge into the bedroom and demand I do something. He learned there was no point. There is no point screaming at the deaf to hear, the paralysed to walk. I could only say, 'Your dad will have good reasons, darling.'

Now, he reached out and held my hand.

'If I pay £50 I can get the job in Roblox without the interview,' he said. 'Then I could watch the film with you.' He smiled his cute, snaggled smile. Oh Nicky, well played!

I stretched out the contact on my hand for as long as possible, knowing that it would, of course, vanish the second I turned him down.

'I'm not working. I've got no cash. You'll have to ask your dad.'

'You know what he'll say,' he whined.

'It's more fun to work for something like that anyway,' I said. He drew his hand away and there was a silence while he fiddled with his phone.

'Can I go to Louis's house? For a sleepover? I can do the interview there.'

'Of course!' I said. 'But…don't you want to invite him over here? We've got the extra consoles.' My words petered out. I'd blown the deal. No £50, no son in the house. I'd made my choice.

'He's got the computer version, which is better,' Nicholas said.

I sighed. 'Shall I help you pack?'

'No, it's fine.'

'Just take your phone, okay? Text me later.'

He nodded and closed the door behind him. I unscrewed my tranquilisers, popped a couple. I curled up, the picture of Frank and me on the *Innisfree* in my arms, and I slept.

*

My husband's shirt had sweatmarks and splashes of tomato sauce on the sleeve. His hair, like mine, was an unwashed mess. I noticed he had not clipped his eyebrows. He was not himself at all. He was sitting on the bed where Nicholas had been, softly shaking me awake.

'Come down, would you, Helen? I want to talk to you.' He gave me one of his professional smiles.

Frank was a photographic agent, with, now, his own successful agency. His clients were increasingly glamorous, headlined by Ruth, who was beautiful, and French.

Frank sold his clients' photographs everywhere and all manner of projects – fashion, causes, news – used the images to sell themselves. Certain Instagram hashtags were almost entirely populated by his clients. Other agencies were struggling in the digital age when, in theory, anyone could make an image. But not Frank. He had embraced the algorithm on behalf of his clients. Insatiable demand met high-quality supply via my husband. No wonder he was smiling. Although, to be fair, he'd be smiling even if the business was in the gutter.

'Okay,' I said, groggy and slightly put out by the feeling of being scolded. Clutching the picture, I shuffled down the stairs after him. Actually, I had an agenda of my own! This picture was solid proof of *us*. Of *me*. Perhaps we had lost a future – but we had a beautiful past, the kind of past that can sustain a whole life.

The sides of the stairs were piled with objects on their way up. The carpet had not been hoovered in some time. I had an odd sensation that I was leaving, descending the stairs for the last time. I peeped into the sitting room. The sofa I hated – could I leave it? But I was going to. It was a fact as insurmountable as a car crash. From room to room I wandered, overwhelmed by premonition. *Dear James, I'm rubbernecking my own life.*

'Helen?' Frank waved me into the kitchen. The table had candles on it. There was a delicious smell of garlic and basil.

'Sorry. I should have got dressed.'

'It's fine,' said Frank.

The sink was full of pans, the work surfaces littered with containers full of cooling sauce. Evidence of my stubborn failure to recover was mounting everywhere.

'I've started batch-cooking. It's the only way to keep up.' Frank waved at the containers.

He laid a bowl of spiralised courgette and sauce on the table and another of salad. Frank had started a low-carb, intermittent fasting regime a couple of years before and absolutely nothing made him deviate. Not even the loss of his child and a convulsion in society could make him denigrate the temple of his body. It was impressive.

He said, 'I let the cleaners go – I didn't want anyone coming in,' and poured me a glass of my favourite red. He smiled professionally again.

'Remember that episode of *The Sopranos* where Tony and Paulie take Pussy who has snitched to the FBI out on a boat to kill him?' I said. 'And they all have a drink together before they shoot him? They keep going with the social niceties, right up to the end even though they *all know...*' I twirled courgette and sauce round my fork in the silence. 'Have you put chilli in this? It's delicious.'

'Helen, we need you back,' Frank said.

'Oh.'

He offered me the parmesan. I shook my head and he grated some over his own plate. 'I know you are devastated, I do get that,' he went on. 'But, the truth is, I can't do this alone. Your son…needs you. *I* need you.'

I looked round the grimy kitchen.

'I'm doing my best but—' He waved around the room. 'I have to go back to work. I've got meetings and bills you wouldn't believe. You have to…get a grip.'

'Get a grip?' I spluttered into my wine. 'Look, I didn't ask you to babysit me, Frank. If people would just let me sleep!'

He shook his head. 'You can't stay in bed for the rest of your life!'

'Why not?'

Frank took a deep breath. 'What about Nicholas? The constant gaming? Do you care?'

'Of course I care. But what can I do?'

'He needs his mother!'

'He has a mother.'

'I'm the only functioning adult in this family,' Frank snapped.

I sighed and pushed my plate away. I could only really face sweet things anyway these days. 'Do you realise, you haven't asked me once how it was, what happened down there that night?'

'I thought it was better you spoke to Romy,' he said. 'You needed a professional.'

'What a cop-out,' I said.

He leaned back, looked at me. 'You also haven't asked what it was like to get the call from the hospital and have

63

no way of knowing if you'd be alive or dead when I got there. And not knowing how to ask or talk about the baby... which...I...' The breath caught in his throat. 'The doctors said you'd be depressed, that you'd be changed. I just didn't want to make everything worse. I'm worried for Nicholas now he's vanished into all that Discord stuff. Why aren't you worried sick, like me?' He downed his wine.

I wasn't supposed to drink this much with my medication, but I sloshed more wine into my glass.

'I felt my baby die inside me. I don't know what to say. You and I are in different worlds,' I said.

'You didn't turn to me, Helen. You've turned to this James bloke!'

'You weren't fucking there!'

'I've apologised for that. I feel terrible.'

I stared at him.

'Helen, I've never stopped loving you.'

'I believe you,' I said.

'What more can I do? What more can I say?'

'Where were you that night?' I asked.

'I told you. A client meeting with my photographer. Ruth Martin.'

Her name emerged from his lips as if in huge gentle parentheses. It was terrible to see, terrible to hear. And yet, there we remained, holding our forks, sipping our wine, in our normal, unexploded house. I marvelled quietly at the marital physics.

No amount of lying would destroy our edifice. A single vocalising of the truth would. *I can't survive it. More destruction. I can't.*

I held the picture out to him, trembling. 'We were in the same world here.'

He took the picture from me and stared at it, lost in it as I had been. 'Where did you find this?' he said, softly.

'Under all that baby stuff.'

'We were out there such a long time, weren't we?' he said. 'You know… I actually forget about it all most of the time. Like it was a dream.'

'See the lure?' I said.

'Oh!' He touched it with his finger. In so doing he covered my young hand with his.

'Frank,' I said, laying down my fork. 'This was when I was happy. Before everything.'

'That's the bomb talking, Helen. We were happy just two months ago. You love this house, and London! You like your job. We were just…young.'

'The bomb woke me up, Frank. My life is a sham.'

'What are you talking about?'

Was that one of the reasons people got married, so they could have a safe space away from the truth? It is so hard to say what you mean, to face the truth.

But something was changing within me. My evolution was the strange, multiple-mutation sort, arriving swiftly after catastrophe. Up to now, Frank's was the incremental, inevitable kind that no one exactly notices and is simply progress. Explanations of my changing feelings seemed so complicated, requiring great parentheses of history to make sense. But here we were, with spiralised courgette and a necessity for me to explain myself. I was going to try.

I poured myself some water. 'Remember when I got

pregnant with Nicholas and we decided to come home? I know we talked about it, how we could buy the *Innisfree* from Corin and make a life and business of it. Perhaps I should have insisted, because I think it could have worked. You see them all the time now, the families on Instagram and Youtube. But there wasn't the blueprint then, was there? Frank, I agreed to the choices we made. I'm not complaining that we made them. I'm just saying… I was adapted for that simple life at sea.'

Frank was scanning what I was saying for indications that I was about to blame him for something. He nodded carefully.

'Remember you said we'd go back one day? I think that was the only way I could imagine a life on land. And do you remember when we were sailing home, so that Corin could drop us in Portsmouth and we could catch the train to London, and I cried the whole journey? I didn't want the life I was choosing. I didn't know how to say no to any of it. Part of me knew we only really worked on the *Innisfree*. We were equal somehow.'

'But you wanted a family. We had Nicholas!'

'Like I say, I agreed to the choices we made. It's just, I didn't understand what I would lose.' My voice caught in my throat at this. *You. I lost you.*

We'd left our watery innocence and walked onto land to become adults. But I now saw that the moment we did marked the first diverging branch on our evolutionary tree. For Frank's adaptation to London life had been extraordinarily successful. It was as if the new element unlocked something in him that propelled him to evolve spectacularly. First, despite having no experience in the field, his photographs from our time sailing demonstrated a keen visual eye, and this, along with a sensitive artistic taste, and a self-deprecating confidence which was immensely attractive to a certain kind of powerful woman, secured him a job as an assistant at the global photographic agency Lumina, straight off the sea.

'Helen, do you resent my success?'

'I resent that you didn't give anything up. You got to grow up *and* get what you want. Growing up for me was giving up what I wanted.'

'You didn't say a fucking word about it at the time!'

'No, I just cried all the way from the Med to London!'

'Has it occurred to you that I missed the sea as well? And that getting to where I am actually demanded a lot of hard work and, dare I say it, talent?'

It was true – Frank had soared. The rules that we had spent the years aboard the *Innisfree* avoiding did not trouble him as he had feared. They did not seem to touch him. The bars he had imagined turned out to be a mirage: he drew near them and they melted away. He appealed powerfully to the woman who became his boss because his declared ambitions were not the conventionally masculine sort. He had no wish to climb a corporate ladder. When he left after a few years to set up his own agency, she was not surprised, and nor was she pissed off that he took a top client with him. She simply took annual leave over the period of his notice, texting him a picture of herself in a swimsuit posing at the wheel of a yacht in Madeira. I had found this on his phone, quizzed him on it. He had been genuinely bewildered by its meaning, denied any affair, pointed out that he was gone from the company. We had a three-year-old son and I had no realisable dreams of my own. I decided not to rock the boat.

'Frank, you left me behind.'

'You left yourself behind. You've never really been here with me.'

We looked at each other. I did not say *Ruth*. He did not say *James*. I was suddenly very sober.

'Do you love me, Helen?'

'No,' I whispered.

His jaw softened, and I was suddenly reminded of the grainy film of Neil Armstrong's foot touching the surface of the moon that first time. The slowness of the impact, the ancient dust rising, the imprint there for eternity.

He said, 'I see.'

My mouth was on its own mission, deciding on its own what I would ask, what I would tell. 'Were you going to leave me? Before the baby?' I said.

He sighed. 'Yes.'

I gasped, and brushed my fingers over the image of us in the glass, my eyes brimming. 'But Frank, I *did* love you. With all my heart. I have never loved anyone else like you.' Tears fell onto the glass and smeared when I tried to wipe them away. 'Until the bomb, that was enough for me. We had the baby, we had a new chance.'

Frank picked up the picture again. 'Do you want a divorce?' he asked me.

'I don't know,' I said.

'I don't want one,' he said.

The picture lay on the table between us, our young faces

smiling up at us. Frank took my hand.

'Helen, let's set two things aside for now. Who loves who, and who was going to leave who. I don't think we can do anything with those hanging over us. Okay?'

'Okay,' I said.

'How about this? Let's promise each other. We're going to try and do what will make us happy again, as a family. We could sell up, get a new house if you like. Get away from these journalists. Get away from these memories. I do think you'd be much happier back at work. Feel more like you.'

He was getting into his stride now, imagining all kinds of additions to our dream life. 'I could go back to taking photographs instead of flogging other people's. We could get a sailing boat. For weekends. Wouldn't that be great? I mean, Nicholas should know how to sail, shouldn't he? Get him off that fucking computer.'

I left my plate and curled up on Frank's lap, clutching the picture. He stroked my nape. 'Let's be in the same world again,' he said. 'Or better yet, let's build a new one.'

7

DEAR JAMES. IT CAME TO ME in the middle of the night when I was awake and looking at the stars out of the window in Cariad's nursery. I want to find you. Are you looking at the same stars as me?

It was morning, a couple of weeks after our dinner. I was fighting the autocorrect to send this text to myself when my phone rang. It was a new phone. No one had rung me on it. But now, Frank's name was scrolling across the screen.

'Helen, I'm coming home and I want you to get dressed – I'm picking you up to take you out.' My husband sounded very pleased with himself.

'What are you talking about? Where are you?' I mumbled. I was barely awake, having surfaced just enough from sleep to try to write to James. He was my first thought on waking, my last before I dropped into medicated sleep, and the backdrop to every thought in between. My only pleasure, my only real animating activity, was writing to James.

'What about Nicholas?' I protested.

'Nicky will go to Louis's house after school.'

'But I don't want to get up,' I whined. 'I'm tired. I have stuff to do.'

'I'll be home in half an hour. Wear something warm.'

'If you're hoping for a romantic weekend I will disappoint you!' I snarled. But he had hung up.

*

Outside the air was cold, with the seething edge of the British spring. I pulled my coat firmly round my pyjamas and darted from the house to the car. I had no socks on and my wellies were too tight. There'd better not be any walking.

'Pyjamas? Really?' Frank sighed.

'I'm here, aren't I? Anyway, what's this about?'

'You'll see soon enough.'

We drove through the leafy streets, then on through wide industrial boulevards. We were leaving London. I had no idea where we were.

Since returning to work, my husband's appearance had gone back to its previous high standard. Hair cut, clean shirt, sleeves currently rolled up to reveal an expensive sports watch of some kind, sitting squarely amidst the golden hairs of his strong arm. Round his neck was his camera. We were both taking his advice to think about what we wanted. To put into action more things that would make us happy individually and as a family. How I longed to be satisfied in the normal

71

way, in Frank's way, by a camera, a car, a new watch. By an explanation, a spa weekend, by something that does not require a new world order to be possible.

'That's a new watch.'

'Nice, isn't it? A sailing watch. I got it after we talked about the *Innisfree* the other night. I always admired Corin's.'

'Got' can mean 'receive'. And it looked like a present to me. How I wanted to be satisfied with the meaning of 'got' as presented by my husband. Instead, I said, 'I *got* a card from the kids at school in the post. I forgot to mention it.'

'Oh, lovely!'

The card had a cartoon puppy with a bandaged head on the front and 'Get Well Soon'. Inside, the signatures, drawings, and tags of dozens of my students. I had returned it to its envelope and placed it on the chest of drawers in the bedroom. I could only deal with my pre-bomb life in phases.

'Food for thought, isn't it?' said Frank. 'They miss you.'

Did I miss them? I was worried about them, most of all Sindi. I missed the small miracles of teaching, my Interventions, my classroom. But not with a force strong enough to tilt me out of bed.

From its holder in the dashboard, Frank's phone sang its tune.

'I should take this,' said Frank. The name scrolling across the screen wasn't familiar to me. He pressed his earpiece. 'Joanne! Lovely to hear from you. Did you get the files? Of course. I know. Amazing, aren't they? I thought of you especially with the one of the boy surfing.' I guessed from his enthusiasm that he was discussing Ruth's photographs.

'We are down to the last two? Well you said Terry has a

love for those big waves! Abso-*lu*-tely. Hmm-mm. Oh she's right here!' He looked at me, laid his hand over mine. 'I'm taking her for a surprise trip. You bet.'

I stared out of the window. I don't like surprises, I thought. Surprise parties, surprise trips with my husband wearing a surprise watch. *Dear James, Did you know the Andean civilisations mummified their dead kings and treated them as living leaders, with a woman to speak for them, translating their dead wishes? Am I speaking to you? Or for you? What is it about absence that makes the one left behind pour words into the space?*

'Gotta go, Joanne. But I'll call you later and we can set up a meeting so we can arrange a time to come in and present to you. Unless you want to save time and appoint us now? Ha ha! I know, cheeky, but only thinking of you! Take care. And you.'

Without comment, but still smiling from the conversation, Frank switched back to the satnav. 'That was the marketing head of a certain pharmaceutical giant, seeking to appoint an agency for all its advertising! Honestly, Helen, if we get this deal then we really are into the big bucks.'

Frank touched things and they turned to gold. Almost as if he heard my thoughts, he turned and smiled, 'Only as good as your last miracle in this business though!' and I wanted to tell him about that last day at school, the day of the bomb, when my baby was healthy, a brand new life unfolding inside me. And now she was gone, and I was no longer miraculous in any way. It was impossible to express this to Frank. Our worlds were different and so were the wonders in them. One thing was common to them both though. I, too, was only as

73

good as my last miracle.

'Now...here we are!' We slowed and pulled into a large car park, with coaches, surrounded by parkland, and in the distance, a stately home. *Welcome to Stonyfin Park.*

'You could have said we'd be in public,' I grumbled, wrestling my way out of the car.

Frank was consulting his phone. 'This way,' he said, and set off down one of the paths that branched across the estate.

'Frank, what is going on?' In spite of my dislike of surprises, excitement flickered in me. Frank was a salesman. He knew how to please people. If he'd brought me here, it was not to disappoint me.

My husband took my hand. We followed the signs to *Woodland Walk* and *Stonyfin Lake.* Trees with painfully tight buds enclosed us. A woodpecker was battering a tree trunk. Groups of schoolchildren belted past us, or filed neatly in crocodiles.

We passed through a long stretch of towering rhododendrons, weighted with white blooms, then the wood opened out into a clearing, full of joyful screaming.

'Oh my God!' I cried.

There, in the middle of the clearing, upon a trailer, was the *Innisfree.*

She was painted black, and emblazoned on her fifty-seven-foot side in white was a new name: *Pirate Queen.* Children were pounding up and down the decks, banging her rails with sticks. Their shrieks echoed through the trees. A boy swigged a can of Coke, stamped it flat on her deck.

Frank pointed his camera at me and snapped furiously. I held my hand to shield my face. 'No!'

'What's wrong?' he cried, as I ran towards her, my wellies sucking through the mud. My coat flapped open, heads turned to see a madwoman in pyjamas careering through the play area. Not caring, I clambered up the steps nailed to her side, and ran my hands along her scarred flank. Was it really her?

From her mast, cut in half, drooped a tattered skull-and-crossbones flag. A fake crow's nest had been installed, and children, like cockroaches, like rats, teemed up to it. I hated them all. She was tilted to port, as if she had drifted to the seabed and landed almost true. Every single surface was peeling and dented.

In the cockpit I sank down among the dirt and fag ends. Mould had collected in the corners. A woman, a teacher, I realised, in her emblazoned hi-vis jacket, looked at me nervously. 'Are you all right?' she asked.

'I...I...' I left her and fled down the steps where the hatch used to be, down into the bare saloon. Feet rattled past the gaps that used to be portholes. Alone in the gloomy forepeak, I fell to my knees, searching. I knew it was her but I had to be sure. There in the corner, just above the floor, carved in small letters, *H + F.*

I huddled into the corner. For a long moment I could feel the *Innisfree* seeming to breathe, slow and deep. We used to imagine this as we lay crushed together in this cabin. Jonah and his love in the belly of the kindly whale. I ran my hands over the panelling. Did she know it was me?

'It's her all right!' Frank arrived in a cloud of cold and crouched beside me. Clumsily missing my cheek and pressing a kiss to my head, he leaned over me and aimed his camera at me beside our initials. 'Nicky should see this,' he said.

'Stop taking pictures!' I cried. A girl appeared with a laser gun and shot us, giggling, before running away.

'Why?'

'I can't breathe! She feels like a coffin!' I pulled myself away from him back through the saloon, waiting behind two smoking teenagers who ostentatiously ground their cigarettes into the floor.

'What are you looking at?' one of them scowled at my pyjamas. 'Psycho!'

'This is a Swan,' I spat. 'The most beautiful sailing boat ever made. You should be ashamed of yourselves.' I pushed past them up onto the crowded deck.

'Helen, wait!' Frank cried, grabbing me. 'What's wrong?'

'She's...destroyed! How...how could you!'

'But she's being enjoyed...she's full of children! You can come here whenever you want... I thought you'd be thrilled. Our names are still there!' He trailed off, gazing at me, stricken. I shook him off, stomping back towards the car. Behind me, Frank pulled out his phone and spoke forcefully to someone on the other end.

'Someone's coming,' he called. 'To talk to us. Helen... Wait!' He ran after me, gently pulled me to a standstill. 'Helen, just hang on. I'm going to sort this out.'

A young man with a downy moustache came marching down the path, took in the pyjama-clad vision that was me and waved.

'This is Mike,' Frank explained. ' We've been chatting about the boat. He runs the...play area.'

'I actually sourced the boat,' said Mike, proudly. 'Project-managed the whole transformation! What do you think?'

A loudspeaker blared across the deck: 'Ahoy me hearties! Stone the Crows!'

Mike grinned. 'That was my idea. The kids love it. We're thinking of getting actors next, you know, with patches and peg legs and so on and having re-enactments…'

I pressed my hands over my ears.

'What's wrong with her?' I heard Mike say.

'How much?' Frank replied.

'What do you mean? It's not for sale.'

'Everything is for sale,' said Frank. 'How much?'

'I'm confused,' Mike said. 'I thought you were looking to hire the space.'

'I want the boat.'

My hands dropped from my ears. 'What are you doing, Frank?' I asked.

'We can't leave her here. Like this.'

I looked back at the *Innisfree*. She held no hope about this encounter, she was a heap of blackened fibreglass and steel, teetering like a condemned housing block. But then – did I imagine her straightening a little, her prow nosing the air? The dignity of being recognised through one's debasement? Did she sense us there?

Mike smirked. 'Three hundred thousand,' he said.

'You're a bright kid,' said Frank. 'So I'm going to let that pass.'

'I think this boat is very valuable to you. Judging by your wife crying.'

'Should I call your boss to have a sensible negotiation?'

Mike was unperturbed. 'I am the boss as far as this is

concerned. We've invested heavily in the *Pirate Queen*. She's the star of the adventure playground. I'm not sure we'd easily find the right boat again. All things considered, 300k would set us on the right path.'

'I'll give you fifty thousand.'

Mike started to walk away. 'Two eighty-five,' he said over his shoulder.

'What are you doing?' I hissed.

Frank smiled down at me. A non-professional, excited smile.

'Don't walk off, Mike,' he said, amiably. 'I know you got this boat for next to nothing because the owner died. And you've gone on to destroy one of the most beautiful sailing boats money can buy. I think we should get some journalists down here, do a big before-and-after piece. To show what happens when no one wants a valuable sailboat any more and it falls into the hands of people who don't care.'

'Go right ahead.'

'I don't think it will do your reputation any good to have a feature about this travesty in the press. Plus, my wife here, who loves this boat so much, is a survivor of the London bombing. We have not given a single interview, but I think now would be the moment. Do I need to add more reasons why it makes sense to just come to a sensible arrangement with us?'

Mike slowly turned round.

Frank went on, 'Like I said, *forty* thousand. I'll still send the journalists round, and some photographers, but this time it will be the story of the *Innisfree* and her kind custodian.'

Mike stared at my husband. Then he smiled and extended

his hand. I marvelled at how Frank negotiated. A simple, impersonal battle using all weapons at his disposal, and then when victor and loser were established, an agreement with zero rancour.

Mike said, saving face: 'Actually we've been trying to get rid of it for a while; too old-fashioned... The kids want a funfair...'

And Frank nodded along because the secret to all good deals, as he had told me too many times, was that all parties, in the end, should feel great about them.

I grabbed his arm. 'Have you really done what I think you've done?'

'We've just bought the *Innisfree*! All those years we couldn't do it, dreamed of it...'

'But Frank, we need to talk about this! The work she'll need!'

'We'll sell the house. Whatever it takes.'

'This is insane!'

Mike grinned, with a mouth full of what looked like baby teeth. He began walking off, talking into his phone.

'You've lost your mind!' I said to Frank, my heart soaring.

'It's about time I joined you,' he said.

*

And this was how the *Innisfree* returned to our lives. We went into the Stonyfin House café and Frank stayed on his phone for the next two hours, finding a space for the yacht in South Dock Marina, an HGV plus driver to take her there and a long conversation with the bank about money. The sun was out. I sweated manically inside my coat. I could hardy believe what was happening. I began text after text to James, but I didn't know how to finish them. And then, suddenly, the thought occurred to me.

Dear James, I don't need you any more!

I was pure adrenaline, grinning in my pyjamas. Not need James any more? Because I had, as Romy would say, *excavated to the real loss*, the *Innisfree*? And now she was back? Bringing *us*, Frank and me, with her?

But what an absolute mess she was. I could not imagine how much it would cost and the time it would take to restore her. And what then?

Reading my mind, Frank said, 'We'll sail the world. We can do anything, go anywhere. All the places we couldn't go to when she wasn't ours.'

'But the agency, Frank…'

He shrugged. 'We'll work it out. Hey, maybe the pharmaceutical giant will buy me out!'

'Are you going to wake up tomorrow regretting this?' I said.

'Look, I said we should get a sailing boat, didn't I? I've just…you know, taken the idea a bit too far.' Frank laughed. 'To be honest I feel really alive.'

It was a different kind of journey home, bathed in possibility. I lay on the back seat and wound down the window. I pulled my wellies off and stuck my feet out, waving them. George Michael was singing *And you gotta have FAITH*, and I joined in. The sun flowed over my feet; it seemed like the first touch of the elements on my skin in years.

'Nicholas is going to freak when he sees her!' I said. 'I can't wait to see his face.'

'This is just the beginning, Helen!'

The hairs on his arms shone gold. It was as if he was made of gold; we both were. I could not believe what had just happened, and that I was married to this man, who had just made the impossible happen. I'd remember it as one of the happiest days of my life, flat on my back with my feet out of the window, singing along to George Michael with my miracle-maker husband, deleting hundreds of text messages that I just didn't need any more.

8

A FEW DAYS AFTER OUR discovery of the *Innisfree*, still on a high, we were gulping fizz and milling around the sitting room to Frank Sinatra's *When I was seventeen, it was a very good year*. I had not been this drunk in years. Partly this was because I had not been out in years to anything that was not either school- or agency-related, and getting drunk was not really on the cards. But the main reason for my engrained restraint was the unwitting police force of one that Nicholas had become, that perhaps all children in a family become, scrutinising parents for moral failures, observing and judging any and every perceived violation of, in particular, motherly norms.

But I was sure as hell drunk now, and Frank's mouth was sharp with bubbles as I kissed him, properly, for the first time in ages. In that facsimile of the kisses we used to share, was a portent; a good one. With his gesture Frank had not only saved our marriage, he seemed to have turned back time. There was no terrorist bomb, there was no lost baby, there were no intimations of a terrible future. Frank and I were not disappointed in each other. Ruth, James, even Cariad; their ghosts did not come.

We had tried to tempt Nicholas out from gaming in his room. He refused, saying he would join us after the thing he was trying to accomplish in Roblox. I didn't feel like remonstrating or persuading. Frank and I were more like husband and wife, mother and father, than we had been in years. I was enjoying myself.

A wind was building outside but I could not hear it yet, only see its effect as the angle of the drops sharpened. The streetlight outside gave them life, as if they were tumbling swarms of fireflies. Our floor-to-ceiling windows were like huge screens upon which a dramatic screensaver was playing. Leaning together, Frank and I watched as rain began to spatter against the window, increasing in vigour.

'Oh I love this…' I said, recalling how I used to play recordings of thunderstorms to help me sleep. Some people recommended wave sounds, but I had found myself tensely awaiting the next wave to arrive, very much awake. But the growl of thunder, the crash of rain, all of it far away, produced a strange calm in me. The storm playing out beyond the window was similarly mesmerising.

Rain rattled against our faces reflected in the glass, like handfuls of gravel thrown by a lover below.

'Remember the squalls in the Med?' said Frank.

'The rain was always so warm, or at least I remember it

that way.'

'Ready to experience it again?' he said.

Just then the street and the sky flashed like an X-ray. There was a second of profound quiet and then an explosive rumble. I grabbed Frank's arm as the lights in the house flickered. They steadied almost immediately however, and Sinatra pressed on into *The summer wind came blowin' in from across the sea…*

Frank turned to me. 'I'm so sorry I wasn't there that night, Helen. I hope this… I don't know…atones? You know, I've been thinking a lot, and those days on the *Innisfree* were my happiest too.'

I gazed up at him. 'We are really going to have a new start, aren't we?'

Peace spread over his features. Sometimes you don't know if something is true or not until you say it. Sometimes you have to say something to make it true, or start the process of it being true.

Energy bounced along my nerves. I danced to the bedroom, singing, and lifted the photo albums from on top of the wardrobe, laying them out on the sofa. Page after page of Frank and me on the *Innisfree*.

'Muuuuuum!' Nicky's voice came from his bedroom. 'The wi-fi's gone!'

'The lightening must have knocked out the signal,' said Frank. Then louder, to Nicholas: 'Come on out, Nicky!'

My son sulkily presented himself. 'I was right in the middle of something!' he whined. The rain smashed against the window but he did not flinch. 'Can you fix it, Dad?'

Frank was poring over the albums. 'Look at these,

Nicholas. Your mum and dad on the *Innisfree*.'

Page after page of images of the sea, and the boat and the sunsets, and all the crew who had come and gone and we had lost touch with.

Nicholas gave them a quick glance. I imagined them through his eyes, and recalled the photo albums my mother had very occasionally thrust upon me. Tiny pictures of solemn people whom the 60s and 70s had passed by, and a dark-eyed baby laid on the rug in front of a gas fire, very occasionally in the arms of the solemn man. I had disliked the pictures, which seemed to cast me into a distant past. Sometimes sunlight had bleached the figures out altogether. Nicholas had countless hyper-real and 3D moving images that must make these photos seem like relics. He wasn't even in them. What kid cares about his parents before they were his parents?

He was staring at me. 'You're drunk,' he said.

'We're having a parteee,' I said, swaying over to him.

He put his arms out to push me away.

'We're celebrating!' I protested. 'Come on Nicky!'

'No!' he said, and I glimpsed in him the same exasperation his father had shown towards me. 'Why can't you be like everyone else's mum?' he went on. 'Why does it have to be *my* mum who's drunk in her pyjamas, spending all day in bed, writing letters to men!'

'Apologise to your mother!' said Frank, but it was too late. I looked at my son and all my pent-up frustration exploded.

'I've barely drunk anything in years, Nicholas! And anyway, before you set up camp on the moral high ground, why does it have to be *my* son who cheats at swimming?'

Gratification swooshed through my veins, almost knocking me over. 'I've raised a little liar and a cheat, taking medals he didn't earn!'

'When did he cheat at swimming?' asked Frank.

'I did not!' Nicholas cried fiercely.

'You're a Bell, Nicholas,' I said, pointing at him. 'One of us. I'm a bad mother, your dad is…' I had no idea why I was voicing this certainty to my son in front of Frank, but I was doing it. '…An adulterer! And you're a cheat! Hurray!'

'I hate you!' Nicholas yelled.

'Who cares?' I yelled back.

'What the hell?' cried Frank.

The window rattled in the wind and we all turned to it in silence.

'You cheated on Mum?' Nicholas asked.

Frank downed his fizz. 'No!' he said, grimacing. Then, 'Did you really cheat at swimming, Nicholas? Was it the gala?'

Nicholas shrugged, unable to confess. I giggled. I was aware I had spoiled the mood for everyone except me. It felt good to be angry, disruptive instead of perpetually smoothing everything over.

'Oh come on, you two. I'm just having a laugh.'

Father and son stared at each other then at me. Then, slippery as his father, Nicholas changed the subject. 'What about the wi-fi? On the boat?'

'No wi-fi, Nicholas,' Frank said.

Nicky gawped. 'Signal?'

'No signal either. There'll be a satellite phone for emergencies. That's it.'

'You can swim with dolphins though!' I slurred grandly.

86

'Your dad and I swam with dolphins a lot, when we were young. Your Artificial Reality headset can't beat that.'

'The thing is,' explained Frank, turning down the music. 'We're not moving house, Nicky. Or going on holiday. We're going to be together – just us – after everything that's happened. A family, away from all these terrible influences. We're going to be very happy, and your mum is going to be sober.'

'But I can escape all the bad stuff on the internet!' said Nicholas. 'I don't have to leave.'

'We're talking about real life!' I said.

'The internet *is* real, mum,' he said. 'It's as real as the sun… or the ocean.'

'Um, that's nonsense, darling,' I said. 'The internet is…just a concoction of the human brain. You'll be out exploring our planet, for real, alongside real creatures.'

It was as if we were Darwin's parents, blinking at fossils, unable to absorb their implications; or Galileo's parents, frowning at the stars, trapped by the evidence of our own eyes that the sun moved *round the earth*.

'The internet has only been around for thirty years, Nicky,' Frank sighed. 'And in its present form, about five minutes!'

'Just because it wasn't invented or discovered doesn't mean it wasn't there!' protested Nicholas. 'We've just learned how to use it. Like…fire! You're dinosaurs… You'll go extinct because you haven't adapted. It's better for me, more adaptive, to be here understanding the technology and the future than out on a boat!'

Away from questions of personal morality, Nicholas grew in confidence, on sure ground. He turned to me, as I wafted happily round the room. 'Didn't that bomb destroy your world, Mum?'

'My world, yes, but not *the* world.'

'*The* world is just a collection of individual worlds!'

'For God's sake Nicholas, have you forgotten what happened a few months ago!' cried Frank. 'That young man destroying so many lives!'

Nicholas said, 'You can't blame the internet for that!' He waved his arms round the room, taking in my photos, which now seemed flat and irrelevant, as if I'd wheeled out some daguerreotypes or lockets with little portraits. 'The internet is linking every human brain…into something bigger than them all put together. One day, the whole planet will be like one giant brain…made out of all our brains! You just don't get it — you're still analogue, and the world is quantum!'

Nicholas looked from one to the other, desperate to be understood. There was silence once more, made deeper by the howl of the wind outside. I was, in truth, stunned by how articulate Nicholas was on this. However, it is difficult to applaud the brilliance of your child when you are horrified by his vision of the future, and when you are pissed. Also, I didn't deserve to be called a dinosaur. And anyway, there was no question of him staying behind.

I said, carefully, 'Pardon me if I am wrong on this, but what you seem to be saying, Nicholas, is that if we leave you here with your computer, it will be just as real an escape as if you came with us?'

'Yes,' he said, but he sounded a little uncertain.

'I know you're very advanced and you probably do know best…but I really do think that being on the boat is an experience you will be sorry to miss. You'll learn to sail and fish and understand all about meteorology and astronomy and navigation and we can learn all kinds of other things through that. You'll be with your mum and dad, we'll be a family. Imagine – your classroom will be a sunny deck, and you can do your homework in a hammock…'

Nicholas stood unconvinced, phone in hand. The doorbell rang.

Frank went to the door, holding his glass, smile in place. I leaned against the hall bookcase watching him go.

He opened the door and stepped back. A burst of chilly wet air tumbled in.

'Sindi!' I cried.

My student shuffled awkwardly on the step. She was soaking wet. Her hair was oddly short on one side – was it *singed*? An acrid smell surrounded her. Her eyes were red-rimmed. She was wearing a grubby sweater and ripped jeans and carried no bag or coat.

At the sight of me, her face opened. Her arms went up like a toddler wanting to be lifted up, and she rushed into the hall and flung herself upon me.

'It's okay, it's okay Sindi…' I said, patting her sodden head, and raising my eyebrows at Frank over her shoulder. I could feel her heart pounding against me. Her fingers twisted themselves in my hair. She was sobbing incoherently into my neck.

'Sindi..?' I held her away from me and looked into her face. She gulped and wiped her nose.

Nicky drew possessively close to me and eyed her.

'Oh, hi,' Sindi sniffed heavily.

'This is Nicholas,' I said.

'And I'm…Frank.' Frank held out his hand.

'Hi, Mr Bell,' said Sindi. She did not even notice the proffered hand. Her arms wrapped around herself, and I realised she was shivering.

'How about a hot chocolate?' I said, leading her into the kitchen. Frank and Nicholas hovered after us. And I found myself irritated by my husband's presence, and even by Nicky's, because of the clash of worlds that now presented itself. Recently bombed dinosaur Helen, failed wife of Frank and inadequate mother of Nicholas, currently unable to get out of her nightwear, and also quite drunk, was a completely separate person from Intervention Helen, respected bearer of the miraculous pregnancy and fawn-receiving teacher. Wife Helen and Teacher Helen even moved differently, burdened by different abasements and calculations. Damn this bomb, blasting the lines that separated all my Helens!

The hiss of the barista machine drowned out an awkward silence. I handed her the foaming mug.

'There's been an accident…at…home. Clint and Donna,' she said.

'What kind of accident?' asked Frank who had followed us in, with a gawping Nicholas.

'Um…well he's got these oxygen tanks for his cancer? And he won't stop smoking and well, he was really worked up, really shouting and there must have been a spark or something and…' She gave an almost apologetic demonstration with her fingers.

'They…blew up?' I indicated that Sindi should sit down, and sat down myself.

'Well there was definitely a bang. I…left. I didn't know what else to do. I came… here. To you, Miss.'

'How did you know where we live?' asked Frank.

Sindi murmured into her chocolate foam. 'Accidentally saw your file in the school office one time.'

'Fuck me, is there no bloody privacy any more?'

'Shut up, Frank,' I snapped. To Sindi, I said, 'Are they all right? Is there a fire?'

Frank got out his phone. 'We need to call the police,' he said.

Sindi's voice grew smaller as she gazed round our kitchen.

'Please…please don't send me back there,' she said, her eyes full of appeal.

'Okay, this is what is going to happen.' I dredged my thoughts together. 'You're going to go upstairs and have a bath, and we will take care of everything, call who needs to be called. Sorry Sindi, I'm a bit drunk and a bit slow. We were celebrating.'

'Is it your birthday, Miss?'

'No. We bought a boat.' I waved my hand. 'Not important right now. Now follow me, and we will get you into a nice hot bath and take it from there.'

*

'That's the famous Sindi, then,' Frank said in the kitchen. A faint sloshing could be heard from upstairs. Sindi was in the bathtub, humming to herself.

'Yes,' I snapped. I had a headache, caused by the waning alcohol in my system and the series of phone conversations

I'd had with the police. The upshot was that Sindi was staying with us for the next few days. There had been a fire at her foster parents' flat, swiftly attended by the fire brigade, and Clint and Donna were in hospital.

Frank had carried on drinking throughout this, and now he was in a bad mood.

'It's like she owned you or something, just flinging herself on you like that.'

'She's got nowhere else to go! Actually I'm flattered she thought of me. Still remembers me.'

'Don't you think her story is weird? Oxygen tanks and him smoking? I don't buy it.'

'She's fifteen years old, Frank. And traumatised. She probably isn't the best at explaining herself right now.'

'I'm just saying. I mean how is it your problem? You took sick leave three months ago.'

'Frank, keep your voice down! You have no idea what that girl's gone through! Her mother *killed herself*. Can you imagine?'

I leant over the table to hiss the potted version of Sindi's tragedy to my husband. 'Her dad died in some kind of drug fight thing. Those two, Clint and Donna, fostered her, but they fucking hate her! I hate them too. Clint called her a fucking slag in front of me at parents' night...'

'Whoa, steady!' Frank held up his hands. 'I'm just saying, we may not be the right people for this job. It needs professionals.'

'You and professionals! What happened to kindness?'

Nicholas appeared in the kitchen, drawn from his gaming. He was more animated than I had seen him in a long time.

For the first time in ages he didn't seem to want to go to someone else's house or disappear into his room.

'How long is she staying?' he asked.

'A few days,' Frank and I said, in unison.

9

MY CHRYSALIS PERIOD WAS, at last, drawing to a close, in that the sweaty, wriggling, wet-faced preverbal thing that had wrestled with itself for so long in the dark seemed to have solidified and reached a conclusion. A new me, post-bomb, post-catastrophe, was finally emerging. Sadly, that unfolding creature was a highly developed, nuanced and shimmering liar. I was, with every step I took and word I spoke, lying, as my mother used to say, through my back teeth. Barefaced lying to my husband and to my child about my whereabouts, my feelings and my secret, shameful inner life. I was sorely disappointed to discover that this seemed to be my core personality, the kind revealed by Alzheimer's or hallucinogenic drugs. Don't we all hope we are more than this, when stripped back to our essential selves? Like we all wish to be the happy drunk, and hope we would join the resistance rather than collaborate? How ashamed I was that, when the innocence draped over me was swept away, this was the sculpture beneath. I was fake, empty, as lacking in substance as an avatar. But no one seemed to notice. My improvement was cheered by all.

Frank was back in the marital bed, where lies were both hardest to maintain and most deeply entrenched. I was the one to take my husband's hand as he placidly arranged the sofa, saying to him, *come to bed*. Men as big as Frank do not thrive on sofas. They wake scrunched and crumpled and, despite their best efforts, become surly. It was not as if I was sleeping soundly without him. I was easing off my medication. There was a momentum to my recovery, I could feel it.

What had once been a comfort, Frank's solid presence beside me, now seemed vast and indifferent, like the lichen-covered memorial stones upon the Victorian dead in the cemetery nearby, their names long worn away. I lay like a slab beside him, the room shaking at each bang of my heart. How could Frank not hear it?

Second after second that *should have been hers*... My heart thumped its fist upon its pulpit. The baby did not even have a grave, for she did not live long enough to achieve personhood and therefore memorial status. She was cremated – or rather incinerated – as hospital waste. Her non-life was coughed out of the hospital chimney, too small even to make an impact as ash. Puff! Waiting on the precipice of each beat, I longed for my heart to stop, for this place of conception to be where I might finally rest. And then, when the beat came, my blood flooded me with shame, that I should feel so, when I had so much to live for. *So much*. Why could I not forget?

In preparation for the renewal of my marriage, I cleared away my letters to James. I did not throw them away, of course, just hid them in a drawer beneath my thickest jumpers, as if to muffle their desperate longings. I confined myself to writing them when I was alone, and did not leave them out where they could disturb anyone. I did understand they were not helping, I did understand that. The bedroom must be returned to us – Frank and me; it had to be, we were *husband* and *wife*, *father* and *mother*, and this was the temple of that truth. It was practice and remembrance for the intimacy we would share on the *Innisfree*. What made sense was Frank smiling and throwing the sofa cushion over his shoulder as he followed me upstairs.

Frank had pictures on his phone of the *Innisfree* beginning her renovations and we scrolled through them in bed. Together we recalled our times aboard her, the spot where we had sneaked a first kiss on night watch; the forepeak cabin where we had first slept together. In these times in bed together I was able to glimpse an existence bigger than the immediate devouring past. It was as if our talk of the ocean and of our forthcoming escape into it swirled over the rocks I had been strewn upon, covering them with brand new blue. Although I wasn't ready to go the boatyard to see her yet, despite Frank's promptings, the time was coming soon when I could face the *Innisfree* broken because I would be able to visualise her as healed.

In the meantime, I was taking part as energetically as I could. By day I pored over my photographs for details to give Frank. In group shots of us smiling and tanned, I scrutinised the equipment at the edge of the shot, the colours of the paintwork. Sometimes I ended up gazing at a photo for a long time, lost in the memory it provoked. In one, of Frank on deck with his arm around Corin, laughing, I was accidentally included in the corner. Across the years and the fading of the image I saw the love in my expression towards my new husband. Love untainted by experience. Around us, the kindly embrace of the *Innisfree*. Behind us, the timeless blue of the sea with the distant islands, now faded to white by my poor storage of these photos. Additionally, I camped online buying items and sending them to the boatyard. The marital bed was transformed into an office, and Frank would video-call me with questions or things he found. I was, as I explained to Frank, gathering my energy to participate fully, in person. In the meantime I was finding my niche, doing what I could.

After our gentle interludes together in bed, Frank kissed me and rolled away and left me to my pounding, sleepless night, as roiling as any night of passion. I wondered how long this could go on, this chaste soothing. This is not how a man and wife are. It was not how we were on the *Innisfree*.

At last, when I judged the moment right I rested my hand on his arm to stop him rolling away. It was time for us to operate correctly with one another. He smiled and embraced me.

But in that moment, I slammed against the lie that now constituted me, the lie whose substance was unutterable, but was as unforgiving as a crag beneath the surf. The lamplit room reverberated like a crowded town square, condemning me. My husband kissed me and, in the chamber our kiss created, the voices multiplied.

Frank lifted away from me.

'You're still thinking about him, aren't you?'

'Who?'

But as I spoke I realised that the fact that neither of us needed to utter his name confirmed James absolutely as right there, centre stage.

'If you aren't in the mood, you only had to say.' I rolled over and put my back to him, blinking in the glow of the lamp.

'It's going to scupper our chances, Helen. If you can't get over it… *Him*.'

'He's on your mind, not mine!' I wrenched myself to face him. My nightdress was awry and my face burned.

'If you were really over him you'd throw away the letters.'

'You snooped through my stuff?'

'No…not snooping. Well, all right then, yes, when I was wondering what had happened to all the letters my deeply depressed wife was scrawling and leaving everywhere declaring her passion for another man, and I thought I'd take a look, so that when we talked about it I'd be informed and I'd say the right thing—'

'I can't believe you did that!' The old fury was returning, creaking through my bones like a coffin lid being raised. I dreaded it, my helplessness in the face of my own anger. Why didn't he stop, why didn't he just let me do what I had to do?

'Take the plank out of your own eye, Frank,' I said. 'I've been doing some thinking of my own and I know what you were up to on the night of the bomb. But you don't see me banging on at you for an explanation, do you? You hypocrite.'

I was pleased with my deflection. Even in the midst of a

battle for possession of your very soul, you can still admire a decisive parry. I glared at my husband, and enjoyed his discomfort. 'You're the one who's not really here,' I went on. 'You haven't been – for a long time.'

'What are you talking about? I got us the *Innisfree*!'

I shrugged. 'Yeah well. My baby died but I didn't kill myself. I think I win the commitment stakes.'

I braced myself for fury. Instead his voice was quite small. 'I *was* seeing Ruth that night. But as a client. You have to understand, you must understand what I'm saying – her latest pictures are astounding. I mean, game-changing. They're going to get us that deal. But…' Here he rubbed his forehead sadly, his face softening to the way I imagined it was when he was alone, thinking about this. 'But *even so* – I am leaving it all behind. Her pictures. The agency. For *us*.'

'You're in love with her, aren't you?'

Under the duvet, my feet wriggled towards each other as if for comfort. My clever deflection had backfired.

Frank looked at me, making no attempt to hide his sorrow. 'Nothing's enough for you, is it?' he said.

It was far worse than if he had just said 'yes'. He was so in love with her – this fabulous photographer – that leaving her was an almost unbearable wrench. I began to cry. He didn't reach out to comfort me.

I was aware that what I was going to say next was unconnected to what had gone before. It was a truth from underneath, somehow, like a deer that bolts across the road in the beam of the headlamps, and you realise later, afterwards, *that* was what caused it all—

'The *baby*. I feel her *all the time*, around me, here in the

99

bed. All the time. I look at you and I think of her. It's terrible. I can't make it stop.'

He said softly, 'I know … In the silence that followed, where I rubbed the lace edge of my nightdress between my fingers and wept, I could tell he didn't know what to say, how much to say, that I was at the limit of what kindness my husband could offer me. For he had, to his mind, already made his sacrifice and his magnificent gesture, neither of which had proved to be enough.

Finally he said, 'There's a kind of hope she took away, isn't there? I…wanted to bring it back. I am willing to do anything, give up *anything*…' and here he looked me in the eyes and squeezed my hand. 'But I've failed, haven't I? And if I can't, I don't know what to do.'

We were holding hands on the rumpled bed. It was the first time since it had happened that we had admitted our feelings of helplessness to each other. Was it a distance between us, or was it a kind of growing up, that made me suddenly feel sorry for my husband, to grasp for a fleeting moment what he had done to try and save our marriage? But also to see how, finally, to gain an advantage in our remorseless negotiation?

'I want Sindi to come with us on the trip.'

'What? Why?'

'I'm really fond of her. And she doesn't have anywhere to go. We can't abandon her. A leg or two of it at least. Nicholas wants her to, as well, as it happens.'

Frank sighed. 'I want James out of our lives,' he countered.

'Agreed.' I knew what I had to do.

I sprang eagerly to the task. Isn't that true freedom? The

only possible freedom for mortals on this earth? Desire aligning with duty, so that they cannot be told apart?

I went to the drawer and I dragged my jumpers out onto the floor. I scooped up my letters to James in a great armful, new tears springing to my eyes as I realised I was cradling them. Even though I had almost stopped writing them, there were many, many more than I could hold. 'Help me,' I said over my shoulder, and Frank appeared at my side. He piled the rest into a dressing gown open on the floor.

'What now?' he asked.

'Bin.'

He followed me as I went downstairs and we pressed the lot into the paper recycling. I eyed them scrabbling at the sides, full to bursting with strange life. I scrunched up the ones that poked out, as if they were rats and I was wringing their necks. It didn't seem enough. I'd have liked to burn them, or shred them, but this would have to do. Still, they made me uneasy. I heard them creaking together inside the bin.

'They're like zombies,' I said to Frank. And it was true that they were not truly dead and gone; it troubled me that they were there, still rescuable, still crying out with all their unmediated pain and need. I pressed the lid down hard and scoured the passageway for something heavy to put on top. Seeing the tool box buried in dust in the corner, I wrestled it on top. It was heavy and left a smear of dusty cobwebs down my front.

Frank looked puzzled at my fervour, but as we returned to the bedroom, he stopped on the landing, turned me to him and said, 'Thank you for doing that.'

'Fair's fair,' I said, and reached my arms around his neck

and kissed him. My jumpers looked desolate on the floor, as if they'd held armfuls of birds that had flown away. Frank lifted me away from them and laid me on the bed.

Beneath him, I gorged on relief, on the ecstasy of having no secret. But then I realised that Frank's hands upon me, which I sought, which I pressed against, and which I wanted, were making me feel cold.

'Is it a betrayal?' I whispered. 'Of the baby…to do this again, without her?'

My husband took on the thoughtful look I remembered from when we were young. Frank had always been a ponderer, his eyes would squint as if trying to see the problem at a more granular level. It made him look like he needed glasses.

'We are husband and wife,' he said. 'Adults…*parents*… Carry on. I think she would agree.'

I nodded. Weariness swept over me.

'And remember everything that's coming, darling. Just wait till you see the *Innisfree*.'

There was just one last unutterable truth that hovered at my lips: *It's over between us.*

I pressed it fiercely away against his mouth. No no no. Look what we have sacrificed for each other. Look, look, we have proven how love can survive anything. The husband knows the wife, he knows how to comfort her, he promised to do this, to *comfort*, and he has fulfilled the promise. And the wife, she too made promises: *all that I am I give to you.* She lifts the nightdress so that the husband can reach her, there is no barrier between them any more.

Except for my own rigid numbness, inside my skin. How strange it was that I should urge my husband to take me to bed, and now that he had, and our secrets were out and the letters were gone, I felt absolutely no desire at all. Just do it, voices caroused in my head. Just do it until you feel like it. The act of doing will make you want to do it. Lying gets easier the more you do it. One day you will evolve into the most perfect liar you can be.

But the cold was spreading, it was starting to turn into repulsion. Frank would detect it. How could he not, when I flinched at his touch. My movements against him were now to try to carve out breathing space, a gap between us; a pause in which he might agree to stop because I wasn't ready, I just wasn't ready for this—

'Helen,' he whispered. 'Stay with me.'

The image of James swept over me, his face close to mine in the tunnel, as he tried to keep me in my life. I so wanted to exit that life, because I knew it was over—

Helen, he had said, *stay with me*.

He saved my sorry little life.

It wasn't a sorry little life to him.

A wave of feeling, sharpening inside me, like fear. *James* unpeeled me from my numbness, painfully unpeeling me from the inside.

I bit my lip to stop myself crying his name.

Frank felt my response. He kissed the tears from my eyes and whispered how much he loved me.

'I thought I'd lost you,' Frank said. 'I thought…'

10

It was two weeks after my reconciliation with Frank and the morning of Sindi's sixteenth birthday. We were having a little party before school and before Frank left for work. We were all in the kitchen. On the table was a magnificent, intervention-worthy cake pierced with sixteen candles. Before it sat Sindi in her nightdress, delight suffusing her bleary features, and beside her stood Nicholas, gazing in little-boy wonder at this glamorous new addition to the family. Beside the cake sat two wrapped gifts.

It was important to mark Sindi's turning sixteen, because this meant she now had some say in where she lived. Her foster parents, who had demonstrated their unsuitability to care for her by blowing up their sitting room, also never wanted to see her again. Clint was in a coma now: cancer, shock and smoke inhalation had done for him. Donna was grimly by his side at the hospital, job abandoned. Which left residential care – and us. For of course Sindi had not just stayed for a few days. She had moved in. She had asked just once what would happen to her when we all went to sea, and my answer, that we would find another foster family, so appalled us both that we each began to cry. Frank had crushed the idea of her coming with us so absolutely at first that it had been dropped until I insisted on it, trading in James.

Sindi reached out and ruffled Nicholas's hair, and my little boy flushed bright red.

Bless you, Sindi, I thought. I moved the cake closer to her and the burning candles sent soft shadows over her face. How I loved her, how perfectly she fitted in; her wrongness our wrongness. She belonged with us.

Happy Birthday to you! Sindi's lips parted impatiently waiting for us to finish so she could blow them out. The moment we started on *hip hip! hooray!* she found surprising depths of puff and extinguished them all.

'Have you made a wish?' Nicholas asked.

'I'm not telling you,' Sindi said.

While Nicholas carved the cake into massive slabs, Sindi unwrapped the smaller of the two gifts, which was a packet of twenty Embassy Regals. She could smoke legally now, so there seemed no point fighting her habit.

'Promise I'll only smoke outside,' she grinned.

She pulled the paper from the second parcel with a gasp. It was a new phone. This had been Frank's idea.

'It's got a great camera,' he said, pointing out the lenses front and back. 'I can show you how to use it if you're stuck.'

Sindi turned the phone mutely in her hands. The humiliating fact was that Clint and Donna had not provided her with a phone at all, either because of cost or indifference. Of all the injustices in Sindi's short life, this was the one Frank homed in on. 'It's not normal for a kid her age to be without a phone,' he'd said. 'I can get a good one through work at a big discount.'

Sindi never asked about the *Innisfree*. She was bright enough to know when she was beaten. As Nicholas dished up our slices of birthday cake, and Frank poured out glasses of Coke to toast Sindi, she smiled round at us all.

'I have an announcement to make, or, rather, an invitation to extend,' said Frank. I was surprised by how much my promise to relinquish James had cheered my husband up. 'Sindi, we would love it if you would join us on our trip on the *Innisfree*.'

'What?' Sindi stared at him, her mouth falling softly open.

'What?' said Nicholas, joy splitting his face.

'Really? Oh my god. You know what – I literally just wished for that! I would love that. I would love that. Do you mean it, Miss?' She rushed round the table to hug me. 'Thank you, *thank you*,' she said into my hair. She said to Frank over my shoulder, 'Will you teach me to sail? Oh my god, I can't believe it!'

'We'll all go and see her in the boatyard this afternoon,' Frank said. He was basking in the adulation that comes when you simply give people what they want. Nicholas wrapped his arms round his father's waist, grinning happily. The kitchen rang with chatter. Tears filled my eyes. This was what a happy family should look like. But even as we all laughingly re-orientated ourselves so we could have a group hug, and Frank and I fielded excited questions from Sindi and Nicholas about the *Innisfree*, I was impatient for them all to go so I could get on with my demanding parallel career of finding James. For of course I had lied. In fact my efforts had escalated. They involved notebooks now instead of letters, and a Walter Mitty-like disappearance from the house during school hours. Though I hated myself, nothing on this earth could divert me from what was both my sickness and my salvation – James.

*

Today I found myself loitering beside an entrance to London Bridge Underground Station. The station had reopened a few weeks ago, and although I knew I could never go down there again, never even go on the Underground again, perhaps James did not have the same fear. He had told me he was going to catch my train, because he was going into King's Cross. I had guessed from this that he lived somewhere near London Bridge, perhaps in one of these smart apartment blocks with their walls of glass. Perhaps he lived in a shiny penthouse bachelor pad overlooking the river. Sometimes I simply picked a street and waited on it, scanning the crowds, but today, now that the station was open, I gravitated towards the Tube entrance.

How strange that all these people, despite their haste, were not running, nor were they screaming. They were *hurrying*. Each of them was a separate person, expressing their singularity, despite the crowd, in the acceptable margin of air around them. How could that be? How did they not explode those flimsy boundaries of jacket, of skin? How was their fear contained?

How strange it was that the flow of humanity closed over any disaster, rendering it like a sunken wreck that soon no one, except historians, would even remember. I loved this about the city, even as I stood outside the flow, unable to forget, unable to move on.

Of course I was panicking. Crowds made me panic. Desperately I dredged up Romy's advice for controlling myself: observe your breath, one…two…one…two. Instead of chewing on my pearl, which I knew now was unacceptable, I added a second strip of nicotine chewing gum to the strip I already had in my cheek. The nicotine gave me a hit of energy that could not be smelled on me later; the gum gave my face something to do that wasn't scowling or mumbling. I thought of cud-chewing; of cows who did not question their lot. I could move my jaws from side to side or up and down, or not at all, and no one would know that manipulating this filthy stuff in my mouth was like speaking, all the speaking I could not do.

I needed coffee. But if I turned away from the rush-hour flood, that would be when James made his appearance. London Bridge Underground has several entrances, and the immutable fact was that by standing at this one, he would, if using this station, be *caused* to go to another. This was the problem with reality in the aftermath of a devastating event. The parallel worlds, the alternate universes, the dead, the vanished, appeared alongside normal existence. I was reminded of Nicholas and his spirited defence of the internet's physical reality. Of course there was something in it. I was living at the same strange edges as he was. I was no longer simply a particle of life, conscious only of travelling its own path. I was a nexus. Realities splintered from me, like light through a prism. Or, like a lump of ancient exploded matter from the far reaches of the universe and plunged into a river, reality broke around me like white water. Perhaps, I thought, as nicotine shocked my palate, lying is the only response to that. Honesty requires adherence to one truth. And this fountain of humanity from the Underground demonstrated the impossibility of that.

It takes courage – real courage, the kind no one ever knows about – to turn away and cross the road to Borough Market, knowing that I would, by this action, cause our paths to diverge. But I knew now, with the certainty of a scientist with a controlled, peer-reviewed evidence base, that in the face of many realities, one must continue as though there is only one path, operating independently of anything I might do. This required a letting-go of everything I needed to survive a single second more. The terror of this did not make it past my Herculean mastication to disrupt my calm exterior. Were there any justice in this world or the next, I would be beatified.

There was a little coffee shop within the market that I'd begun to frequent. To get to it I took a circuitous route that took me past the fish stall. That blast of sea-breath, the rows and rows of silvery bodies, their eyes gleaming. This was my childhood laid out; often my mother had sent me down to the dock to help unload the fish, already packed in ice in massive crates. My father drenched in scales, grinning at me from the dockside, pointing here and there where I could help stack, or come by with a bucket for rejects. I was a pilgrim even then, pacing my day along the slimy dockside, immune to the smell and the sheer numberless dead; whole cities of ghosts.

Fish shone with meaning for me. They were valuable. They took my father away, but they brought him back, happy. They taught me everything I needed to know – about pacing, about waiting, about how to be the one who is forever on the harbour-side. How to be the wrong creature, in the wrong place. Fish were so undignified. In their lack of dignity, each and every one was magnificent.

'What can I get you, pet?'

It was early still, not really the time for buying fish. The fishmonger had a beard and a hoop earring like a pirate. We recognised each other; I came here often enough for that. Sometimes I bought something: a pollock, whose dim expression seemed to demonstrate its surprise at suddenly being the species to ascend to the light; occasionally some crabs. I didn't like to eat fish perhaps as much as a fisherman's daughter should. It always felt like eating the stock.

'What would you recommend?'

'Oh the langoustines, most definitely. Fresh in today. Just off the coast there. The langoustines. Ten?'

'Okay,' I said, and wondered how I would fit them in my bag, but I was feeble in the face of any reminder of those days, no matter how slight. He nodded and wrapped them up, and said, 'Till next time, pet,' and I moved slowly past the shop. I missed my father then, or I remembered missing him, which is much the same, and I remembered how much

I loved him, and how helpless my love was in the face of the sea.

'Small, black Americano!' squeaked a hairy young man in the coffee shop, touchingly free of indifference. His eyes scanned the cluster of us at the end of the bar. 'For Jane!'

I nodded, confirming my coffee-buying identity. I took the mug, trembling so hard that the coffee sloshed against the rim. At a high stool at the window, I took out my notebook, in which were impressively laid out my rendition of the Tube map and my careful street maps, showing where I had waited, with sketches of things and people I saw while I did so. I hadn't intended to draw the Tube map, but as I had waited here and also by King's Cross, I found myself thinking of the stations in between. Might he go to one of them? I spent whole days at some of those entrances. What started to happen was that the possible stops for James began to multiply in my mind. I researched which stations had vents, in case he would be minded to visit them. And so it evolved, my own strange Tube map that was all about James, all about where I might find such a man as James.

In these idle moments between waits, I let the details of him fill my head. His clothes, for instance. I recalled vividly my face crushed against a wool sweater, its colour impossible to discern in the dark. The fibres seemed to contain oxygen as I gasped against them. The sweater smelled of lemons, even through the smoke. Running my nail over my immaculately straight rendition of the Central Line, I remembered that. My eyes brimmed as if a lemon had been cut before me.

My coffee encountered my chewing gum and the ensuing bitterness almost made me retch. I slipped the gum out, pressed it absently under the bench. My new project was all-encompassing and full of colour and creativity, lacking only the teacher to give me a gold star. My next move would be to describe him to taxi drivers in case anyone remembered picking him up. It was hopeless, but what else could I do? I couldn't explain anything at this time. I had no words for what I was doing; the pointlessness of it, and the necessity of it. I was an explanation-free zone. Zone 9¾. Going nowhere. Lines I would never take again, to find a person I would never see again. That thought, that I might never see James again, was not one I could look at squarely. I had to see him again. I could not envisage a life where I did not.

My wonderful rendition of stations and routes rivalled the diagrammatic brilliance of the Underground map. I considered having it printed. Framed. But then it would require explanation at home. And I knew, even without Romy's *feelingsarenotfacts*, that it could not be properly explained at home. It is impossible to inhabit your madness fully when you have a family. It remains tightly confined by the inquiring gaze of your child. It whirls faster and faster, unable to resolve, like a rat on a wheel. At home I would abandon myself to lies and sanity. Here, with my notebook, I pursued the truth at all costs.

A woman with a buggy burst into the tiny aisle, bumping into my high stool. There were squeals, apologies; marshmallows toppled from an enormous hot-chocolate confection in the hands of her muscly toddler railing against his straps.

'*Give it a rest!*' she hissed at the toddler, who glowered toothlessly.

'Please, sit here. I have to go anyway.' I gathered up my things, under her desperate gaze. 'Have to be somewhere....'

How easy it is to slip away when you are unencumbered. All I had was a notebook, its mad pages, a bag with fish in it. I waved myself out of the shop, towards my waiting place.

At the zebra crossing, my phone rang. It was Frank, excited. 'Where are you?' Of course – we were all going to the *Innisfree* today. I'd slipped out for a couple of hours, and now I realised I'd been gone all day.

'I forgot the time. I'm coming back now.'

He sounded surprised at the normality, the ease with which I seemed to be moving around. I was still fragile according to current orthodoxy.

'Do you want me to meet you?'

'No, really. I'm not far. I'll be along.'

And I was quite happily turning back, with a new acceptance of my hopeless situation, that had been gifted to me anew in some way that I didn't quite understand, when a waft of lemon touched me. For a fragment of a second I continued: revelation travels only at the speed of pain after all. I had a vast nanosecond in which a whole future wavered, and in it I continued towards the bus stop, with my notebook tucked away and a thought of Nicholas and Sindi and their joy that morning at breakfast. My continuance was heroic in its momentum – I was able to imagine, down to the finest detail, a time when I didn't do this, when I could live with the isolation that is the price of survival.

But then, the smell of lemons, and every fibre of my shrivelled heart opened and vibrated with pure feeling, like a cello. I stopped and gently spun with the grace of a ballerina

(I was sure of it). In that moment I was whole, I was perfect, because for all its multifarious pain, my world – the mad one with its relentless pursuit of the utterly impossible – was proven to be the real one – the world in which James came back to me and I wasn't alone any more.

11

WE WERE STANDING on the zebra crossing, facing each other. How had we come to be like that? I had no recollection of stepping onto the crossing, nor of time passing.

'James!'

Glee romped through me. I forgot my scribblings and the langoustines sweating in my bag. I gave no thought to the bomb, or the baby, or the traffic nudging the edge of the crossing. This is the magic of the city. This can happen. It happens every day. You can be blown up on the Underground, or bump into the person you have been longing for.

My fingernails fizzed in their cuticles, eyelashes rattling in their follicles. My eyebrows threatened to lift off my face. He caught my hands. We stepped in unison – I'm sure we did – clumsy as teenagers, able only to peep at each other sidelong.

'Helen!' he said, and, ignoring any etiquette or grace to our meeting, I barrelled into his arms.

There was a moment of pure rest, where I felt the soft lemony wool on my cheek. The moment rocked me, like a boat in a misty dawn. Once, my father took us on holiday to the Hebrides to show me a place he loved from his own childhood, a place where the Gulf Stream deposits its scavengings from the bottom of the sea for miles upon the shore. On the only walk we ever took alone together, he led me for many miles through the close-cropped boulders to a headland. And there, when I looked up wearily from my boots, an astonishing beach of tropical shells was laid out, glittering and private as though it had fallen from space. The exquisite peace of that moment returned to me now, in James's arms.

People were jostling us. The bumper of a car was now about six inches from my thigh.

'Let's get a coffee,' he said. 'Do you have time?'

I nodded. I had time. The brimming notebook and the langoustines attested to the time I had.

*

We laid our hands out on the coffee shop table as if we were comparing features, as if we were related, long lost. Neither pair was in good shape.

'Anti-depressants. Sedatives. Puffed up like a balloon,' I said.

'*Itchy*. Nails bleeding. Can't stop chewing.'

'I sleep at the drop of a hat,' I said. 'But it's like death, like tunnels.'

'No sleep.' He pointed to the shadows behind his glasses. 'I rang the hospital. They wouldn't tell me anything, or let me in. Not next of kin.'

'You tried to find me?'

'I rang every day. Why didn't you contact me, Helen?'

'You vanished. You weren't in the paper; nothing!'

'I wrote my number down and put it in your pocket!' he said. 'With a J, so you'd know it was me! I made sure the ambulance guys had you and then I got the hell out of there. It was chaos, easy enough to give a false name and slip away. The thing is, Helen, I knew how it would all go down, the endless raking over it all. Once I knew you were safe, I didn't want to be part of it. When you didn't call me, I started on the hospitals. Then I saw the mention of…a baby in the paper and figured out what had happened. I guessed you had decided not to get in touch.'

'I've thought of you every day. Every minute,' I said. 'There was a box they gave me when I left the hospital. With my clothes and an ultrasound. I threw it away. Your note was in there, I suppose.'

His itchy hand slid to my puffed hand.

'The baby…was a girl,' I said.

There are stock responses to the news of a dead baby. *I'm sorry. I'm so sorry.* Fear flashes over people's face that they will fail, somehow, to show the appropriate anguish. I never judged them for it, for I suffered from it in relation to myself. My flat, comfortless tone. My shoulders stiff, my face alabaster.

'Helen, not a day goes by when I don't wish I had got to you sooner.'

'It's all right,' I mumbled, as if he were apologising for being late for an appointment.

'No, it's not all right. I had a moment's hesitation. I didn't know if I could get you out at all. I thought maybe I should just run. I stood there. Perhaps those seconds would have made the difference for your baby—'

'Don't say that.'

'I have to. There can be no silence between us, Helen. Nothing that we have not said. Can you forgive me? I would understand if you can't.'

A waiter in a shiny black shirt delivered two enormous coffees, piled with cream and sprinkled with chocolate and cinnamon. Despite ourselves, we grinned like children and each tipped sachets of sugar in.

I said, calmly and with certainty, 'James there is nothing to forgive you for. You gave my baby the only real chance she had.'

His eyes reddened, and he ran a hand through his hair.

'Thank you,' he whispered.

We spooned cinnamon cream with our long spoons.

'I'm starving,' he said, devouring his accompanying biscuit in one bite.

'Me too,' I said. 'But my teeth don't work. Like I've regressed. Only gooey stuff, sweet things…'

'Sugar puffs,' he said. 'Remember those? Bulk-buying them now.'

'But are you hurt?' I said, sitting back, looking at him.

'Deaf in one ear. Eczema all over my body.' He shrugged. 'Nothing, really. I'm back at work. Somehow keeping on the straight and narrow. Sort of.'

'Which ear?' I said. My hand rolled next to his hand, sunning itself in the joy of proximity.

'Left,' he said. 'Music's not quite the same to listen to, but it's nothing in the grand scheme, is it? Do you have people telling you how lucky you are all the time? To be alive?'

I rolled my eyes.

'I feel it now, though,' he said. 'Lucky to be alive, that is.'

'How did you get me out? I don't remember anything after being in the vent.'

'Oh, it wasn't too hard,' he smiled. 'I crawled up there and yelled until someone heard me. The top bit was all enclosed. We had to get wire cutters from the fire brigade. The ambulance guys were nearby and they sent someone down and between us we pulled and pushed you up. Then they used the vent to get to others. You were out cold. I was glad you were. You were very brave in there, Helen.'

The James of my imagination had finished coalescing from fragments and was now real in front of me. He was a little older than I'd thought. Long eyelashes. Dark hair, greying at the temples. He smiled at me, shyly, and then my hand and his twitched toward each other, like animated shrapnel. With a magnetic leap, they snapped together, snug as two lost jigsaw pieces.

I knew I could tell James anything, and that I must, because time was short.

'I need to show you something,' I said, reaching into my bag. My notebook. 'There were letters too,' I said. 'And a lot of text messages.'

He opened the book up, carefully. He studied a page, with its lists (whose neatness I was proud of), and the first map.

I blushed furiously. I was possessed by opposing feelings, like a current opposing a wind and producing rogue waves. My maps pleased me. My lists pleased me. My absolute dedication was sublime. But these maps and lists served no purpose. I was, in this regard, a disgrace.

My phone was ringing. I was late for the boat appointment. I reached down and, with deliberate pleasure, turned it off.

James turned the pages very slowly.

'Helen, these are beautiful.'

'There were letters too… I…threw them away. My husband, my husband…'

Itchy hand over puffed hand. 'You did this for me?'

I nodded.

'Funny you should have. I did this.'

He unzipped the laptop, set it before himself. His inflamed fingers tapped with abandon. He tilted it round, expanding the image which was an incomprehensibly intricate diagram consisting of tiny dots, lines and numbers. He pointed to a dot at the top left of the screen. 'Rho Oph J162249.8-243838,' he read. Then he smiled at me. 'Or, *Helen*.'

I pulled the screen to me. 'What's this?'

'It's what's known as a Young Stellar Object. This whole nebula is a star nursery – you've heard of those? – where stars are created. I'm into all this; sorry. Matter is created out of the mass of dust, and then flung out to begin its life as planets and stars.'

'You named a star after me?'

'Well, I had to do something. A bit like you and your maps, I guess. I knew you were out there somewhere, possibly looking at the same sky as me. It's pretty easy. You can just do it via a website. But I know a bit about it so I could really get into choosing the right star. I'm a bit of a nerd. I spent a bit of time…' He bit his lip thoughtfully and tapped some more. 'How about this one for…your baby? What's her name?'

'Cariad.'

'That's unusual.'

'It means beloved, in Welsh.'

He turned the screen back to me. This time there were great swirls of orange, blue and purple. 'This is the whole nebula. Isn't it beautiful? Your star, Helen, is over on this ring here. And Cariad, this star, next to you. Over the next billions of years you'll move out together to begin your own constellation.'

'You can do that? Really name them?'

'No problem.' He tapped some more. 'It's done.'

*

'Are you afraid of the Tube now?' I asked him. 'I haven't been down since. I don't know if I will ever be able to.'

'Well you know, statistically, after an attack it's the safest place to be. That doesn't help, I know.'

Our second huge coffee was nearly finished. I was scrabbling for topics to keep us here, to defy time. I was so late for the appointment. I didn't know how to say, 'I have a family and we are taking a boat that my husband and I used to love out onto the ocean and we are going to sail away from all this. I'm leaving and I don't think I will be back.'

So, I just said it. The words as they were in my brain. Blunt. Plain. As if I were alone. And then I found that I added, 'I do not want to go.'

Itchy hand, swollen hand. 'Let's do it now,' he said.

'Do what?'

'Take the underground. The station's right there.'

*

Outside now, we were face to face on the pavement, exactly as we had been when we'd met earlier.

'What are you talking about? I can't.'

His fingers around mine grew warmer and more certain as I shook my head. Terror and recklessness converged inside me.

'What if I panic… What if…?'

'I'm here.'

'What if the train breaks down or…or…'

He interrupted by lifting my hand to his mouth and kissing the pearl of my engagement ring.

He said, 'I was there, remember? You were chomping on this thing like it was a gobstopper.'

'I've been told not to do that any more,' I mumbled. 'It's disgusting. Frank doesn't like it.'

'That doesn't matter now,' said James.

*

The tunnel clawed people pitilessly down its dark throat, spat others out into the light. My teeth chattered as if I had fallen into the river and every muscle was trying to save itself.

'What…if it happens again…and we can't escape…?'

'Then...we will join your baby, wherever she is, won't we?'

I understood then that my heart was cut in half between the living and the dead. And more, my foot lowering onto the first step showed me that in this moment I was willing to give up the living for the dead. James was beside me as this truth unrolled over us both. I straightened myself and took a deep breath.

James said, 'Try not to think about it. We jump on the train, then we see where we are. Okay?'

And then we were running, down the steps, down the escalators, pounding with a speed and exhilaration that brought to mind, for a second, being young, when running was for itself, not an attempt to outrun a nightmare.

On the concourse we paused for breath. 'How about the Jubilee?' James said. 'The train you were supposed to get! And they've got those nice sliding doors on the platform.'

Parting briefly to press our cards to the barriers, we set off again. People blurred around us, our footsteps mingled with the melancholy words of the busker growling 'Suzanne', and it seemed we were swirling in an invisible current down, down. A train pulled in as we swept deeper, and we leapt straight onto it. The carriage had just a couple of people in it who sank behind their papers as we plonked ourselves breathlessly down.

'Where are we going?' I asked, scanning the map of the network above the window opposite me.

'Stratford... You realise between London Bridge and there we zigzag under the Thames twice? We are deep down, Helen.' James smiled at me. 'Think you can do six stops and back?'

Blood beat in my skin. My hand in James's was slippery with sweat. The air was heavy and stale, and I was sure I could taste smoke and darkness buried inside it, but perhaps I always would. The doors sealed shut and I thought of the vast torso of the river writhing above us like a corporeal sky, the whole of existence inverted. I said, 'Frank will have called the police by now. They must think I'm dead.'

'Don't worry about that. You had to make an emergency visit to Stratford. We'll be under your boat soon!'

At Canada Water, a neon-clad group of police offers got on. It was hard to differentiate them as separate people. They stared as one around the almost-empty carriage.

'You all right, madam?' one of them asked.

'Yes, fine,' I said. Didn't I look all right?

'Where are you headed?' another asked. 'You know we're still on high alert, don't you?'

'Stratford,' I said.

'Stratford *and back*,' James added. 'We're survivors of the bomb, Officer. We're trying to overcome her fear of the Underground.'

The PC came closer and I saw that he was very young, even allowing for the feature of middle age that suddenly everyone was young. He leaned over us, hanging onto the rail above. He seemed almost Sindi-young, though packed in a huge, reinforced body.

'We lost colleagues that night. I came on duty right after. Posted outside to bring up the bodies. Never seen anything like it. Will never forget it.'

'Don't start, Pete,' said the first officer gently.

'You've got the look,' he went on. 'Pale and sweaty. Survivor panic. Survivor guilt. But we have to keep on going, don't we?'

'We do,' said James.

Not far away, Frank, Nicholas and Sindi were all wondering where I was, and yet I was here, underneath them.

The officer turned to go. 'You take care now,' he said.

The separate officers became a neon clump again. One said, 'Stay safe!' Another chimed in 'Stay free!' and laughter echoed down the tunnel. The door wheezed shut and the carriage lurched forward.

I leant my head against James and closed my eyes.

Gently, reassuringly, his chest rose and fell beneath my cheek. I was sure I could hear his heart too, the steady call to life.

I said, 'I love you, James.'

'I love you, too,' he said, and softly kissed my hair.

*

We were giggling like drunks, clinging to the railings at street level outside London Bridge. 'I did it, I did it!' I said.

'You did!' he said. 'The power of the mind.'

'*You*,' I said.

We were face to face again. But closer this time. I pulled him to me and kissed him. We were an island around which people flowed. An oxbow lake, the blue centre of a flame.

His arms around me he murmured, 'What now, Helen?'

I thought of my phone and what would happen when I switched it on. Messages from Frank moving from furious to desperate. I thought of Nicholas, who would be asking questions.

I thought of the *Innisfree*. The magic of her, that I no longer felt.

Sindi, homeless without me.

'Maybe I could come to your place for some courage,' I said.

James shook his head. 'We're going to do this right, Helen. We're not going to be cruel or secretive or weak. Here. I'll put my number in your phone.'

'I don't want to switch it on yet, James. There'll be so many messages…'

'Okay then, we'll try this method for the second time.'

He jotted on my hand his phone number and his address. 'I'm ten minutes walk over there. You can come any time. Later tonight if you want, or as soon as you're ready. Tell Frank about me. Tell him you don't want to go any more. You've done nothing wrong.'

'Wait—' I grabbed his hand. 'This really happened didn't it? We found each other?'

He smiled and nodded. We were face to face, though the distance was growing, as he backed towards the crossing and I backed towards the taxi rank. A car approached on his newly deaf side. It was an expensive car, quiet and fast. It encountered an enchanted pause in traffic that allowed it to go too fast. Once a nexus of converging realities, always a nexus. James stepped right in front of it.

There were many things I had and would turn away from. I did not turn away from this. I watched him sail up, up up, smack onto the bonnet, roll up, up, up the windscreen, down down, down. I saw his face open and close in surprise. He smacked onto the ground in front of the car, which slammed

126

to a halt.

James was trembling – fitting? – on the road. Already people were clustering, pulling out their mobile phones. I pulled out mine. It took an age to switch on. And when it did it was, as I knew it would be, so alive with messages I could not key in a number. A huge man beside me barked, 'I'm doing this. I've got this,' giving a precise location to the emergency services like it was a meeting and he was ordering refreshments.

'James!' I screamed. I barrelled into the road and knelt beside him. His laptop was smashed beside him. Blood was pooling from his head.

'No, no,' I whispered.

'Out the way, miss. Out the way.'

People, pulling, pushing, standing, phoning.

'Don't leave me,' I begged. 'Don't leave me, James.'

His glasses were long gone. He had blue eyes. They looked right at me, and through me, and beyond me. I laid my head upon the lemony wool. Behind my closed eyes, the endless beach, alive with glittering shells.

12

THE PARAMEDIC CRACKLED inside a plastic apron. 'Miss, I need you to move back now.' A heavy accent, Spanish? Full braces which gave her the look of a fierce adolescent.

The road was heaving. I was on my knees, coughing in petrol fumes and the taste of blood. Round me, in a gladiatorial circle, shuffled shoes and coats. Some of the shoes pointed away, raring to go, but restrained by their owner's compulsion to watch. To take out the phone, dial that top number, say casually: *I just wanted to check in with you. No reason...*

I was frisking James determinedly, his neck, his hair, his wrists. My fingertips uncovered tiny pockets of warmth on his skin and dragged them out in triumph. *Dear James.* My brain sparked, a cog on its old track. *We beat time my darling. We did it. It's going to be all right.* His lips were open. I breathed into him as best I could, but my breath was juddery and wet with tears. His tongue was cold and slack and his head lolled away from me. I saw the individual bristles where his beard was growing in. And the hair at his temple, fine, like a child's. *No... No...*

I glared round the crowd.

'Who did this?' I snarled. My hands sprawled on his bloody chest like paws. There was an uptake of breath in the circle. A shuffling back of the shoes so that the car was revealed behind its curtain of coats. The driver was spotlit, a long-necked young man, frozen beside his fender.

'Look what you've done!' I screamed, and I realised that what felt like grief was rage, condensing in my muscles, streaming down my face. I leapt at him, tripping over James's body, which rolled gently, encouragingly, and I grabbed his hoodie, slapping and punching.

The driver put his hands up and stepped back. His face was twisted and red. 'My girlfriend is in labour!' He seemed suddenly to understand what had happened. 'Oh my God.' He pushed me away and tore round to the other side of the car, yanked at the door.

And now, the paramedic gripped my arm. I strained from her as if on a leash. I scrabbled and spat at the driver.

'You killed him!' This time the murderer was here, in front of me. It was a strange distorted miracle. Last time I lost everything, there was no one to see, no one to blame. This time I was getting my eye for an eye, my tooth for a tooth, my life for a life.

'What was he doing in the middle of the fucking road?' the man yelled. Then, easing the woman out of the car, he forgot about me. I saw it happen. He quite simply forgot that I was there, that James was dead in the road. Nothing mattered but the woman and the baby. 'Help me!' he cried, as the woman groaned like a bull and collapsed in his arms. Blood was running down her leg. Confused, I searched the faces in the crowd. They too had shifted, it seemed, to follow the new moral centre of the drama they were watching. The paramedic gently tugged me, as her colleagues rushed to the labouring woman's aid. She placed a hand on the space between my shoulder blades and she rubbed it, as I used to do with Nicholas when he was a baby.

'Miss, come away now. Are you a relative?' She was very patient. She must have seen it all, people turning to statues at the scene, lost to themselves forever; or babbling like the insane.

'I'm his wife,' I whispered. I sobbed into my hands, feeling the pearl of my ring against my lip.

The paramedic stroked my cheek. We were friends now. The dreamlike, eternal friends only strangers can be.

'Okay, Mrs…' She pulled out his wallet. 'Capelin.'

'He's James…'

'Move back now, Mrs Capelin, so we can look after him. The police will be here in a minute and they will sort out what's happened.'

The remaining paramedics fell upon James like hyenas. Slicing off his jacket, his sweater. One of them balled the sweater in his hands and threw it to one side. It rolled to my feet and I scooped it up, stuffed it in my bag. We widows are ravenous for souvenirs.

The burst of activity confused me.

'Can you...save him?' Hope opened inside me, like a monster's eyes.

My new friend paused and looked at me sadly. 'You are in shock,' she said. 'You need to come with us to A&E.' She pointed with a bloodied latex glove. 'Go in the second ambulance. Oh no – wait. I think we are taking that lady in that one. You'd better come with us.'

But in hospital I would not be his wife. I would be no one at all to him.

Activity over James had stopped. Braces stood, unpeeled her gloves and threw them into a plastic bag, pulling on a clean pair.

Someone was zipping a sheet around James.

The crowd was starting to disperse as the police arrived, blue lights whirling, a siren snapping off mid-wail.

Two officers climbed out slowly, huge neon arachnids, a shocking reminder that justice would not be served; not now, not ever.

I shuffled into the crowd, eyes down. Soon my new friend Braces would betray me with a look or a gesture. Soon the people of James's life would materialise, brought in to identify him, cry over him. They would overrun the world James and I had imagined, which he had now quit, and where I stood alone. They would have no idea who I was. I would cease to exist as part of James, and he as part of me. As if we had never been. And in a few hours, a new baby would be born and life would go on without us.

My notebook! It was tossed a few feet away. Could I reach it without the officer seeing me? Carefully, I darted out, grabbed it – catching a memory stick that fell from inside.

Such treasures! My love's ransacked tomb. Then I slipped back into the crowd. No one noticed me. All the activity had shifted to the woman giving birth, leaving James alone in the back of the ambulance.

How small he looked, how lonely. I heard his voice in my head, repeating the promise he had made at the top of the stairs leading into the Underground. If it all went wrong… James and me and Cariad. *Wherever she is,* he'd said. *Together.*

'I'm bringing you back, James,' I whispered. 'I don't know how, but I am.'

Pedestrians bumped into me as I ran. It was vital to catch no one's eye. I was negotiating a very tricky sliver of reality now. I talked myself through it. *Dear James. Dear James.* Bargains to be struck. What will Romy say when she hears about *this*? This isn't therapy material. This is reality shattered. It will violate her protocols. She will be rendered mute and backing out the door. She'll send an email. *Should I be worried about you?*

If you go back exactly, if you trace your steps exactly, if you wish hard enough, move fast enough, you can change time. I had proved my powers over reality, this very day. My lungs ached as I ran. Einstein talks about the train that travels at the speed of light. The observer on the train is also travelling at the speed of light, and time stops for him. Stopping wasn't enough for me though. The speed of light wasn't enough. Only my own powers of wishing could turn time back. Before I knew it I was running down the stairs into the Underground. *I am cured, remember?* Card on the gates, people jostling, down the escalator, where so recently James and I had been.

Wheezing for breath, I pulled out the scrap of James's sweater and inhaled it, and *wished*. I appealed for time to slow and stop and go back, more fervently than I had wished for anything.

When I opened my eyes, I looked across to the ascending escalator, and there we were. Oh!

I was on the step above you, your arms around my waist. Something was settled between us. See the relaxed slope of my shoulders. The smile on my face. Let no man put asunder. Has it been sundered? Why am I covered in blood?

'Are you all right?' The couple that was James and me called from across the aisle. They morphed into lovers, entwined round each other, impossibly young. Their innocently voyeuristic eyes widened.

'Is that...fancy dress?' asked the boy. He had glossy black hair in a topknot, and lovely red lips. He was looking down at me. Soon they would be gone.

'Banquo,' someone with my voice cried. Someone with my face, but who wasn't heartbroken, smiled.

The girl waved her cowboy hat at me. 'Have a lovely night,' she said.

At the bottom of the escalator, the busker who'd been playing 'Suzanne' earlier had been replaced by a man who was playing nothing at all. He sat hunched against the wall in the designated semicircle, a crude penny whistle abandoned by his side. Our eyes met and in their bewildered gleam, I saw how it was when all hope leaked away. The calcified angry body, left behind, its blood retreated to some core vestigial organ of life that kept the body upright, though not alive.

Fucking Jubilee Line with its sliding screens. Preventing

me from hurling myself onto the tracks. Stopping me choosing once and for all the dead over the living. In that moment I'd have done it. Nicholas or no Nicholas. Instead, I was herded into the carriage, clutching my bag, and sent roaring back to the living.

13

INSTEAD OF HEADING HOME, I stumbled from Canada Water station and headed along the spotlit path beside the Thames to the boatyard at South Dock Marina. James and I had travelled hand in hand beneath where I was now walking just a few hours ago. I imagined our faces looking up from the speeding carriage, up, up, shining through all that earth. To my left, the river flashed, on a fast ebb, cantering out to sea beneath the full moon. Something splashed. A swan took off in a slick of moonlight.

The river does not know him. The sea does not know him. The Innisfree *does not know him.* Could I escape what had just happened?

But deep inside my mind, a terrifying wave rose. It was made of emptiness and dead stars. It was racing towards me. If it ever reached me, it would destroy me. It was a wave of unimaginable pain. I didn't want to live, but I was afraid. I dug my nails into my palms and picked up my pace.

Arriving at last at the marina, I paused for breath at the dockside, beneath the looming blue crane used for lifting boats in and out of the water for repairs and cleaning. Suspended from the crane in a cradle of straps was a small canal boat, its hull just dipping beneath the surface of the marina waters. I imagined it was being tested for leaks after being blacked and painted, before going back to its berth. Fanning out beyond, hundreds of houseboats of all kinds shifted in the waters, watchful and strange, as if I had come across a herd of whales, suspended at the surface.

The boatyard at South Dock Marina, sandwiched between the marina and the river and enclosed by tall railings, is the last surviving yard of its kind in London. The marina residents, or berth holders, have on their doorstep specialist tradesmen who can maintain and repair their floating homes. The extent of the *Innisfree*'s refurbishment demanded a whole team, which Frank had managed to bring from Plymouth.

I had not yet visited her and had no key to get into the yard. Leaving the crane behind me, I crossed to the gates. A dazzling security light forced me to shield my eyes as I peered through the bars to see her. The wave, for a moment, receded.

The boats inside were all on stilts, raised high enough for the people working on them to walk underneath. They were like statues in the moonlight. Slowly, my eyes grew accustomed to the shadows. A slim silhouette nosed between two canal boats at the far side, adjacent to the Thames Path. *Is it her? The* Innisfree?

I took out my phone, ignoring the notifications. I sent Frank a text, ignoring all of his to me.

I am at the Innisfree. *Please come.*

*

There was something I needed to do. I turned back from the boatyard gates to the canal boat suspended from the crane. Carefully I peered into its dark windows. It was definitely empty. Checking that no one was around, I jumped the short distance from the side onto the flat roof and tip-toed to the open deck space at the bow. In a corner among some tools was a bucket and beside it a coil of mooring line. Easing down onto the deck, I lowered the bucket over the side, as silently as possible, and filled it from the marina. I splashed the icy water over my face and hands to wash away the blood. My coat also had blood on it, so I took it off, dried myself with it, and threw it overboard. Finally, I took out James's sweater, pressed it against my face one last time and threw that overboard too. Teeth chattering now, I replaced everything as it was on the canal boat and clambered back onto the dockside, returning to the yard gates to wait for Frank.

If my eyes fell on the marina, or the sky, or my own trembling hands, then the wave in my mind gathered strength and fragments of the evening's events reeled before me. As long as I kept my gaze on the *Innisfree,* there was a chink in the shattered dark of my brain. When I looked at her, I forgot James! It was only a second, but I forgot him.

'Helen!' My name carried over the marina.

In the floodlit darkness, Frank was running towards me.

I stood helplessly, unable to move or shout back. Reaching me, he hesitated, taking in my battered appearance, my lack of coat. 'My God, what happened?' he said. Then, 'Are you hurt? Come here.' He pulled me to him and I sighed in relief against his shoulder.

'I was mugged,' I said. 'He took my coat.'

Until this moment, I didn't know I was going to lie. But I uttered it with conviction and proceeded to embellish it. My lie was going to save me, here in the land of the living.

'I was so shocked, Frank, I didn't know what to do. Massive guy. In a balaclava, on a bike.'

'Where did it happen?'

'London Bridge. I go there sometimes. Romy's idea, gradual exposure to my fears. I should have said, I know, but I wanted to… It's something I had to work through myself.'

'London Bridge? Are you mad? You should have told me!'

'I had to do it on my own. Anyway, he grabbed my coat, kept going on his bike, trying to pull me over. But I managed to wriggle out of it and I ran.'

'Helen, you could have been killed! We must go to the police.'

'No. No. I wouldn't recognise him. It's only a coat. I… Please Frank.'

'Let's get you on board. We can talk about it there.' He took out a fob with a golf ball-sized cork float attached and unlocked the gate. 'I bet you knew her straightaway,' he said, hauling a set of ladders to the side of the boat.

The moment I placed my hand upon the gunnels, calm coursed through me. She was warm and smooth to the touch, the knocks and dents of her recent past sanded and varnished to mere undulations. Many more were probably older, perhaps caused even by me. How careless we were back then, with our lines, our chains and ropes. Chucking them over the side with abandon, never thinking of damage. But each injury was part of her now. She had absorbed us into herself.

I quickly pulled off my shoes and socks so that I could feel the wood of the peeling deck on my soles. The magic of wood is that, unless it is freshly doused in freezing water, it is warm. The planks gleamed, reminding me of the baleen of the blue whale where it strains the seawater for plankton.

We were some twenty feet above the ground, and close to the railings that bounded the Thames Path. The river was running past us, bursting with shadows; from the far bank, the skyscrapers of Canary Wharf stared unblinking.

Frank turned on the deck light and took me in properly for the first time.

'Bloody hell, what have you got in there? It stinks!' He eased my hands from my bag and lifted out the fish I'd bought so long ago.

'I went to Borough Market.'

'Think we'll give them a miss, don't you?' he said, flinging them over the side of the boat. They sailed high into the night sky and into the river.

'What's this other stuff?' He had his hands now upon my notebook. I yanked the bag away from him.

'No Frank…it's my diary. Please.'

'What are you talking about?'

Crying now, I sank to my knees. I couldn't bear it, to have lost James. All I had now was my notebook and I was never letting it go.

'We should go to the police,' Frank said again.

'No,' I whispered. 'I just want to be here now, with you. Please.'

'Helen, what on earth were you doing? Why did you ignore all my messages?'

He eased me onto my feet and led me to the cockpit, giving me valuable seconds to think of an answer.

'I turned off my phone. And then outside the market, this guy grabbed my coat and I just ran. I was so frightened I just didn't think about being scared of the Tube. I just did it.'

'You actually took the Underground?' Amazement spread over his face. 'Wow, Helen! Hang on a moment.' Disappearing briefly below, he reappeared with a blanket which he wrapped around me, and a mug of neat gin. 'I was going to surprise you,' he said. 'I'm reinstalling the gin barrel. Remember?' The original Swan had a tank especially for alcohol, rum or gin. It was the source of many parties when we were young. 'But I think this calls for a drink!'

I gulped the gin and pulled the blanket tightly round myself. I laid my head against his shoulder. Overhead, the red and green moving lights of a plane passed.

'I went back and forth on the Jubilee Line,' I went on. I knew I should stop my embellishments, but I was exhilarated by how plausible this James-less, painless, conflict-free version of events was. 'I thought for a while I'd faint from the terror.'

'But you still haven't said – why didn't you call me?'

'Well I did, as soon as I'd got myself together...'

My husband grabbed my hands. 'Helen, please, I have to know you won't do something like this again. I had to make up an excuse to Nicholas, some crap about you going to find halyards – it was a word he didn't know, so it worked. I had this feeling that you…were seeing James. I don't know why.'

'I promise I'll never see James again,' I said. The truth of this fused with my lie. How different loss is when no one knows about it or will ever speak of it! It was the perfect crime. I'd got away with breaking my own heart, and no one would ever know. I wasn't even crying any more.

Frank got up to clear away our cups. He paused, said, 'This has been a terrible day, Helen, for all of us. But it proves we are right about what we're doing. We have to get away from here. Terrorism, crime, the fucking internet!'

'I agree,' I said.

As the minutes passed and I realised I would never be questioned about James again, never hear his name again if I did not utter it, a kind of terror gripped me. Perhaps I should have confessed to dragging him from his life into mine, placing him in the situation that allowed a car to hit him. Perhaps I deserved the punishment that would have been forthcoming if I confessed, which would have been Frank ending our marriage, abandoning the trip. But confessions do not belong in the land of the living, where a miraculous boat was preparing to take us away from death and violence, where a child believed in me and the plans we'd made, where a husband had proved his love for his family with a magnificent gesture.

I did not know who James's family were, except for the father who had the hip flask. Perhaps they had been notified by now. Perhaps they were tormented with questions about what he was doing to get knocked down like that. Or how he could possibly have been so unlucky as to survive the bomb, and yet die anyway. Probably he had a mother still alive somewhere who must have just learned of the loss of her child, and howled, as I had howled over mine. *I'm so sorry*, I whispered.

Waiting for Frank at the rail, I watched the Thames plunging on her journey out to sea. Though my husband was near I knew I was alone. No one could ever know what had happened tonight. The price of having a life to come back to was excising James from my heart. As if it had never happened.

An extraordinary creature I had not thought about since my studies at university swam into my mind. The European eel begins its transformational existence far away in the Sargasso Sea. The eggs drift across the Atlantic, arriving in Europe as transparent glass eels. They enter the Thames estuary, where they develop into elvers which migrate upstream, navigating through locks and tributaries to find suitable habitats within the Thames basin. They even leave the water to travel short distances overland until they find a home, where they change again, this time into yellow eels. They live for up to twenty years like this, before the urge possesses them to return to the Sargasso. To make this arduous final journey they transform one more time, into silver eels, and they leave under the light of a new moon.

The sea was calling to me now. The *Innisfree* was preparing herself to carry us. Like Frank, I longed to go, to return to a place before all this, to be a different creature, the one who had not made my choices, the one I used to be.

14

My glasses were thick with dust and I could no longer see the angle grinder clearly. But determination kept my hands clamped around its vibrating body. I was mesmerised by its the blade whirling off the old decking. My success made me see more success, even while the dust gradually obscured my vision. I wanted to press on, to the bone-cleanliness beneath. I was good at this. My focus narrowed, tighter and tighter. I could see through the particles on my lenses. I could see *between* them. It was like when Frank and I took magic mushrooms in port one time, and the microscopic details of things revealed themselves, and set us giggling, probably on this very spot.

The grinder hit a protruding screw and slipped from my hands, squealing like a piglet. My thumb sprang from the on switch, and the fierce little engine died, an instant before it would have sliced into me. I gasped inside my mask. Trembling on my knees, I shook my gloved hands to get the circulation back, and woke up to my surroundings for the first time in what seemed like hours. The deck was covered in a layer of the same moondust as my glasses. It filled my hair and the cuffs of my boiler suit. It was actually fibreglass dust, and I would have an evening of itching to look forward to wherever it had reached my skin. But I didn't care. Careful as an astronaut, I lumbered further along the deck to where I could see a plastic bag, and I rubbed the lenses with its dust-free handle.

The Thames Path below me was busy with weekend strollers. Some were in couples and groups, but many more were alone, tramping with head down or face blank. These individuals were as slow as I was in my dust with my aching limbs. I felt for them. I recognised them, even as I recoiled from them. Each was imprisoned inside some form of *I can't live without you*. I could see rage and pity pulsing in their veins. They stared out at the Thames, just as I had done.

I thought then of the boats and buildings surrounding me, all the labour poured into them. People I'd never know, whose lives were expended without record upon these creations. My plan was to expend myself upon the *Innisfree*. I would labour every second, thinking of nothing else, until she was restored. Then my life would be part of this beautiful structure. It would be part of history. Something beautiful, for Nicholas. Something meaningful from all this mess.

The boatyard was busy with tradesmen and boat owners, some of whom, having nowhere else to go, were living on their boats while they were being worked on. Squirrels darted up

144

steps and ropes and used the boats as highways to the trees. Clustered beneath the hulls or creeping over the decks were the scarce tradesmen themselves, patching, filling, painting or standing back to admire each other's handiwork beneath clouds of cigarette smoke. There were never enough skilled people to do the work these boats needed. There was no end to the work, no end to the hours and the money that could be spent on a boat. As boat owners often joked, having one of these craft was like standing in a shower shredding £50 notes.

But working on the *Innisfree* brought such solace, and I was sorry I had hidden from her in those early weeks. In the scraps of original paint uncovered by sanding, in the way Frank's voice met mine across the deck, in the smell of fresh wood, the taste of salt water in the air, glimpses of the past were coming alive, melding how we were then with the present moment, with nothing in between.

It was an unspoken pact between us, the *Innisfree* and me. In healing her, we were healing the fabric of time itself. Sometimes, I dreamed that I told Frank the truth about what had happened to James, and he held me and was kind to me, and I woke with a gasp, to find Frank's massive, innocent form beside me, isolated from me by what I could never share. More often in the dream, he grew cold and furious; or even, in one recurring nightmare, pushed me over the side of the *Innisfree*. Worst of all was the dream where he gathered Nicholas and Sindi into the car and drove them away, leaving me standing alone. These reminders cemented my lips together, but always, the longing to confess, to have the truth heard non-judgementally, was there, like a stone around my neck.

'Morning Helen! Fancy a cuppa?'

Among the *Innisfree's* neighbours in the boatyard were a devoted ancient couple living aboard their narrowboat while it was being repaired and blacked. They impressed me with their fearless scaling of the ladder up and down to the ground. They accepted uncomplainingly the lack of running water and wi-fi, and the abolition of all privacy for the long weeks of renovation. They liked to come out on their deck with a cup of tea and watch me work.

'Thank you! I'm due a break.'

I climbed out of my boiler suit so as not to scatter too much dust upon their deck. I called to Frank, who was going through some tools to find the sander: his plan for this weekend was to begin sanding the hull. He waved me away, engrossed in what he was doing.

Clambering up onto their deck, I accepted the sweet tea and Club biscuit gratefully and began with my carefully rehearsed, abbreviated questions about their boat and comments about mine. They were called Marvin and Jessica. She smoked a pipe which he said affectionately was repulsive. He had wispy blue hair, claiming his granddaughter had demanded he dye it, and which she said he liked too much. We squeezed together on the tiny bow deck, Marvin and Jessica both sitting on the very rim of the boat to make room for me to sit on a chair. We had a friendly moan about the inconveniences of boatyard life, but how wonderful it would be when the work was done.

Jessica inquired gently about the bomb, tapping her pipe on the side of the boat, scraping it out with a little tool she kept in her pocket. I was ready with my reply. I was very lucky. I had a wonderful family. Hopefully the *Innisfree* would be finished soon and we could start our new voyage. It was a very polished intro to 'Helen', nicely proportioned, dovetailed like a good cabinet, I thought. We all agreed that renovating a boat was the hardest thing we'd ever done. But I could tell they wanted more. They were the kind of people who could answer for themselves, and they assumed I was too. More probing about the bombing turned me into a blushing robot. There was no way to talk about it without talking about Cariad and James and it was impossible for me to do either. They moved the conversation onto other atrocities that occurred, the difficulties of forgiveness. I realised they were probing for my position, and would never understand that I did not have one, or not one that they would recognise. I could not explain that the bomb had obliterated my soul along with the baby. Suffering had not made me a better person. I was worse, and I had not been that great to begin with. I clammed up, dragged up some platitudes to defend myself.

But when my tea was done, I found I couldn't bring myself to leave, to end on a light note. My judgement was off; this well-meaning pair had unleashed my tongue and I began to talk about finding the *Innisfree* in the playground. I went on and on, describing every aspect of that day, right down to George Michael on the speakers and my feet out of the window. I didn't know why this was the story that unravelled from my lips, but it seemed that if I could only tell it, I might be understood. Marvin and Jessica were looking at their watches, so I broke my tale with questions, desperate to keep their interest, feeling a terrible lonely panic rising round my throat, realising that I was, now, simply a walking, breathing malfunction. They were never less than kind. They scanned the yard, searching for rescue. I was horribly divided, able to see that I must stop talking, that it was time to leave, but also trying with my story to remain there longer, to achieve in this torrent of words some kind of absolution. Finally Jessica's phone rang and they apologised but they had to get on, and my face burned because they'd cut me off mid-sentence, but I didn't blame them. I simply gathered up the remains of my composure, and I thanked them for the tea and castigated myself as I crossed back onto the *Innisfree*.

'Miss, do you need some help?'

I paused in pulling on my boiler suit and looked down at Sindi. Her hand shielded her eyes in a salute. Sindi had discovered the joy of deep baths in a proper bathroom and spent hours submerged in bubbles these days. Her hair gleamed. Her toes in her flip flops were painted green. In her hand, instead of a cigarette, temporarily, was a scrap of rope. She was watching YouTube videos on how to tie knots, waving the results in front of Frank or me for approval.

I got the same feeling looking at her now as I had that morning of her birthday. Sindi was a light. That's how I felt about her. I loved her. When I looked at her I had the unequivocal feeling that I had done some good. My frown unrolled from my face and I waved her up.

'What would really help is if you hose down the deck. But you'll need to wear a boiler suit, Sindi. The fibreglass will drive you crazy.'

I watched her tenderly as she pulled on the suit. Don't

carry a lie with you, Sindi, I longed to say to her. The weight of it skews everything. You can't tell what your face is doing. Other people's faces become questions to be answered under pressure. You become a codebreaker frantically tapping inside your own brain. I pointed to the pressure washer and, while she pulled on some boots, I got the machine powered up.

'Holy shit!' she grinned as I showed her how to operate the gun at the end. A spout of water shot across the yard. 'Hey! Nicholas!'

She aimed a jet of water over the fence, splashing next to Nicky, who was filming a swan on his phone.

'Stop it! You'll frighten it off!' he cried.

The swan was out of the water, neck outstretched, and had fluffed out the sails of its wings. It advanced massively upon him, slap, slap, slap. Nicholas moved slowly backwards, continuing to film. Passers-by paused to watch. Sindi stopped the flow of water and watched too.

He was becoming so confident behind a camera, just like his father. Increasingly he looked like him too. I squinted to see in him the little boy who had so recently, it seemed, depended upon me for everything. I could not summon him up. It was almost as if my heart could not stand the weight of all these histories around me, the past and the present that refused to disengage, that kept me existing in a paradox. My heart was trying to protect me, choosing where I should see the past coming alive in the present, so as not to plunge me back into thinking of James, sailing up, up, up, surprise on his face. Then still warm beneath my frantic hands, as if he could be summoned back from where he had fallen. Perhaps my heart chose badly. Still, it chose, and choice is life. Choose. Choose Choose, it banged, as the Thames shook the pier, and the swan rattled its plumage.

Frank appeared at the top of the ladder. He waved at his son. 'Hey! David Attenborough!'

Startled, Nicholas looked up from the screen and saw that the swan was very close to him now, and angry. *Then* I saw the little boy inside him, animating his expression, as he realised that he had strayed beyond the limit of parental protection, and, briefly, he was afraid. His eyes sought me out, locked on mine as if he were in a river and I was pulling him ashore with a rope. I was a mother again, electrified with purpose and certainty. It was only an instant – the boy vanished, and a familiar showman smile spread across Nicky's face as he backed smoothly away from the bird.

The swan extended its wings, like Icarus in a different story where everything turned out fine. Nicholas took a final shot and grinned over at us, before striding towards the yard, intent on his phone again. He would make the footage into a TikTok video; he would show his father; Frank would appreciate the finer details, give him some pointers on how to lift an image here or there. They would consult intently, heads close like atoms bonding as a molecule, then they would simply spring away from each other, separate elements again. I didn't know how they did that. I could only connect with Nicholas now through giving permission for his gaming, a dark and needy adventure which I understood. I didn't care about these curated images. Watching them made me think of Ruth. Or of pictures in general; fraudulent by nature. Of course I was tormented to have no picture of James. Nothing

I could produce to prove, to myself or anyone, he had ever existed.

'What's going on here, then?' Frank asked.

'Sindi's going to hose down the deck,' I said. 'OK. Ready? Not too hard or you'll just spread the stuff around.'

Sindi set the motor going and began to gently corral the piles of dust, gripping the gun with two hands. Dust gathered beneath the jet, moving obediently towards the corners. As she drove it towards the drainage holes, she suddenly flipped direction and sent a wave of watery dust over Frank, drenching his face and upper body.

'Sindi! That's fibreglass!' Frank flailed vainly on the ladder.

Sindi stopped the gun. 'Oh God I'm sorry! It slipped!'

'Could have gone in my eyes! What's the matter with you!' He clambered blindly down to go into the toilets and clean himself off. Sindi calmly set the motor going again and continued faultlessly. Her back was to me and I couldn't see her expression.

'Sindi?' I asked.

'It was an an accident.' She shrugged, continuing with her work. I turned off the motor.

'Sindi, when we're out at sea, Frank is skipper. He's in charge. He'll give orders and stuff like that. There has to be respect on board a boat.'

'I'm sorry,' she said glumly.

'When we're away from here, there can't be accidents. You can't know because you've never done it, but it's dangerous.'

She turned to me, pleading all over her face. 'Please don't be angry with me, Miss.'

'I'm not,' I said. 'But you didn't just cover me in fibreglass.'

151

'Frank... Sometimes I just don't like him!'

I sighed. 'Join the club, Sindi. Just say sorry to him. It will all be forgotten.'

*

The cabin right at the prow of a boat is called the forepeak, and traditionally it was where the crew would sleep. It is also where the anchor chain is usually housed. When the anchor is dropped from the prow, it pulls the chain up from the locker. The *Innisfree*'s forepeak cabin, as well as being where Frank and I had carved our initials so long ago, was the site of some catastrophic damage which the surveyor had pointed out to us. On the ceiling of the locker were several huge cancer-like lesions, the result of leaks from the anchor winch and the cleats. Her deck was constructed in the form of a fibreglass sandwich, with a core of wood or foam between two sheets. Water penetrating the core had rotted the wood or foam, causing this destruction. 'You'll have to cut that out from the deck above, replace the whole area,' the surveyor had explained. The list of areas of essential repairs on the *Innisfree* was massive. The surveyor had valued her *Innisfree* at £8,000 and calculated the work would cost at least £150,000. The numbers made no sense, but we were resurrecting a dream and therefore they possessed a dream logic. The surveyor thought we were mad.

Boats, of course, are the repository of dreams. People see beauty in their boats like they do in their wives and generally they don't like to hear that they are worthless or beyond saving. Boats encounter boatyards not when they are at their best, parading on the water, but when they are at their most vulnerable: skeletons on stilts, blistered and broken, faded with UV, their glory days behind them. Nevertheless, loved enough not to be scrapped but salvaged. And their owners, especially naïve ones like us, are made vulnerable by association. Perhaps that was how I knew I loved this boat. I was vulnerable to whatever verdict was passed on her by experts. I was vulnerable to inflated prices, shoddy work, or no work at all. And, indeed, catastrophe.

Crouched in the forepeak, contemplating the damage, I had the urge, suddenly, to call Romy. I hadn't seen her or spoken to her in months, and so I didn't expect her to pick up, but she did. The soft voice echoed from the terrible place I had been, would soon be no longer. 'Helen, it's good to hear from you. How are you doing?'

'I'm in a boat! We're taking a trip across the Atlantic!' I knew as I spoke that I wouldn't be telling her about James. I babbled excitedly; I wanted to try some different words out in the world, the good words, the words of adventure, of healing. I told her that Frank, my wonderful husband, had found a boat that we had met upon long ago and we were renovating it. 'In fact I'm sitting right inside her right now!'

'Helen, that sounds magical.'

'And we're bringing along Sindi. You know, from school? Oh – and I'm cured of my fear of the Underground. I went back down, faced my fear – I…' I stopped then, because that was somewhere I couldn't go. I changed tack, told her about the renovations. 'We're about to do some major surgery on the boat.'

'I'm so happy for you, Helen.' I found myself waiting

hopefully for a platitude. It gave me something to fight against, something to cling to, test my contempt against. She didn't disappoint me. 'Marriage is an edifice. Which can be remade endlessly for all of your life. In fact, what you seem to be manifesting is Build It And They Will Come. Congratulations, dear Helen.'

'Thank you, Romy.' I felt the press of confession in my throat. I needed to get off the phone before she asked any questions about Cariad or James. I would not be able to resist her. I never could.

Romy said, 'You're a lucky woman, Helen. Do you feel that now?'

'Yes,' I whispered.

'Have a wonderful trip.' Romy sounded so far away, as if I were calling her on the satellite phone. I felt distraught as I ended the call. We'd never speak again. Stupid, pointless Romy. *Thank you.*

Back on deck, I assembled the tools for the job. Frank appeared beside me with the saw, followed by Sindi. Frank pretended to flinch when he saw her and grinned broadly as she started to apologise again. Then Nicholas clambered up, phone in hand, scanning the boat with the camera.

'I'm worried about the camber,' I said.

Cutting a big section from the deck would make it difficult to repair in such way that the delicate curve of the deck was restored.

'It's okay,' Frank said. 'The team said if we secure it with ropes and cover it, they will be able to sort it on Monday.' He knelt and marked the shape I should cut. When he had done so he stood up and leaned in to whisper, 'You know we definitely screwed in that very spot. Don't you remember?'

I whispered back, 'Remember it was raining? And we didn't care?'

We each wore goggles, and both pairs ever-so-slightly misted up. We pointed at each other and sniggered softly. Nicholas focused his camera on the blade and Sindi and Frank stood back.

Revving the motor I pressed the blade into the *Innisfree*'s screaming flesh. Fibreglass sprayed around us.

'Whoa!' Nicholas cried excitedly.

I focused hard, absorbing the jolts of the saw as it traced the line. The *Innisfree* shuddered, mute, beneath this medieval surgery. The saw moved with agonising slowness. After what seemed an age, there was a moan from the boat, Frank placed his boot on the section, and with a shriek it collapsed in a shoddy mass of splinters into the forepeak cabin. I looked up and saw that our neighbours had come out onto their boats to watch. What would be left of the original *Innisfree* after all this excavation, all this painful reimagining? Perhaps only our dreams of her.

I stepped back, my part done. To my surprise, Frank's arms found their way around me, holding me from the back. He was so warm, always. It was comforting. He kissed the top of my head. I might be undeserving of his affection, but I didn't push him away. Why would I do that when my heart was breaking and I could never say why?

Dear James, Would we have grown old together? Sometimes the dead let us go; they do not want anything more from us. Cariad for instance. I had never touched her, nor seen her – except in the shadowy ultrasound that I threw away. She had lived in me as the future does, not real but at the same time the realest thing there is. In Frank's arms I thought of how she had arrived and paused at me, she had chosen me for that pause, as if I was, say, a stopover in Bruges on the way to somewhere more glamorous – Málaga? – or like a friend of ours once, from the boat days, on his way to France from Vancouver, and he broke the journey to spend a weekend with us, even though it made the trip very expensive, and we had a wonderful weekend, and he left and we knew, somehow, we'd never see him again. But a necessary intersection of past and present had taken place.

But what do we do with the dead who are not done with us? *James*. In the metamorphosis of the *Innisfree* I saw my answer. *Do not accept the loss*. Create inside yourself the one you loved, who died and left you. Allow yourself to be cut open, transformed. To become a new person with an open cavern for a heart, ready to meet again.

15

'Okay, Columbus,' sniggered Nicholas as Frank unrolled two brand new Admiralty navigation charts on the dining room table. Sindi looked intently at the ceiling, trying not to laugh.

'Come on, you two,' Frank sighed. He weighted the corners of the charts. They covered most of the surface of the table. I wondered why we were doing this now, right after breakfast, but Frank was in no mood to be opposed.

He was upset. That morning he had signed the papers to sell his agency. But it was not the sale he wanted – to the pharma giant. It was instead to the old agency, Lumina. Discussions about the sale to Zentron had been exhilarating. They wanted to keep the agency name, FRANKLY, and Frank himself in a consultancy role. They were also hinting at huge numbers. There had been dinners, meetings, awaydays to which I was not invited. They were courting Frank. They seemed to love the whole idea of the sailing trip – especially his return. But for some reason, the exhilarating discussions did not conclude. Then, unexpectedly, Lumina stepped in. Frank's old boss, who had rejoined the company at a higher level, rang him with a decisive, immediate, and good, if realistic, offer. It was, however, for the client roster, not the brand.

I was relieved, but Frank was unhappy. 'It's my life's work,' he said, in our one discussion about it while Sindi and Nicholas were at school. 'I want to see my agency in good hands, not subsumed. I mean, I left Lumina to do my own thing!'

'But you'll be free,' I reasoned. 'Well and truly starting again, like the rest of us.' After all, the *Innisfree* had been his idea, and he had never wavered from it, despite James, despite Sindi, despite the need to give up the agency. I pressed on, believing myself able to offer insight. 'I don't think Zentron are going to conclude in time for us to go,' I said. 'And they're so big, Frank, who knows what would happen? You don't know anyone there – not really.'

Of course, I wanted rid of the agency. I was surprised by my determination that he should take Lumina's offer.

'This is about Ruth, isn't it?'

'No! It's about us actually changing our lives rather than half-changing them. You can't sell the company and keep it. You can't have an agency and be out at sea with your family. Look, we are all giving things up. Nicky was going to start secondary school in the autumn. This is Sindi's exam year. All our lives are turned on their head for this.'

'I want to hang on…' he said. 'It would be more money, and safer hands.'

'Zentron will be flirting with loads of agencies. They'll string you along and then drop you. Lumina is solid. You know them. And they're an agency themselves! They know how to look after clients.'

'Would you expect Michelangelo to sell the Sistine Chapel as parts?'

I laughed, and then realised he was serious.

'I'm not saying I *am* Michelangelo, but the principle—'

'Frank, you bought the *Innisfree*. We three are all ready to go. You've made promises. Just sell the bloody agency to Lumina!'

'Bloody agency? So that's what you think of my life's work.'

'Hardly a life's work, Frank. Seven years.'

He stared at me with loathing, got up from the table and walked out. I remained alone in the kitchen for some time. It is so hard to insist on what you want. When, overall, it isn't even what you want. I wanted James, another life. But I couldn't have that. Now that the *Innisfree*'s position as destiny had been cemented into all our minds, my determination was visceral.

We had not returned to the subject over the intervening days, though I had tried. I'd also tried to make up but, as I wasn't going to change my view, my cups of tea and thoughtful meals were perceived as insincere. Around the house Frank was frigidly civil. I absented myself as much as I could at the boat. Nicholas and Sindi seemed not to notice and I was thankful for their self-absorption, which kept everything normal.

Then, this morning, he shook me awake early and slapped the signed papers on the duvet. 'Happy now?' he spat, not even waiting for my reply before walking out. Blinking, stunned, over the fact of getting my way, I wondered how much resentment the structure of our marriage could stand. The dramas of love and hate were one thing, giving our relationship a dangerous energy. But resentment was uglifying, like a boat being made over by cowboy builders, emerging less than it was, after draining years of your life and all your cash.

Frank's mood aside, the charts were spectacular. Sindi and Nicholas were no longer smirking. Before us lay the world in reverse. The land masses were blank spaces. No mountains or cities interrupted their yellow expanse. No human settlements appeared at all. At first glance the charts were like maps that had not been finished, or documents from a time before humankind, when everything on earth was nameless. It took time to process that the white space *between* the continents, which on a map is empty, was dense with information.

Currents and ridges, abyssal plains, trenches, sea mounts and basins. Gridlines, contour lines, compass roses. Fantastical names arranged this way and that – but above all the ocean was filled with numbers; hundreds of numbers, each a measurement of depth. Sometimes the numbers were packed densely; sometimes where the ocean floor was still uncharted, and no one knew what lay there, there were several centimetres, or hundreds of miles, between them.

To see a chart for the first time is always confusing. All that empty blue of our familiar globes, all that featureless two-thirds-of-the-surface from satellites, is revealed to be its own dimension, with a comprehensive geography, a secret planet hidden right there inside our own. It is confusing, in the way that revelation is confusing.

'How…do we even use these?' Sindi asked.

'Mostly we won't,' Frank said. 'We'll use GPS and electronic charts. But this is clearer for us all to see now, and we will have these on board in case the electrics fail for any reason. Helen and I are both trained to read them.'

'Some of these depths date back more than a hundred years, when people used lead and line to measure fathoms,' I said. 'The landscape underwater doesn't change that much, but also, it can change *overnight*.'

'Nah…' said Nicholas.

'It's true,' I said. 'Underwater volcanoes can produce new islands in hours. And then, earthquakes and other volcanoes below the surface can take them away. There are cases of disappearing islands which made it onto one chart, but not the next.'

Frank and I had both delighted in the charts back then, for different reasons. Frank was restless for open waters, but I looked at them as a way to find home. My father used them back in his day when there was no GPS. The shape of the north-west coast of England was part of him, like his own boat, and he did not need to use the chart when he was inshore. But he had it there, the lamp over it, laced with pencil, when he headed out into open sea to find the fish in their deep shoals. By the time we got to the *Innisfree* first time around, technological advances meant paper charts were for checking and emergencies.

'Okay, so… Mid-Atlantic Chart, and South Atlantic,' said Frank. 'The two together give us our entire route from the UK.'

Nicholas was busy on his phone. 'How tall is Everest?'

'About eight thousand metres,' Frank said.

Nicky said. 'There's a bit here…' He scoured the chart, pressed a finger on the sea off Puerto Rico. 'It's deeper than Everest is high!'

'Are we going there?' Sindi asked, nervously.

'The Puerto Rico trench? No,' I said. 'But you can't have a skeleton down there. You're all gelatinous. And you make your own light.' I flapped my arms, like a squid.

She smiled, the friendly light-filled smile that was uniquely hers. I thought then that someone needed to tell her about that smile of hers; she needed to know how beautiful it was.

Frank said, 'OK, where we are now on here, Sindi? Where's London?'

She squinted at the map, pointed.

'Good. So, this is what we will do. We set off as soon as the boat is finished and we head from London to Falmouth, here.'

Sindi's gaze wandered to a photograph of me wedged in the bookcase. It was from the early days, curled at the edges, slanted in a clipframe. She lifted it down. 'You were pretty, Miss,' she said. She held it up. I was windswept and grinning, my hair French-plaited to keep it out of my face. The hood of my sailing jacket was blowing round the back of my head. I remembered when it was taken. My first sailing exam passed, the skipper of the *Innisfree* had just taken me on as crew. My expression showed me fully present in my life.

'She's still pretty,' Frank said. 'But... Earth to Sindi, can we get on please?'

She replaced the photo and returned to the chart.

Nicholas, still engrossed, said, 'So after Falmouth? Where do we go?'

'Across the ocean!' said Frank. 'The whole Atlantic! Your mother and I never did it when we were aboard the *Innisfree*. We took charters around the Mediterranean, here, and we went round the Canaries, here. I wanted to, but it never happened.'

'I think Corin was worried about the impact site,' I said.

'That was just an excuse,' Frank snapped. 'I mean, yes, there was an impact, but it was repaired.'

'It was more than that. It knocked his confidence. Well, everyone's confidence except yours.'

'The boat crashed?' Sindi asked, wide-eyed.

Frank sighed. 'We were going to cross the Atlantic. There was an informal race set up. And, well, the skipper, Corin, decided things too late, picked up crew from some stragglers in harbour. And one of them, this moron – Grainger, his name was – well, he lied about his experience; he had no experience, and day two of the race, wham, he sailed us right in front of another boat that had right of way and she—' He demonstrated with his fists. 'Race over. Water leaking in. So we went back to port and we spent most of the summer repairing her. By which time it was too late for anything.' He sighed. 'And after that, we were always working up to it, as I remember, always next season. But now...' He grinned at Nicky and Sindi. 'We are doing this for the *Innisfree* too. A boat like her shouldn't be pootling around the Med. She needs to be out and crossing oceans.'

To my mind, the salient point about Grainger was not that he was a dangerous fool, but that he was only nineteen. Hardly older than Sindi. And we were not much older, inexperienced young people, just like him. He'd left the boat in disgrace. How judgemental we were.

'So, first step is we cross the Bay of Biscay,' Frank went on. 'We will time it so that we have the best chance of good weather. Now, usually people would stop at the Canaries, but I think we should carry on to Cape Verde, here. Less crowded, and Cape Verde is the best jumping-off point for …this!'

He swung his finger out across the densely featured expanse of the Atlantic. Instead of crossing to the Caribbean, specifically to St Lucia, which was the usual route, he swung down towards Brazil and stopped at a speck off the coast.

'Fernando de Noronha. The paradise archipelago.' He tapped the creamy parchment triumphantly. 'Well, go on then,' he said. 'Look it up on your phones!'

'Charles Darwin went there!' said Nicholas.

'They close the beaches for turtles?' said Sindi, doubtfully.

I said, 'It's unspoilt. Unpopulated. Most sailors go across to St Lucia. In fact there's an amateur race every year crossing the Atlantic with hundreds of boats all ending up there — what's it called again, Frank?'

'The ARC — Atlantic Rally for Cruising Yachts. But we are going to do something different, and see exactly what Charles Darwin saw.'

'So, crew,' I said, 'that's the adventure.'

Sindi was puzzled. 'How long will it take?'

'Well, we'll set off no later than September, and we'll reach the islands, including a stop, by Christmas,' Frank said. 'And it will be warm and beautiful and we can think then about where we go next.'

'Can we carry on to Antarctica, Dad?' cried Nicholas.

'It's a thought! We will all be expert sailors by then.'

'What about…the danger?' Sindi paused. 'I mean, I don't understand the chart or anything but it's a long way, right? And if these are depths? And I have never set foot on a boat before. And I can swim, but…in a pool. I mean…' She gazed uncomfortably at the chart, then at Frank. 'I could… drown.'

Frank said, cheerful now, 'The first rule of sailing is that you have to respect the sea. So this leg here, from London to Falmouth, will be a shakedown cruise. We're near the coast, we can test the boat, and you two will get to familiarise yourselves. You'll be competent before we go into open water.'

This was not reassuring to Sindi.

'I've only ever swum in a pool, right?' she said again.

'Lots of sailors are not great swimmers,' said Frank. 'It's not that useful a skill. The cold of the water will finish you off pretty quick. And if you fall from high up, there's impact. Then currents and waves. Better to be good at staying on board.'

'I need a ciggie,' Sindi said.

Nicholas said, 'I forgot, I promised to go and see Louis.' He shuffled beside the table.

'But we haven't finished!' Frank said.

'It's enough for now, Frank,' I said. To them both, I said, 'Back at lunchtime, okay?'

When they were gone, I turned to Frank. 'There's only so much they can take in at once, Frank. They're kids! But did you see their faces?'

'It's not too much to ask that they concentrate for more than two minutes! We're making big sacrifices for them.'

'They don't need to know about our sacrifices.'

'Every single thing I fucking say, there you are, questioning, undermining, taking someone else's side.'

'They are just *young*, Frank. Like we were. Like Grainger was.'

'Oh. Like the bomber too? Stop making excuses for people, Helen! You're so fucking…fake!'

We sat in shocked silence. It never occurred to me that my lying was detected on some level by my husband. Moreover, it had never occurred to me that he might hate me. Just as my lying to him did not mean I hated him. This was, surely, the paradox of marriage, that it abstracted, transformed and confused the once perfectly delineated notions of love and hate.

Frank unexpectedly banged the table and stomped out of the room. A chart skittered into my lap. Glasses in the cupboard tinkled. A small original painting I really liked (of an oak tree with hundreds of slightly differently shaded green leaves), which Frank had bought me long ago for my birthday, fell and the glass cracked.

An argument ensued in my brain. A voice like mine sobbed and blamed Frank and another one explained minutely the reasons it could not possibly be his fault and how it didn't matter anyway, as we were leaving. The argument raged for long minutes, during which I sat quietly. Then I picked up the picture carefully, running my fingertip gently along the crack. A shard fell onto the floor. I noticed, now that I was close up, that the picture was really quite amateurish, quite clumsy, and I wondered why I had liked it so much.

16

THERE WAS NOW AN unstoppable momentum to our leaving, and it was all happening quicker than we expected. The ease with which we had acquired the *Innisfree* seemed prescient of the sale of the agency, and in its turn, the sale of our London home. The house sold in three hours. We may have been convinced society was disintegrating, but all of London seemed to fizz with moneyed house hunters who clearly did not agree. I thought of the people pouring out of the Tube when I went searching for James, how they flowed into any vacuum left by disaster. There were always more consumers, more developers, more investors; more warm bodies queueing up to spend their money right where rage had recently been given monumental expression. Not even the common knowledge that our house was the home of the Youngest Victim deterred them. Our buyers were a well-heeled couple our age who spent just twenty minutes in the house. An hour after they left, the agent rang to give their offer, which was well over our asking price. We thought we should think about it. An hour later, the agent rang again. They had upped the offer. Would we accept it and keep the house off the market? We said yes.

Our lives were commodities that others wanted to buy. This was a novel experience for me. I was not used to being valuable. Also novel was that we were funnelling our realised wealth into two non-assets – the *Innisfree* which was a wildly overvalued and subsequently depreciating asset, and a trip, which was no asset at all. We were, to the outside eye, throwing our success away, on a boat whose worth would never match the money spent on her, and on a voyage that would consume, not generate, cash. Our buyers wanted space, and paid handsomely for it. We were downsizing into almost no space at all. To the outside eye (everyone we knew) we were irresponsible. To us, the lack of hold our land life had on us was confirmation that this was right, or at least destiny.

Our mortgage was huge, obtained in those heady days when proof of ability to pay was not required, and dreamers, the self-employed and geniuses from left field like Frank could buy homes with a teeny deposit and a promise to take out an endowment plan to repay the capital. Where others might remember with unspeakable fondness their drinking or cocaine-fuelled glory days, I remembered the decade or so of financial insanity, where *I am what I say I am* was enough to buy a roof over your head. Neither Frank nor I had any capital. We were both from that most uncherished demographic, the lower middle class, and the generation after the one that hit the societal jackpot. Had a large deposit been required, we would never have been able to live in London.

Our land life had been created from dreams, bluster and ambition. And now these had been transmuted into hard cash. Not loads of hard cash, as the mortgage was so huge and the expenses of the *Innisfree* so vast, and the endowment plan we'd taken out had made consistent and catastrophic losses as well as being depleted by huge management fees. But there was enough left over to put some into an account for Nicholas should the worst happen. In other words, if there was a system, we had profited from it. Gamed it. Did that make me just like the traders and hedge-fund players the bomber had scorned so thoroughly?

Painstakingly constructing the *Innisfree* and one life, we simultaneously dismantled another. It made me think of the speeded-up old cartoon footage of Road Runner or Bugs Bunny laying train tracks in front of them as they escaped pursuit. Our rocketing towards our new life had a fanatical quality. I had started to dream of wandering in an empty house, through a series of ducts and tunnels, held together with nothing more than epoxy and tape, rattling and leaking both water and light. It was as if my brain was trying to connect these entirely incompatible existences to make sense of the transition.

Our belongings were being given or thrown away, or put into storage for that faraway time when we might come back. So, a month after the sale of the agency, and the end of a professional life, Frank and I started packing away our domestic life. We began in the sitting room, loading books and ornaments into boxes. I was grateful when, after a time,

Sindi joined us, lifting a bronze nymph from the shelf and holding it aloft.

'This is super-valuable, I bet,' she said. She ran her fingers over it. 'Where'd you get it, Miss? Is it solid metal?' She then eyed the painting of great fiery roses over the sitting room mantelpiece. 'Someone would pay a lot for that as well, I bet,' she said.

'Do you think so?' I said, leaning back to take it in afresh. Frank had started collecting art when he got a bit of money. He liked still lifes: intricate baskets, bruised fruit, lurid flowers. And this particular artist who did only these. I wasn't sure about it.

Elbow deep in packing books, Frank looked up. 'Yes, we need special storage for all the paintings. I'm not selling them. Ah Jesus, this entire Thomas Hardy collection. Are you sure, Helen? I mean when will we ever?'

'I feel about those like you feel about your flowers,' I said. 'I mean, it's kind of all or nothing, isn't it?'

'We're coming home though right?' said Nicholas from the doorway.

'Ah you're back!' I smiled at him.

He gave an abashed, sloppy smile and gripped the door. It swung from his grasp and he fell to the floor.

'You're drunk!' Sindi squealed.

'Am not,' he mumbled, still smiling weirdly and attempting to pull himself up by the doorframe.

Frank strode over to Nicky and hauled him up.

'Sorry, Dad,' Nicky began, holding his hand over his mouth. 'It was…Louis…his mum's vodka.'

Frank raised his eyebrows at me. I steered Nicholas to a

chair. The smile had started to sag. His eyes were closing. 'I feel sick.'

Sindi knelt before him. 'Hey squirt, how much did you have?'

Nicholas slumped sideways. His face was pale and slack. He said, so quietly that I almost missed it, 'I don't want to go. I'll miss Louis…'

Sindi said, 'But we're the two musketeers!'

His eyes opened blearily. 'But, school… Everyone thinks this is weird.'

'You were set for the Heights, right?' Sindi looked up at me. 'I can tell you straight up that the Heights is rubbish. It's no loss at all not to be going there. Since your mum left… well, it's beyond crap. Come on Nicholas, don't back out now. I can't go if you don't.'

'You're gorgeous, Sindi,' Nicholas mumbled, his eyes closing.

'*In vino veritas!*' said Frank, scooping him up and carrying him to his room. Nicholas flopped over his shoulder, waved blearily at me, setting Sindi off giggling. Frank's frustration echoed down the hall: 'We have *got* to get out of here.'

'I'm going to call Louis's mother,' I said when he returned. 'I don't appreciate her getting my kid pissed.' But Frank rested a hand on my arm.

'We're gone soon. There'll be no drinking at sea anyway.'

'No drinking at sea?' Sindi's eyes were wide.

'In harbour, yes, but not out in the ocean. It's dangerous.'

'Fun times,' Sindi said.

Some time later, when we had packed as much as we could in the sitting room without making it uninhabitable, and we were sitting drinking some hot chocolate, the door opened and Nicholas appeared. He was in his pyjamas.

'Ah Nicholas, you know what we can do a lot of on the *Innisfree*?' Frank lifted his camera from a box. 'Pictures! We could document the whole trip. Father and son. What do you think?' He smiled at them both. 'You see, this is why I get impatient. I want you to understand how *fantastic* this is, what an *adventure* it is.'

'Sorry, Dad,' said Nicholas wearily. 'I just got sad about leaving Louis.'

'He could fly out to see you at Cape Verde,' Frank said. 'There's no need to drink yourself to death.'

Sindi stared at this display of family tenderness. 'When I got pissed for the first time at nine, Clint went mental because it was his beer. I got a belting.'

*

Later, I stood helplessly in the middle of the bedroom, defeated by the scale of what must be decided upon. There was so much we had never properly unpacked, including boxes of childhood things from Fleetwood which my mother had sent me when we first arrived in London, as if she wanted to be rid of it all. My old jotters and photo albums. Clothes from when I was a baby. And cuddly toys, grown aged and stiff, staring from their boxes brightly, as if they could fool us, turn back time. I knew my mother had not sent them to me in a spirit of love. They were packages of anxiety, of loss; each one saying, Okay then, you're all grown up? Here's all your stuff! If she could have flung it out of an upstairs window like an abandoned wife I am sure she would have.

With a ruthless sigh, I turned from them to a more recent box in the corner, whose contents I knew I would not be parted from, no matter the shortage of space on the *Innisfree*. Inside, among the few newspaper clippings I had kept, was my notebook. I felt a pang at the sight of it. I tipped the box out and searched through the contents, wondering about the memory stick. There was no sign of it. My mind, and my memory, were not what they were since the bomb. I was just about to take the notebook into bed with me when there was a tap on the door and Sindi shyly put her head round it.

'What do you think?' she asked. Her hair was in a neat French plait, just like mine on the *Innisfree*.

Frank used to love my hair in a plait because he could undo it. He loved to unravel my handiwork and run his fingers through the strands. I had not worn my hair like that in years. When not pinned up, it fell around my shoulders in thick, peppery waves.

'It suits you,' I said.

She moved to the mirror, beckoned me over. I went to her side and our heads were reflected together. She was wearing a big shirt over her leggings.

'Did Frank give you that?' I asked.

'Oh, this? He was going to throw it out, but it's so warm and comfy so I asked if I could have it.'

'You're welcome to go through all my stuff if you want. We need to buy you sailing gear, but if there's anything in there that you'd like…? There's loads I'll need to throw out. You won't believe how little space we'll have.'

With an alacrity I hadn't seen since the Intervention, she

shot to the rail and began pulling garments off, holding them against herself, throwing them on the bed. There were so many clothes I had not worn since long before the bomb. I was a bit embarrassed by them now: my overly feminine dresses, blouses and skirts. Once on land, after years of waterproofs and shorts, I'd taken pleasure in dressing the part of woman, wife, teacher. Sindi frowned, skimming a small hand over the maternity dresses bunched at the end, moving past them without comment. She grabbed a particularly silky floaty dress and twirled.

'You're not really a dress sort of girl, are you?' I laughed. Sindi's look was sexy because of skin exposure, but increasingly I was coming to believe that it was not so much a 'look' as lack of clothes. I'd noticed that since dressing gowns, jumpers and warm shirts had become available, she had begun increasingly to wear them.

'Not a dress girl? Why not?' In a second, she undid Frank's shirt, wriggled out of it and slipped on the dress, standing in front of the mirror. We both stared. It fitted her perfectly, far better than it had me.

'I never wore anything like this.' She turned to me, hands on hips. 'Listen up, kids!' she said, with a toss of her head. 'Chalmers! Explain xylem and phloem!'

'Ha ha!'

She tilted her head to the mirror, grinning.

'Those clothes belong to a woman who's gone, Sindi,' I said. You don't want those. *I* don't want them.'

She slipped out of the dress, put the shirt back on, buttoning it thoughtfully.

'You know, you're starting to look how you used to at

175

school. Before all this,' she said.

'That's nice of you to say, Sindi, but she's gone.'

Between my eyebrows was a deep vertical frown line. It was a new development. I was sure it had not been there before the bomb. I pressed my thumb into it, but it didn't disappear.

'And in a way, I'm not sorry,' I added.

'What do you mean?'

'I liked who I was on the *Innisfree*, back in the day. Maybe I can get her back.' I smiled at Sindi in the mirror.

'I think we have the same face shape.' She blew out her cheeks, stuck out her chin. 'See? Heart-shaped.'

I burst out laughing. But it was true, uncannily so.

Sindi began to French-plait my hair like hers, her fingers tingling on my scalp. She said, thoughtfully, 'You know, we both have it.'

'Have what?'

'Clint said, when I was about ten or something, "One day you're going to be able to twist men around your little finger. You'll be able to get whatever you want from them." I didn't understand what he meant. He told me, "You know exactly what you're doing. You've known it since the day you were born."'

'That's a horrible thing to say to a little girl,' I said.

'It's the nicest thing he ever said to me!'

I sighed. 'One time on the *Innisfree*, Frank went out onto the foredeck and he kicked the anchor winch when I was chatting to another guy in the crew. I didn't know he had; I wasn't paying him attention at all. He told me about it later, showed me his nail turning black. He'd hurt himself because of *me*.' I paused, looked into her eyes in the mirror. 'It's not love, Sindi.'

Her hands waved about my head and colour came to her cheeks. 'Don't take this wrong, Miss, but I think you are doing everything all wrong with Frank.'

'You mean, he'll go off with someone else if I don't buck my ideas up?'

'I just mean, you could wrap him round your finger if you wanted to.'

'Well, I appreciate your marriage advice,' I said.

She seemed to want to say something. She wrestled with it, while she finished plaiting my hair. With every twist, our reflections became more and more alike.

'The intervention, Miss? That you did on me? I want you to know, that was the best day of my life.'

'It was?'

'I mean, it made me think about things, what I could be, maybe.'

'And?'

'One day I'd like to have a beautiful house and a rich husband, like you.'

'Oh?'

She nodded. 'Your life is amazing, Miss... All the books you have! And your art, and your garden, and having no worries – I mean I know there was the bomb and everything, but I mean no worries about money.'

'Sindi, it's not what you think it is.'

'Me and my husband, we'd have a pool, and parties and a really big house.' She flung herself upon the dresses strewn on the bed, sighed happily. 'I can't get over how soft these

177

beds are, Miss. But not squishy.' She spread out, testing the surface like Goldilocks. 'You know, at Clint's we all slept on foam. He had a mate worked at a factory cutting the stuff up. Clint sent him sizes and he'd do it at night. Everything from boosted foam. Sofa, chairs; everything.' She closed her eyes. I thought she might be asleep. 'Springs are the business,' she murmured.

'I've got bad news for you, Sindi,' I said. 'On the boat the bunks are foam. And your opportunities for meeting rich men to marry are nil.'

I eyed the bed. I wanted to get back in, suddenly. Curl up with my notebook. Sleep and sleep.

'I'm just dreaming, Miss, that's all.' She looked over at me, her eyes full of something unspoken. 'Because…I can have dreams now, right?'

17

IT WAS CLOSE TO TWO WEEKS since I had been to the *Innisfree*. There were so many tasks that surround leaving a life. Endless packing, selling and giving away; trying to keep the news from getting out too far, but of course it was impossible to sell an agency and a house and withdraw children from school without having to explain. We were in the grip of a heatwave, day after day, that melted roads and made the plums in the garden ooze and wasps fizz against the windows. It was impossible to sleep and so one night I decided to cool down and calm my mind by going to the *Innisfree*.

Creeping down the stairs to leave the house, I saw a glow in the sitting room. Nicholas and Sindi were side by side on the sofa, backs to me, peering at her phone. The sound was turned low, but a shiver of recognition drew me closer.

Careful not to disturb them I tiptoed a little way in.

On the screen the bomber's video was playing. The words were too tinny for me to make out. I could just see his red curls and button nose and the straps of his home-made suicide vest over his shoulders. I had never watched the video all the way through. It was, apparently, over an hour in length. Why were they watching it? In particular, why was Nicholas watching it? Frank simply reported that the boy was a waste of space and that was all I needed to know. I had glimpsed him on the news that one time, and otherwise kept him at bay in my thoughts because what threatened to overcome me was the fact of his youth. The age that my own child and Sindi would be approaching soon. The age of a life opening up, of excitements, and joy.

Sindi and Nicholas sniggered in unison, then burst into suppressed, hysterical laughter. Shocked, I almost ran into the room to drag Nicholas out. How could he laugh at that video? How could he even watch it at all?

But what good would it do? Perhaps this was simply another shockwave from the bomb. It had sent us all mad in our different ways, an insane event unleashing inappropriate reactions. I forced myself to tiptoe past them, slipped out through the door and walked, shaking, to the end of the road, where I called a taxi.

The peace of the marina enveloped me, just as it had the night that James died. This time I had my own key fob and I let myself into the yard, the hulks of the boats cast into shadow by a floodlight. Occasionally the silence was broken by a hoot or a splash where a moorhen stirred from its slumber under a pontoon.

We were leaving within the month: the jobs now were getting supplies on board the *Innisfree* and getting her into the water. She was all but finished. What I needed was to be given the strength to keep my mouth shut about James. I believed in the *Innisfree*, her power to reassure me that the past was strong enough to contain me.

Her new teak deck glimmered black, warm to the touch. I curled up in the cockpit. There was a charge between the *Innisfree* and me, two living things alone together in the night. She seemed to know the reason for my visit, that I had come for guidance. Not Romy-guidance. The kind you can't pay for, or at least not with money.

Taking out my phone, I logged into the new account I had opened on an anonymous talk forum for women. Free from identity, women gave each other advice here. They poured out their problems with husbands, lovers, children, themselves. Troubled by my persistent intrusive thoughts of James, and the fact of having lied so comprehensively to Frank, I had been following the forum and seeing the advice given to others for several weeks. But even though everything was anonymous I had found it impossible to ask for advice about James while in the family home.

Sane discourse could no longer include James. The only emotions available to me, to all of us, within the family were acceptance of the past and excitement about the future. My continued preoccupation with him was so disruptive that I hid it from everyone, including myself, submitting to it secretly when alone, but never acknowledging that he was, to all intents and purposes, very much alive. I did not write my letters any more; my communications operated at a guerrilla level in my consciousness, invisible to all except in the unguarded movement of my lips, like a runner mouthing the songs in her headphones.

Navigating to the forum, I shifted to make myself comfortable and tapped out an account of my fixation. Squinting in the gloom, fighting the autocorrect, I detailed my flagrant inability to get over him or let him go or tell the truth about what had happened.

Articulating the story took ages. I had to keep going back, inserting a detail I'd missed or, more frequently, deleting digressions. Anyone who has tried to speak their secret for the first time will know how it wants to roam, how it grows tentacles of narrative that seek to drag you deeper, away from what you meant to say, to drown you. Dew settled into my clothes, hastily thrown on. I shivered, but I persisted. Under cover of my username *captainspiralise* I told my tale.

The wise women of the forum pondered my story.

> – It sounds like a disaster unfolding in real time, to be honest. What about your husband, your children? Lying to them is very destructive. And how do you know it was mutual? You found him, not the other way around. Men say all kinds of things to avoid conflict. Maybe he was just freaked out, saying what he had to, to get away? Then the accident happened, and kind of froze it all in your mind? Sorry if this sounds harsh. I am just trying to help.
>
> – Captainspiralise, this is not real.

I responded: But he is real. This is why I am here. Please don't flame me.

They said:

– You sound very lonely, Captain.
   – Does he ever talk back?
   – Can I ask how old you are?
I said: 44. No, he doesn't talk back.
They said:
   – You need to close the book on this one. 44 is not
   18 if you get my drift. You will waste your life pining.
   You will miss your child growing up, and give your
   relationship with your husband no chance at all.
   – This is heartbreaking, Captain.

A line of gold shimmered beyond Canary Wharf. My hair
was damp, my clothes soaked through. I was aching. There
was silence but for the hiss of the Thames – its high tide slap
against the harbour wall. The cursor blinked, waiting for my
reply. If you come to the wise women they tell you things you
don't want to hear. *Dear James, is believing in you just a mental
illness? How do I let you go if you are not real?*

The wise women said:
   – Are you there Captain?
   – By the way, all is not lost with your marriage you
   know. You can rekindle a marriage. Nostalgia is your
   friend here. Focus on where you fell in love, how you
   met.

I said: Okay, I am doing that. I am writing this in the very
place we met :)
They said:
   – Go no contact. No Ouija boards (lol)
   – Set down the burden, Captain.
They said:
   – Take all the mementos and burn them.

    – When you find yourself thinking of him, snap a
band on your wrist.

    – Captainspiralise, you are an addict. It's going to
be hard.

I said: Shall I tell my husband the truth about what
happened? He will be furious. And hurt.

I turned over my phone, and closed my eyes while I waited
for replies. The rising sun warmed my face.

'Mum!'

I almost dropped the phone in shock. There in front of
me was Nicholas, still dressed in the clothes he'd been in
yesterday.

He put a hand on my shoulder. 'Mum, are you all right?'

'What are you doing here?' I said, wiping my eyes. 'No, no,
I'm fine.'

'I couldn't sleep. I pinched Dad's keys to the marina.'

I stared at him. I couldn't utter the words, 'How could
you betray me by watching that video? And why were you
laughing?' Instead I managed, 'Okay, well you're here now.
I'm just watching the sun rise.'

He sat beside me. I was acutely aware of my son's soft
breathing. The sky erupted in pink and orange, amplified in
the river. The clouds were streaks of lava. Nicholas took his
phone out and filmed the horizon, then turned the camera
to me.

'Smile, mum! Your hair looks like it's on fire.'

I put my hand up to shield my face and saw my skin was
glowing.

Behind him, illumination was spreading across the decks
of the *Innisfree*. So powerful and strange was the effect, at

first I thought I was dreaming. Like a curtain being pulled back, the light slowly revealed the transformation of the boat.

She was unrecognisable from the wreck we had brought to the yard. The new helm glittered, and the polished hatch blazed white. The top-end life raft in its emblazoned container radiated safety. The external navigation screens were in place, and I ran my finger over the elegant dials. Then I got up from the cockpit and made my way to the bow. Nicholas followed, at first filming but then putting the phone in his pocket so he could take it all in. Heading straight for where I had cut her open all those weeks ago, I searched the spot for a scar, some sense that it had happened. But she was completely healed. Her new rails shone. Looking out from them at the sunlit Thames streaming away it was almost as if we were plunging through a golden sea.

Nicholas said, 'Sindi was watching the video when I left. She's been watching it over and over.'

'*You* were watching it, Nicholas. I saw you.'

'When!'

'Just now! And you laughed! Look, I don't want to forbid you from watching it. I bet you've both seen plenty worse on the internet. It's just… I don't know.'

I didn't want to get into it with my son, that actually I *did* want to forbid him from watching the bomber's video, that I was appalled he would even think of it. It was all right for Sindi, but my own son!

'Do you know why I was laughing?'

'No.'

'They've released the full version now. It was edited before, just clips for the news – and halfway through, the guy's cat

185

wanders into the shot. He doesn't know; he keeps on talking, and it's wandering about behind him. It's gone viral. It's a meme, now.' He sighed. 'I mean the rest of it's not funny, but that bit… I'm sorry.'

'Maybe it would make me laugh,' I said, but my son shook his head.

His honest face glowed in the dawn. Everything was galloping ahead of me, faster than I could reach it, even what was considered funny and what was not. *A bomber's video is so unintentionally hilarious the survivor's son laughs.* I recalled, then, Corin telling us one time on the *Innisfree* about his father who had been a POW of the Japanese in the war, held for several years in desperate conditions in Hong Kong. Long after the war, when Corin was a young man, he bought a Japanese car, because they were cheap and cool. His father begged him not to, tried to make him understand how the experience at the hands of the Japanese had hurt him. But Corin brushed him off. His father never admonished him, and simply suffered in silence. Years later, when his father died, Corin regretted it viscerally. There was no way round such things. The child could not be expected to feel as the parent does. Isn't this just how it is?

'Nicky, it's okay,' I lied. 'Forget it. Look, stay here and enjoy the boat. How about I go and get us a bacon sandwich? The cafe will be open now.'

I swung down the ladder to the ground. I found myself longing, like Frank, to be gone from here. I turned to look back at the *Innisfree*. The sun illuminated every particle of the boat's midnight blue shimmer. She was breathtaking, like the ocean itself at night. I stepped back to try and take her in. She had two silver stripes on top of the blue, one at the water line, and a thinner one near the rails, just as she did back then. Frank had made it his mission to try and restore her to the boat we remembered, and he had succeeded.

She towered over me like a mythical sea creature. I ran my fingers over where the crew had filled some holes in her hull. They were smooth indentations now, emphasising that her body was crafted, mended, created with human hands. Each imperfection made her seem stronger. How proudly she stood, how honest her body. There was no boat in the yard to compare with her. But it was her name that caught at my throat. 'Innisfree' was inscribed in beautiful spare script on each side of the prow, each letter shining silver.

As I walked along the side of the marina to the café, my phone pinged. I was not surprised, expecting Frank to ring or text, wondering where I was. It was indeed Frank. Instead of *Where are you?* Or even *????* he had sent a photo. In the greasy steam of the café I clicked on the photo and gazed at it, puzzled for a moment, until I realised it was of my husband's erect penis. No comment or caption. Just the still life of the flowers in the background, and his blurred toes.

From behind the counter, the server said, 'Hello, madam? Your rolls are ready,' jolting me out of my surprise.

I took the bag absently and turned to go. My heart lifted unexpectedly. I mean, I didn't actually want a dick pic from my husband, and it was out of character, but it was definitely a new kind of communication between us, and I did want that. More than anything I wanted things to be new. I texted him, 'I'm at the yard with N'. I added a heart emoji.

An almost imperceptible breeze spread its interference over

the marina. In one spot, the interference became miniature rogue waves where one set of waves meets another. My heart contracted to remember how Frank pointed these out from the deck of the *Innisfree* long ago when we were cruising off Bayona. How these shivers of the water were exactly, in microcosm, the movement of the waves in open ocean. The same forces, whether massive or tiny. At the time, we were becalmed, a strange haze from a sandstorm wiping out the horizon and leaving us entombed in silence and under siege from these tiny phenomena. Everything is something else. Everything is present somewhere else. It's all linked, all part of a whole. I wanted to find this a comfort.

There were notifications from the forum. I opened it up and saw message after message telling me to come clean with Frank, that honesty was the way to heal a broken heart and move forward. That the only way to get over something that wasn't real was to engage wholeheartedly with something that was.

The *Innisfree* was waiting. She and I dealt in greater truths. I deleted the forum app.

A little later, Nicholas and I had finished our rolls, and he was lying back in the cockpit editing his sunrise film for TikTok. It was 8.30. I heard the gates to the yard clanging open.

'Look Nicky!' I said.

The crew were marching in, carrying between them the *Innisfree*'s new mast. It was enormous, in stunning grey carbonate and its length needed all of them. Behind them came Frank and Sindi, pushing a trolley on which were piled the new sails. Frank waved, with a huge smile. I waved back.

I remembered now that the plan was to go into the water today. A lift and hold. Straps would be placed round the *Innisfree*'s body and she would be lowered into the water and held there overnight to be sure she had no leaks. Then, her mast could be fixed on, her sails raised and that would be the point when she would carry us away.

18

'Are we famous?' Nicholas whispered. Beside me on deck, he was holding up his phone to film the crowds of people lining up at the harbour wall to watch us leave.

'I think it's the *Innisfree*, not us,' I said. The *Innisfree* was about to enter the Thames from the lock. The dockmasters in their life jackets had closed the inner lock gates and opened the outer ones enough to let water in and lift the boat to the height of the river. In a boil of water, she was slowly rising, to claps and cheers.

'We've really done it!' I could hardly believe it. The breeze thrilled across my face. Every part of the *Innisfree* gleamed and shimmered. People were squinting to see the top of her mast, vanishing into the sky. Everything was possible. How close I had come to blowing this whole success story apart, with my childish need to be understood, for Frank to hear my story, for me to have forgiveness. These things are not necessary. You build the life you want. You can integrate past, present, future with your own hands. I was proud that Nicholas could see this. There's more than one life in a life.

Frank was standing at the mast, Ray-Bans on, chatting up to the harbour master, who was operating the controls from a little shelter on the harbour side. Sindi clung uncertainly to the rail in her life jacket. She made a decision to cross to the other side and strode across the deck, arms out like a tightrope walker.

'Sindi, no!' Frank turned to intercept her. 'Remember what I said? One hand for you, one for the boat at all times.'

'Just walking is controversial on this bloody boat.'

Now the lock gates were fully open, the water foaming around them, forming a grand entrance to the river.

'Goodbye!' I cried, waving to Jessica and Marvin, our neighbours in the boatyard, and some other boat-dwellers on the marina with whom we had become friendly over the past few months. Promises to keep in touch were yelled out.

Suddenly in the crowd I glimpsed Romy. I couldn't believe it.

'Romy! Goodbye! Thank you!' I waved.

She tapped her heart and clenched her hands together, mouthed, 'Well done!'

You don't have to be a sailor to be stunned by a beautiful sailing boat jostling in her stall, getting ready to charge. There was a gasp from the crowd as the *Innisfree*'s shining midnight hull greeted the Thames.

Wind ruffled the river as it ebbed. We were going to take advantage of ebb and breeze to get us out of the estuary and into the sea and towards Falmouth as quickly as possible.

At the entrance, Frank turned the helm to starboard. Banks of phones went up to capture the moment. The harbour master gave a sober nod. The dockmasters shared a joke, and waved with big smiles. A boat leaving the marina is an everyday occurrence, but not a boat like this.

Everyone waving us off respected our crazed haemorrhage of cash, our stubborn determination to have a better life and escape the constraints of society. Sailors know what awaits you, but will never tell you that you are mad. They won't quiz you on your safety provisions, or your experience. The sailing highways are not regulated. You need no qualifications and no permission. There are conventions and codes, there to save your life. It's up to you if you want to save it or not. No one is going to stop you. They're going to wave you off, like this.

Frank was in his element. 'OK, let's get the sail up. Nicky, come here. Sindi, go and stand with Helen to keep it running smooth. To Falmouth!'

And now the first great shift of perspective, to be in the river looking back at the land. People stopped on the Thames Path to watch and wave. The motor whirred and the sail rose smoothly, higher and higher up the great mast. Frank altered the winches to orientate the sail into the wind, and the *Innisfree* leapt forward, drenching us in glittering spray. I pulled Sindi to me excitedly, kissed her head.

'Here we go!' I cried.

Sindi, for the first time in all the time I'd known her, was openly astounded. Her French-plaited hair was framed by her billowing hood. She gazed around her, then at me, then squeezed my hand.

And it came to me then that this beginning was purer, clearer and more full of possibility that those launches in the past. The *Innisfree* was new, while containing everything she had once been. In the corner of my eye I glimpsed Corin, checking the way ahead for obstacles in the water; the changing crew of our youth, Matt, Simon, George, even Grainger, their voices carried through the rigging, their shadows over the teak.

'Eight knots!' cried Frank. We're doing well. 'Now everyone – keep watch all round. The Thames is wildly busy, we don't want to sink before we've started!'

Our eyes met, and in that connection, at that ecstatic moment, was a glimpse of something I had begun to think was impossible: a second chance at life.

19

Position: 47, 16'N / 06°, 50'W

No one could find the sea sickness pills, and we were now entering the Bay of Biscay, one of the most turbulent stretches of ocean in the northern hemisphere. Convinced they must be on board somewhere, I turned the cabins upside down, my apprehension growing. After food, pills for sea sickness were perhaps the most important supplies, but I could not, for the life of me, actually remember packing them, and nor could Frank. In a reverse placebo effect – knowing that we had no pills and were far from anywhere where they could be obtained – the first symptoms began to take hold. My vision nudged out of synch with my balance. A sensation like a soundless groan unfolded in my veins. Acid burned in my throat.

Sindi and Nicholas had no idea how bad sea sickness

could be, so they were unconcerned at first. But now they saw me succumbing, they did too. Nicholas spent long hours lying on his back in the saloon, as close as possible to the centre line of the boat, his hands folded over his chest like a sarcophagus. Sindi remained on deck for all hours, taking Frank's advice to fix her eyes on the horizon. Nausea seemed to be the best thing for her smoking: it made it worse and she had to stop. Gradually though, both of them seemed to acclimatise, perhaps due to a combination of youth and the realisation that sea sickness was both awful and boring. Frank, meanwhile, was not affected at all.

But I could not gain a hold on myself; my body seemed to be carrying its own rollercoaster. Nausea shrank our vast surroundings to the size of my own throbbing head. Ginger biscuits had no effect, nor snapping a band on my wrist, though I did it anyway. (Was this the treatment for everything we didn't understand?)

On deck was where the dispute between inner balance and outer horizon was most pronounced. So my days on this voyage of a lifetime were now spent almost entirely below, far from the fresh salty winds and the vast blue curve of the planet. There was so much work to be done and I could barely move to do any of it, guiltily watching as Frank kept all the watches and did most of the cooking. Trying to remain motionless in the cabin or saloon, I ground my teeth in frustration. For want of a few sea sickness pills, there was no prospect in view of when I would be a fully participating member of the crew.

The only state that gave any stability was sleep. I sought it with the blind urgency of the new mother, but it was almost impossible to come by. After several sleepless nights, I was lying bleakly on the saloon floor gazing at the galley and the packets and jars secured in their shelves, racking my brain for something, anything that could lessen my sickness. Then, through my blurry apprehension of my surroundings, the names on the packets and jars suddenly swam into relief. I noticed the distinctiveness of their designs, for the first time in all those years of familiarity. While the others sat out on deck, their voices drifting cheerfully down the hatch, I staggered to my feet and, in a dull trance, boiled the kettle and laid some jars in the hot water, standing over them as the steam condensed on my face. After long minutes of gripping the side of the sink, the water was cool enough for me to peel off the labels and lay them carefully out on the surface to dry. I dabbed them with kitchen roll; when that still took too long, I pegged them to a string hung before an open porthole. This succession of tasks absorbed me completely and, for its duration, I was not sick.

When the labels were dry, I pressed them flat like petals into *The Navigation Bible*. I was entranced by them: they asked so little of my broken circuits to comprehend. Their associations crowded my mind, shuffling out the bare-boned nausea. Fired by this success, I was on the hunt for more.

Waitrose, Gordons, Heinz, Swan. Apple, Hellman's, Hobbs. Faber-Castell. ('Why have you got those?' Frank asked, growing impatient with my incapacity. 'I like branded pencils,' I mumbled. He replied, 'I've never seen you draw... Can you draw?' Familiar ponderous squint. *Diagrams.* I longed to confess. *Route maps.*) When would I ever say these names again, except as a secret psalm to myself? *San*

Pellegrino. Twinings. Green and Black. I understood why they compelled themselves silently to my lips. The earth we moved over now was formless, generic, not man-made, not *named*. Something in me wasn't ready for it; the abandoning of all we knew. The great emptiness over which we had no power at all, and upon which language, history – anything human at all – was insignificant to the point of meaninglessness.

A recollection took hold, of something we'd done as kids. I swayed to the galley and retrieved from the rubbish some empty Walkers crisp packets I'd been eyeing. Instead of simply putting them in the book, I took out a baking tray, laid them upon it and tottered to the stove where it swayed on its gimbal. After what seemed like about an hour of infuriated fiddling with the latch on the door, I slid them into the oven and turned it on. Then it was time for a quick grovel on deck to the victor in the current skirmish between my brain and the cosmos – before summoning Nicholas from the foredeck and Sindi from where she was sprawled on the hammock that Frank had erected between main mast and foresail.

They appeared at the saloon table, a little warily. Sindi winced at my slimy face.

'How's it going?' she asked, carefully, nodding at the labels festooning the portholes like a peculiar Christmas decoration. She picked a newly dried label from the open Boat Maintenance book. 'Heinz! You say Heinz over and over…and it sounds really funny! Heinz Heinz Heinz!' She snorted with laughter, and Nicholas joined in.

'Hellman's! Hell! Mans!' He started marching in small circles. I didn't like the look of it, and called a halt. 'HELLMANS!'

They froze, all of us unnerved.

'I called you down because I think you will like this,' I said grimly, because grimness kept my lips taut, my bile in, no matter how I felt. Manoeuvring carefully, for my sickly body was really little more than a collection of obstacles to itself now, I retrieved the tray with the packets on it and laid it before them. They gasped. The crisp packets had shrunk perfectly – tiny and preserved in every detail, little corporate dominoes.

'What the—!' said Sindi, her grimy finger reaching out.

I brushed her hand away. 'Let them cool,' I said.

The boat took a particularly hard roll and the smell of melted plastic overcame me. I gripped the corner of the table, biting my lips to suppress the gag as the two of them leaned over the minute packets in wonder. They glowed like jewels in the light from the porthole. After a few minutes, when the packets were cool, Sindi picked up Ready Salted, turned it in her fingers. Nicholas blocked the bead of the sun with a tiny green Salt and Vinegar. It cast a shadow like a target on his nose.

Before the packets were fully hard, I pierced the corner of each with a screwdriver. Then I slipped a length of fishing line through the hole and made a pendant. Sindi and Nicholas gazed open-mouthed, like toddlers. Exultant, I observed their wonder. I was a proper mother, homeschooling her children, an alchemist turning rubbish into treasure.

I remembered the kids in my class then; their love of logos, of brands. The elaborate fakes they obtained and paraded: watches, sweaters, bags. Their tags sprayed on walls and doors, the carefully constructed brands of one. I had grown so fond of the colourful skewed poetry, the assertion against formlessness, without really knowing why. Now, however, I understood. And with the recollection, guilt burned in my throat. Had I failed them?

'Here,' I said, with tears in my eyes.

I wove the twine through one of her matted dreadlocks, arranging the pendant so that it hung at Sindi's temple. I fastened Nicholas's around his neck, breathing in the fresh salt of his hair as I did so. His fingertips played along the string as I tied it, brushing mine. We are scavengers now, I thought – of a life that's gone.

*

That night, I was shattered from a brief, grateful slumber by the boat pitching heavily. While asleep, I had rolled heavily into the leecloth, a canvas sheet strung along the bunk to stop me falling out, and its weave was branded into my face. Frank was not beside me.

We were meant to alternate watches so we could rest, but so far, of course, he was on watch almost all the time due to my sickness. In open sea, watches are essential and relentless, twenty-four hours a day. They are also, once you get used to them, the best part of ocean sailing, when friendships form and are deepened. Your watch mate is a companion and fellow witness to the wonders of the ocean at night, and you are jointly responsible for the safety of the rest of the crew, grabbing their few hours' sleep.

I fell in love with Frank on night watch. He lost his gawky shyness, became the warm comforting presence that

I came to trust. And he made me laugh, so much so that occasionally Corin would come up from below and tell us to keep it down. In the end he scheduled us apart for night watches, but it was too late. We'd found each other.

For this trip, Frank had invested in all the navigational aids, including the Automatic Identification System which showed the details and position of every similarly AIS-registered boat in the area. But many vessels, such as little fishing boats, are not on the system, and there are obstacles at sea: containers, whales, stray lobster pots. I was worried about him doing every watch alone. What if he fell asleep at the helm and missed something? I was half-mad with exhaustion; surely he must be too? But more than this, it was time to make amends to Frank. It was time to find each other again.

I would just try to steady myself first. I stumbled into the tiny bathroom in our cabin, paused over the basin.

We had filled the water tanks in Plymouth, and they had to last us until we stopped again, which Frank had decreed would not be before Cape Verde. So – no showers, washing up and teeth-cleaning done with the merest dribble, turned off the second it was not needed. And the toilet flushed with great calculation. I turned on the pump and let water pour onto my hands, splashing it lavishly onto my face. Reparations demanded cool fresh water.

A little steadier now, I rubbed the greasy mirror and was surprised that I seemed to look quite bright. I tied my hair in a ponytail and ran my finger over my lips. It was hard to remember that these lips had kissed James, not so long ago. They had formed the words *I love you*. The image scrolled behind my eyes of us running down the escalators, all fear gone. I gripped the basin. My eyes, open now, panicking, were red and rheumy like a monkey in an experiment. My broken heart was nothing more than a lever which I pressed to deliver a shock. Would I never get over him? Is this what the *Innisfree* was telling me, with her relentless shaking of me, so that I could hold onto nothing real?

'No!' I said.

The boat pitched, almost tipping me over.

I hung on, facing the woman in the mirror. 'He's dead. It's over.'

I knew – this thought being the only solid thing in my world, it seemed – that I had to overcome this. My body rebelled against the knowledge, and instead presented, formidably, its case for *love*. When you decide to fight an addiction, there is no fanfare, no triumph. In fact all you encounter is protest from every cell in your body and guerrilla resistance from every inanimate object around you. A wave of sickness crashed over me. The boat rolled and I banged my head.

Cursing, but determined, I dragged myself up the steps and through the hatch, to where Frank was on watch alone. The sky was brilliant with stars, and the air was soft and cool, quenching my skin. I breathed it in deeply, revelling in the moments before my sickness would return.

It was 2am, and conditions were growing calmer. The barometer showed pressure was rising, which meant good weather ahead.

Frank was at the helm, consulting the screens, his face lit with a tiny glow. He looked up hopefully. 'Ah! Feeling better?' he said.

'I've come to help,' I said.

He rubbed his eyes. 'Good news.'

The moon was full and laid a wide bright train across the ocean. The mainsail was starting to flap.

'A flappy sail is an unhappy sail,' I murmured, repeating Corin's saying.

We both reached to activate the winch to turn the sail better into the wind. Frank got there first, operating, with a kind of muscle memory.

'Does she drive like she used to?' I asked.

'Better, I think. Of course all the equipment is new. But maybe I've improved.' He smiled, looking for approval. 'Not much traffic tonight. A container ship far over there to the south west.'

At night on watch you scrutinise the black waters with the intensity of a new mother looking at her baby's face for a sign, an indication that action is required, and if so what action. I focused on the waters, snapping the band on my wrist automatically to ward off nausea.

'Remember our watches back then?' I said. 'So many hours, just being together. I loved them.'

He smiled at me in the glow of the instruments. 'You were such a chatterbox. Corin ended up pairing me with Matt. The most boring man alive.'

In a world of triviality and small talk, night watches are islands of meaningful connection. Now we sat in a quiet that bristled with experience. There were no more stories to tell. Well, of course there were, but these were the stories we were hiding from each other.

'Frank, I want to tell you something,' I said confidentially, as if it was back then and he was my friend.

My heart pounded. I knew this was a risk, but my sense of what we were to each other felt suddenly strong.

'The whole James thing… I want you to know… It's over.'

The truth was a little different, in that I *wanted* it to be over, I was determined that it would be over. But my new approach was to behave as though words created real change in the physical world. Declaring a state to make it real.

'Oh,' Frank said.

'The thing is, some of it is out of my control. And I want to have control of it, if that makes sense.'

Frank said, 'I'll make some tea,' and got up to go to the galley. It was his way of buying time to think.

I pinged the band on my wrist and stared out at the blackness. A bright light was crossing far in front of us. This was the container vessel being tracked on the AIS, too far away to affect us. There was a splash to my left: at first I thought it might be dolphins come to play alongside the boat, as they often had in the past, but it was simply the curlicues of our wake, rising and falling, living sculptures of water that arose, perfectly realised, and then sank away into a dark trough. I was grateful for the lights in the distance, reminding me we were not completely alone in this unstable vastness. They grew smaller, disappearing into the horizon.

Frank appeared with a mug of ginger tea for me. He wedged the mug in its gimballed holder, where it rocked gently, as if self-soothing.

He sat opposite me, folded his arms as if he was a negotiator getting ready to talk me off a ledge and said, 'This again, Helen? The fact that you even need to tell me that it's over pisses me off. I mean, if it's over, why do you need to mention it?'

'Now that we're here, on the *Innisfree* together, just like we used to be…' I trailed off. 'I want to be really *here* with you. I want us to be honest with each other.'

'I thought we were!'

'The night I said I was mugged… I wasn't. I was with James. I found him.'

'You found him? How?'

'By chance. I bumped into him at London Bridge. I mean I was looking for him, but I wasn't expecting to find him.'

My husband was staring at me. 'So what happened?' he said, his voice uncertain.

'We had coffee. It turned out he'd been looking for me too. Then he took me on the Underground to help me get over my fear of it.'

'So when you said you'd done that…it was with him.'

'Yes.'

'Did you sleep together? Is that what this is about?'

'No, Frank. We realised that we were meant to be together. We decided we would be, and then he was crossing the road and was hit by a car.' The breath caught in my throat. 'He was killed. Right there. In front of me.'

'Helen, that's ridiculous!'

'I knew if I told you then, the whole trip would be off and we'd break up and Nicky would lose everything. Sindi too. So I made up the story about the mugging.'

'I don't believe you. You had no coat!'

'It was covered in his blood, Frank. I threw it in the

marina.'

We looked at each other. Frank said, 'No.'

'What do you mean, no?'

'No. There's just no way that could have happened.'

'But it did!'

'The way to be over something is *be over* it! Not this... endless fantasising!'

'Frank, I'm trying to tell you that James isn't important any more, not even Cariad is. *We* are. You me, the *Innisfree*, Nicholas. Sindi. We've been given such an opportunity. A fresh start, without all that pain.'

There was a shocked silence as the boat moved smoothly beneath the stars. Frank reached over and grasped my hair in its ponytail. He twisted it in his fingers until the roots creaked, pulling my head back.

'Here's what I think,' he said.

I gasped against his grip, tears burning my eyes.

'You've gone batshit crazy. Think about *this*.'

I felt his thumb roughly enter my mouth, grinding something hard against my gums, pressing over my teeth. Chocolate. Sweetness and pain flooded my mouth. It devoured my enamel, my tongue, and even it seemed my brain. I struggled against him and pushed myself away, spluttering over the syrupy morass.

'Don't say his name again,' Frank whispered.

*

The next day, I took myself into the hammock, pinging the band on my wrist and striving for an empty mind. I was

205

avoiding Frank, as far as is possible on a boat, which in truth is not very possible at all. It had already involved a ridiculous squeeze past each other in the galley. We averted our eyes, mumbled "'Scuse me!' like strangers in a lift. I was shocked by his flat denial of what I had told him, but even more shocked at my own sentimentality about our relationship.

To escape him, I commandeered the hammock from Sindi. The second I lowered myself into it, I realised I should have done it before: it operated like a gimbal and kept me steady even as the *Innisfree* swayed. I was also as far as possible from the cockpit where Frank was helming.

Perhaps the explosion really *had* sent me batshit crazy. I found myself asking if in fact I had dreamed James's death. I ran over and over the events of that night, but they resisted my attempts to fictionalise them, and became clearer and harder with each replay until I could not bear to think of them any longer. But Frank was the barometer for public opinion. My version had no chance against his certainty. It would be easier if I could just accept this. After all, if I was crazy, I could, as the wise women of the forum advised, eventually be made uncrazy. And as I would never see James again, what did it matter?

I pinged the band furiously. It *was* time to be over James. It was time to be over *everything*. I felt so sick, as if reality itself was churning inside me.

Behind me, I heard Nicholas come scrambling up from below. He appeared, breathless, at my side.

'Mum! I found them!' My son dropped what he was carrying all over me, with an enormous happy grin.

'Pills!'

'I only just unpacked my rucksack! Looking for my penknife.'

I ripped open one of the ten packets of Stugeron as if it was Christmas.

'I must have stuffed them in there and forgotten. Here.' I held out a couple of tablets. 'Do you need water? Go and get some. Or there's a couple of cans of Coke left in the fridge. Call Sindi, let's get this party started!'

I was babbling in my excitement. I could not wait to feast on stability, on sleep, on stillness astride the wheeling waters. Would this be my reward for renouncing James? For getting over *everything*?

Delighted with himself, Nicholas went to get the Coke. I heard him calling Sindi, then her voice shrieking, 'Who designed these fucking toilets! I can't move in here! Where am I supposed to throw up?'

I lay back waiting for the pills to take effect. In anticipation of being imminently cured, I kept my eyes upon the horizon.

Far ahead of us, wispy clouds had darkened into a fanatical black line. A storm was in full force, miles ahead. The line flashed, shattered by cracks in the sky. We were advancing far too slowly to be caught up in it, so I allowed myself simply to observe the mute display. When Nicholas was a baby we'd carried him one New Year's Eve to the top of a hill in Russia Dock where the Thames was laid out around us and we'd stood with hundreds of others, waving sparklers and applauding, as all the capital's fireworks went off along the length of the river, the sky exploding silently with pink and purple and gold upon gold. This merciless storm that, were we in it, would pound us with fifty-foot waves, determined to smash the *Innisfree*, and us, into our constituent parts, to *start again* and *better* with *particles*… Why should it remind me not of the darkness but of our little family bathed in celebration?

I could not tear my eyes away. I realised that within me resided a vertiginous longing to be within the storm, inside the explosion, to feel myself possessed by forces that sincerely, annihilatingly *are* instead of those that are wished for with lifelong, feeble ardency. These rituals of family, which I now chose decisively over the dead, were my only defence against an emptiness inside me, which pulled at me harder and harder, like a black hole swallowing a star.

20

IN THIS NEW LIFE without Cariad or James, I worked the boat raw and alive as a newly released rehab patient. I filled my lungs with clean, untainted air. The ocean carried it to me in coldly dripping outstretched hands, from the far wilderness where it was made, and I drank it in. My blood prickled with oxygen. Our watch cycle pruned sleep just enough to graft the hours more tightly together, and inside them I felt myself grow stronger, a hybrid of who I was and who I might yet be. My sleep was dreamless, the rocking oblivion of the physically worn out.

The wish to be a teacher again, to connect Sindi and Nicholas to what was around them, grew with my energy levels. I began to put some lessons together, deciding to teach only what I cared about and knew about. From this they could extrapolate to other questions beyond my expertise.

When the moment came that they saw a whale or a dolphin pod or an orca, I wanted them to have an understanding that would make what they saw more astounding, not less.

Understanding did enhance experience; this, I knew. From a young age, I had known that green was my favourite colour. If asked, it was because of its seemingly infinite shades. A walk through the woods in summer could feel overwhelming because of the countless variations of green. And then I discovered that there was a scientific reason for my being able to perceive so many shades of green, less to do with the colour than with me. A human is a predator, and needs to be able to see its prey hiding in the foliage. Humans are biologically sensitive to such differentiation. This, I recalled now, was why I loved the picture of the oak tree with its many different leaves that had fallen from the wall. Not so much for its execution, but for its accurate reflection of my human perspective. Knowing this about my relationship to the colour green had enhanced my love for it. This was the approach I was taking in introducing Sindi and Nicholas, both city kids raised on an intellectual diet of HD and fantasy, to natural marine reality.

We were entering a breeding ground for orcas and I decided to focus first on them. Of all the beasts of the sea that Frank and I had encountered in our youth, the orcas were my favourites, the most entrancing and the most mysterious. Their skin patterns made them seem as if they were made of a watery surface broken by sunlight; their reticence was so unlike the dolphins who would seek us out. They exhibited emotional complexity and teamwork that connected with me in a way that the sight of a single whale, no matter how astonishing, did not.

This morning, relieved from watch by Frank bringing me coffee, I stayed up beside him making some notes. Now that I had accepted *no more James*, my husband had become very considerate once again, taking the pressure of watches from me as far as he could so I could catch up on the sleep I had lost while sick. Sindi, heavy with ennui, emerged from the hatch, took the binoculars from my hands and began, under my direction, to scan the water for fins and spouts.

'Remember, you start from the water directly below the boat and then go upwards until you meet the sky,' I said. 'If you do it from side to side you'll go right over anything that's there.'

My confident tone obscured my disquiet that there had been no visible marine life since we left UK waters. My memory of sailing back then was that the sea was teeming. The present emptiness of the ocean felt like I was persuading Sindi and Nicky of the existence of dinosaurs or sirens.

'It's a desert,' she said. 'Just a big wet desert.'

'Just keep looking,' I said. 'It's worth it.'

Behind me, Nicholas was hunched over, and I thought for a tantalising moment he was reading a book. On closer examination it was clear he was attempting to tattoo a skull and crossbones on his arm with his penknife and a biro he'd broken open.

'What the hell are you doing Nicky! Stop it! You'll poison yourself.'

He ignored me, obliging me to snatch the pen out of his hand.

'Hey!' he protested.

'If you get ill on this boat, what are we going to do?'

'I didn't know sailing could be this boring,' Sindi said. 'At least when we were sick there was something to think about.'

'All right!' I snapped. 'The first person to spot anything gets three Jaffa Cakes.'

Jaffa Cakes were the primary currency on board now. I had brought twenty boxes on board because I knew both Nicholas and Sindi loved them and, in the absence of the internet, I was not confident of getting their co-operation any other way.

'That's not fair though, if she's got the binoculars,' said Nicholas.

'Here's another pair,' said Frank, handing them over. 'But nothing happens until you put your flipping jacket on properly, Sindi! You know this, both of you! The life jacket is the first rule.' He clenched his fist at his chest. 'You need a fist's width between your chest and the jacket. Too loose and it will snag on things and ride up if you fall in. I'm getting sick of telling you.'

Sindi said, 'I like it like this!'

'It's not a fashion item, Sindi,' I said.

I had been so involved with achieving our first proper class that I had failed to notice that Sindi was wearing her life jacket like a cardigan and had tucked the uncomfortable central strap into her shorts pocket.

'What's that?' Nicholas asked, pointing to her knee. A long cut across her kneecap was neatly plastered.

'She broke the second rule,' Frank said. 'Trying to run on deck.'

I craned over to look. 'When was this?'

'Last night,' Sindi said. 'You were asleep. Frank sorted it.' She turned to my husband with a big smile. 'Tell you what, I'll put the jacket on properly for three Jaffa Cakes.'

'Nice try,' Frank said.

Sindi extracted a cigarette and a lighter from her shorts. She turned expertly now from the breeze and lit up.

'When those run out, you'll be gagging for Jaffa Cakes,' I said. 'I'll be able to get you to do anything.'

'I don't need my cigs,' she said. 'I just like them. In fact I'm looking forward to giving up. Watch!' She inhaled deeply and then threw the remaining cigarette over the side.

'See you in three hours!' Frank laughed.

'You'll see!'

Nicholas pulled off his baseball cap to put the binoculars against his eyes properly.

'What in God's name is that?' I asked pointing at his ear.

'Oh,' his hand cupped it. 'Sindi pierced it for me.'

I pulled his fingers aside to reveal a silver hoop.

'Frozen beef burger and a needle,' Sindi said, proudly. 'He wanted me to. And it's not going to go septic. I know what I'm doing.'

'I'm not taking it out!' Nicholas said firmly. 'I paid her already.'

'What with?'

Nicholas murmured, 'The password to your laptop.'

'What?' I spun round to face Sindi.

'Keep your hair on, Miss. I haven't used it. Kind of an easy one to guess anyway.'

'Sindi!'

'I mean, SaveMeJames123!' she sniggered.

213

'That's private!' I cried. I turned to Frank, 'Do something!' Frank shrugged.

Sindi held up a hand. 'All right, Miss! I just thought… you might have something interesting on there. A game or something.'

'How did you find my password, Nicholas?' I asked.

Nicholas said, 'You wrote it down, ages ago, back at home. In that funny notebook of yours. With the maps in it? She said if I gave her the password, she'd find a game for us to play. Also…she threatened to throw my phone overboard.'

Sindi glared at him.

'It's just a password,' Nicholas muttered.

I advanced on Sindi, an unfamiliar feeling taking me over. I pushed my shoulders back. 'How dare you, Sindi!'

'Oy oy…' said Frank, placing an arm between us. I knocked it away.

'He wanted his ear pierced,' Sindi protested. 'I've made him cool, instead of a tragic nerd!'

'Hey!' Nicholas protested.

'Shall we turn this boat round? Drop you back in London, Sindi? Maybe we've made a mistake. As for you, Nicholas, I think I've got some photos in the cabin. Of you as a baby. A lovely one of you in your nappy by the fire. Sindi will love to see that. See how you like your privacy being violated.'

In my newly sober state, without James, I could see people more clearly. They were selfish and cruel. My own son included. I stormed to the hatch and went down into the saloon.

It wasn't until I opened the laptop in the cabin that I realised I didn't want to change the password. The presence of the word James in my life, secretly at my fingertips, was like a little miniature of whisky stashed somewhere once I had committed to sobriety. A safety net. As I was sitting hunched over the laptop, Frank braced himself in the doorway, casting a shadow over the screen.

'Thanks for sticking up for me,' I snapped, not looking up.

'If my password had been revealed as…oh, I don't know… SaveMeRuth, you'd have something to say.'

'The point is, I wouldn't go looking! Passwords are private. You know, like *thoughts*.'

'And that's why they are so revealing.'

Oh piss off! I had a whole class planned, Frank. There appears to be no wildlife in the ocean and my son is being corrupted in front of my eyes. This is just stupid bullying crap.'

Frank laughed. 'Just change the password, Helen, and let's start today again.'

'I can't think of anything.'

'I'm sure something will come to you.' He spoke a little more softly. 'This is family life. This is what you have been missing. You're too hung up on privacy.'

He turned to go and then said over his shoulder, 'Secrets make you vulnerable, Helen.'

This was the other thing about life without James. Rage. It came from nowhere, set my hands trembling. God, I hated my husband.

I changed the password, to NiceTryBitches359. But when I tried to confirm it, it reverted. Time after time I tried, but some glitch or other kept SaveMeJames123 there. It was as if James was clinging to his last worldly mention. I tried everything, becoming more and more frustrated. It seemed that he was frustrated too. In that tussle over the delete key, I felt his presence more keenly than I had since we left shore. He was refusing to be forgotten. I hadn't taken James for being a tenacious soul. And now, in this small point, he was absolutely unwilling to give any ground whatsoever. The password, clearly, was staying. I gave up and left it as it was.

Back on deck, Frank was tightening Sindi's life jacket as if nothing had happened. She was chatting about the cigarette-selling business she had developed at school. Nicholas gazed through the binoculars as Sindi continued with her story. Clint had got the cigarettes from a mate at Gatwick airport; Sindi split the packets up and sold them singly or in pairs. Frank was grinning as he worked. He always loved to hear of a profitable deal. Why had she never told me about this? Finishing with her life jacket, he said, cheerfully, 'The pair of you, get a bucket and a scrubbing brush, and I want the bow deck scrubbed until I can see my face in it.'

Frank tied a rope to a bucket and dropped it over the side, hauling it up sloshing with water. Sindi and Nicholas picked their way to the bow, bucket swaying between them. I loved, despite myself, the sight of their strong, brown toes gripping the deck. They were evolving. I half-expected to see webbing appear. Sindi smiled as she passed me. Her plait was loosening. She brushed her hair from her eyes.

*

'Why am I here? I mean, why did you bring me on your boat?' Sindi asked, yawning. We were all sat in the cockpit

216

for lunch, a massive omelette I'd made, enjoying the fact that I could cook and move freely without nausea. The calm seas and easy wind had been with us for hours, making working in the galley a pleasure. We had some two hundred eggs in the bilge, stacked carefully, and it was Nicholas's job – nominated because he was the smallest for getting into the tight space – to turn them a little every day so that the yolk did not sink. In this way they could stay fresh indefinitely. The deck was scrubbed, hours had passed and I was almost reconciled to Nicholas's earring.

'You had nowhere else to go,' I answered. 'We weren't going to abandon you.'

As I spoke, the sail began to flap and the boat to sway. Frank reached over to the winch and made a swift adjustment. 'See that! We're at eight knots!' he said. Sindi's plate slid as if possessed towards her. She caught it, keeping the omelette on top, grinning triumphantly.

'And also,' said Frank, snatching a cup as it made to leap from the table and slotting it into the stand by the wheel, 'we need the extra crew. So a win-win.'

'That's not a win-win.' Sindi said. 'That's you getting free labour from a homeless person.'

She braced herself against Nicholas and carelessly wiggled the ring in his ear. He shoved her off with a stab of his elbow.

'Oh come on, Sindi, this is hardly a gulag,' said Frank. His words were picked up by the wind, whipped round the table then sent out over the side. 'It's the experience of a lifetime. Plus, we…care about you. You'll always have a home with us.'

A home for Sindi forever? The boat banged into a cross wave, jolting us as if we were on a fairground ride.

'Like he will, you mean?' she nodded at Nicholas. 'Or what other way were you thinking, Frank?'

'Maybe we could adopt you when we get back. If you like. Make it official,' I said.

She stared at me. 'But you don't know me at all. Shouldn't that be the first rule, Frank? Even before life jackets? Don't bring strangers on board? I mean, we're trapped together now. Anything could happen.'

'Trapped is a little strong, I think,' I said.

'They gas the dogs no one wants in the dog's home, don't they?' she went on. 'So I guess I'm super-lucky.'

Nicholas blurted, 'I've got no grandparents or brothers and sisters or cousins or anything. So they let you come with us. For me. To be like a sister.'

'That's not true, Nicholas,' I said. 'Sindi is here for her own reasons, not ours.'

Nicholas said, 'Why don't we see my grandparents? Why don't I have any siblings? I'd rather have a family on land than be out here on this boat.'

'But we are a family!'

'It's better now Sindi's here,' he said.

'Aww, squirt!' Sindi ruffled his hair.

'Your dad's family are all religious nuts who don't like us,' I said.

'And your mum's mum is an alcoholic,' said Frank.

'Hey!'

'Granny's an alcoholic?' Nicky said.

'She drinks a little bit too much since my dad was lost at sea. Mainly, Nicholas, she just isn't very nice.'

'I bet she'd be nice to me though,' said Nicholas.

I sighed. 'Well, she was horrible to me. And she's my mother.'

'Your dad was lost at sea?' Sindi said.

'He was. He was a fisherman.'

'She used to send me birthday presents,' Nicholas went on. 'Why did she stop?'

'Because she's an alcoholic!' Frank cried from the wheel. 'She only cares about drinking!'

'Clint was an alcoholic and he never got me anything, or it was something really crap. Alkies are rubbish at presents,' explained Sindi. 'Sorry about your dad, Miss.'

'But—' said Nicholas.

'Nine knots!' said Frank. 'I don't think we ever went this fast in her before, did we, Helen? Nicholas, that's enough complaining about how terrible your life is. Let me ask *you* a question, Sindi. Why did you come to our house when your own burned down?'

'Helen was the first person I thought of,' she said. 'The... only one. But, Miss, don't take this wrong, but you've changed.'

As she spoke, the boat tipped and my slice of omelette that I had so been looking forward to, with the mushrooms I had lovingly chopped back in those moments of calm, flew from my plate over the side. My mouth opened in an existential scream that refused to become sound. Furiously I reached for Frank's slice, but as if he read my mind he sprang across the deck and ate it. I glared round the table.

'Nicholas, *this* is family. No one cares about anybody else. If we had more members, it would just be more of the same.'

Pinning it with his fingertips, Nicholas pushed his plate

with his own slice of omelette in front of me. The tussle with myself was brief.

'Nicholas, thank you,' I said. 'God, it's delicious.'

'That's what I mean,' Sindi said. 'You're different.'

'Yeah well. We've all changed.' I said, mouth full. 'Except you, Sindi, who will insist on going about the place half-dressed. What's that all about?'

She looked down at her shorts and T-shirt indignantly. 'These are my clothes!'

She stared around the table. Frank looked studiously at the horizon, Nicholas at his hands.

'I'm sick of this!' Sindi said, voicing exactly the phrase in my own head. 'You've got everything – your money and each other and this boat, and all your things. Well, I've got this.' She waved her hand towards her body. 'It's *mine*. I like it. I like how it feels in the air. So why should I wrap myself in ugly sweaty sailing stuff just so you're not reminded how great it is? I didn't see you hiding any of your ornaments or your paintings or all your furniture so I wouldn't feel bad. You're proud of all that stuff! Well,' she went on, cheeks pink, decorations swaying in her hair as she pointed emphatically at herself, '…this body is my…Porsche. It hurts the paintwork to put it in waterproofs. So I'm not going to. And if you don't like it, you can throw me overboard. I don't care any more.'

She sat back, arms folded.

'Life jacket though,' said Frank gently. 'Can we compromise there?'

Sindi shrugged, but smiled at him, sidelong.

I didn't know how to argue against her, or against the alliance among all three of them that seemed to be forming.

'I'm going to wash up,' I said, and lifted myself carefully out of the cockpit. The boat was pitching briskly now. Frank gathered up the clanking plates and handed them to me to take down. Our hands extended towards each other with infinite patience, like God giving the spark of life to Adam on the Sistine Chapel ceiling. *One must be a friend to oneself first and foremost*, Romy said. *When one door closes, another opens.* I felt a pang of missing her, her certainties, her optimism.

I wobbled towards the hatch, plates in hand. As I sank below, Frank moved into my place and began to discuss the life raft and the flares. Nicholas and Sindi leaned in to listen.

Do you ever think your life would make more sense without you in it? I had asked Romy. Had she ever answered me? Deep in thought, I proceeded to break the first rule of boat safety: *One hand for yourself, one hand for the boat.* The boat pitched violently, dislodging me from the steps and leaving me dangling into the interior from one hand. My squeal was drowned out by the wind. I swung right over the sink, where, in different circumstances I would have deposited the dishes. Instead they were clutched to my chest now, condensation and grease from the omelette all over my life jacket. Vainly scrabbling for purchase, I let go, timing my fall for the split second when the *Innisfree* was upright.

I heard a splash, and realised it was my own feet, knees, calves. My cheek against the wooden floor was drenched. A plate spooled away on a minuscule wave. The saloon floor was awash.

A scream began in my throat but I killed it. Getting to my feet, tossing the plates into the sink, I splashed my way through the boat towards the fore cabins, from where the

221

water seemed to be running. Instructions rolled round my brain. Find out what it is. *Information.* Keep calm. Avoid panic.

The passageway leading to Sindi's forepeak cabin was swirling. *Sindi what have you done?* I grabbed the doorframe, slid inside.

There it was. The forepeak hatch wide open. With every dip into the waves, tens of gallons of freezing sea water cascaded in, clattering all over the panelling and floor, seething its way into every corner and then further and further out into the saloon. As I stared open-mouthed, a face full of freezing wet salt drenched me.

'Jesus, Sindi!' I gasped, leaping onto her bunk and pulling the hatch shut, just as a great foaming sheet smacked over it. Stupid, stupid girl. I took in the devastation. This would take hours of bailing. All the sheets washed and dried. The mattresses dried on deck. And every minute it sat there, the salt chewed at the varnish on the panelling, finding crevices and corners to seep and cause damage. I sloshed back through the saloon to our aft cabin, finding it swirling with water too, bits of weed clinging to the rug. The book I was reading bloated and sodden, its pages heaving.

Sliding back to the galley I grabbed a mug from the sink and a bucket from the stow. On my knees I filled the bucket using the mug, then tossed the water into the sink. This would take ages. What was I doing? This was a huge task. I poked my head out of the hatch to summon them all.

Unaware of the turmoil below, the three of them were sat close together by the wheel, Sindi so close to Frank their heads were almost touching. No one saw me. They were absorbed in the flares, the small hand held ones and the rockets. Sindi was turning one in her hands, paying close attention to what Frank was telling her.

And then it happened. She – or was it he – leaned, crossed that infinitesimal distance between comprehensible and incomprehensible. Arm or was it hand or was it leg touched.

I ducked down and refilled the bucket. Breaking the rule about never carrying something up the steps – always pass it up to someone – I stepped into the cockpit, bucket swaying by my side. No one even looked up.

I experienced, all at once, every single time Frank had resisted my wish to have Sindi along. The hungry lion saying, *you don't have to release the gazelle*. The killer whale saying, *no need to place the seal pup on the ice floe above me*. In that instant, it was as if my memories switched in perspective like an Escher picture. All my former certainties were upturned as if by a plough blade through the earth. Frank's gaze upon me, as in the past, before all this, before even Nicholas. His gaze that knew me, and was gentle, now upon Sindi.

I tottered towards them. Still ignored, I stood right before them. I swung the bucket and threw the water over Sindi and my husband.

'We were going to sink because of you!' I screamed.

'Helen! What the—'

'Mum!' cried Nicholas.

'Get down those stairs and start bailing!'

I flung the bucket to one side and clambered past them to the helm. Frank went down into the saloon, followed by Sindi and Nicholas, and I heard his exasperation deep inside the boat.

'Oh my God! Sindi, you must always close hatches out at sea!'

Then the frantic clattering of bowls and buckets for bailing.

Frank called up, 'Put her on auto and help us!'

'You sort it out, Frank.'

My heart pounding, I focused on the waters ahead, holding our course steady. The waves rippled with possibility, and the breeze sang through the lines. The *Innisfree* kept on calmly, unmoved by the activity inside her. Then, from nowhere, slim dorsal fins rose, circling, some half a mile away. I blinked, shook my head in case I was imagining it, but I was not.

My heart began to pound. The ocean was revealing itself not to be empty after all. These were not the collapsed, tragic fins of the captive orca stars of marine parks, but tall and slim as blades. The largest were some two metres in height. They'd reach to my own husband's chin if he were standing on the back of one.

The image froze my brain for a moment, Frank on the nose of an orca, being tossed into the air…up, up, up…

The orcas were stirring the ocean like a great cauldron, and as if under a spell I reefed the main to slow us right down. It was as if the ocean had come to life, an expression of our deepest fears. The *Innisfree* crept towards their devilish whirling. I had never seen this mesmerising behaviour before. My longing to get closer eclipsed everything else.

21

I EASED THE *INNISFREE* into the wind, and pointed the bow directly at the orcas some five hundred feet away. The boat entered the dead zone, when the wind is exactly on the nose, and she swaggered to a standstill on the swell. My plan was to circle the orcas without disturbing them, under engine. The sails would need to be furled, and I readied myself to perform this task.

'What the hell are you doing?' Frank said, emerging from below.

'Orcas!' I cried.

'What? Where?' Still dripping, Frank grabbed the binoculars. I pressed the switch to furl the sails, then turned the ignition. A groan ricocheted through the sea, blue exhaust fading in the air. The *Innisfree* gobbled diesel, and this wasn't use that Frank and I had ever agreed – the engine was for emergencies and coming into port. Regardless, I set the autopilot, and the *Innisfree* began to plod on her circuit, snorting like a horse on a treadmill.

'We're not going near them! There's something going on,' Frank said.

'Fuck off back below, Frank. We haven't seen a single living creature in this ocean since we left. Nicholas needs to see them.'

The sound of the engine brought Nicky and Sindi on deck.

'You go any nearer and I will physically pull you off that helm,' Frank hissed. 'You've lost your fucking mind.' To Nicholas and Sindi, he said. 'OK, quick look you two. Then we're leaving them to it.'

Nicholas rushed to the rail, snatching my binoculars as he went. Sindi sauntered after him, smirking.

'Sindi, you've got one minute,' I commanded her receding back. 'I want all the wet stuff out on deck!'

The breeze was already crisping Frank's shirt and hair. He stood close so that his words were conveyed to me without Sindi and Nicholas hearing.

'You're the one who wanted Sindi on this trip, not me. In fact you went on and on at me until I said yes,' he hissed.

'I've got eyes, Frank,' I said. 'My own husband leering at a barely legal girl in our charge. It's disgusting.'

'I can't help it if she…sidles up to me!'

'Sidles? For Christ's sake.'

He grabbed my arm. 'You're accusing me of things I haven't done, Helen.'

'Did you know, Corin warned me off you back then? He

said you couldn't be trusted. More fool me.'

He squeezed me even harder. There would be marks. 'I was showing them fucking flares. I'm the skipper.' He released me, sending me stumbling, saved from falling by one of the main sheets.

'I know what I saw,' I said, escaping to the helm. 'Hey, Nicholas, why don't you come and help me? I think Dad and Sindi can finish up below, don't you?'

Frank glared at me.

'Go and help your girlfriend,' I said.

Nicholas hesitated, looking from one to the other of us.

Frank said, 'Come on Sindi, let's get the stuff out to dry. It won't take long.'

Shoulders back, nose in the air, she thrust the binoculars at me and followed him down the hatch.

Finally I was alone with my son. 'There's at least fifteen, Mum!' he said, looking at me sidelong, as if to check I was all right. 'That's two pods, probably.'

The fins circled in the sunlight, flashing steel sheathed in black. From time to time an orca breached the surface, revealing its white patches. It was one thing to see them through the binoculars, but now another idea occurred to me.

The *Innisfree* pawed the swells. The wind clinked about her like a harness. I pointed to the mast. 'I'm going up there,' I said. 'Bird's eye view. Coming?'

Nicky's eyes widened. 'Up the mast?'

'We'll be able to see more clearly what the whole group is doing,' I said. 'What do you say? Come on!'

Before he could reply we were interrupted by Frank,

holding out the drone to Nicholas. I had forgotten we had one. Nicholas gasped in delight and the two of them got to work getting it going. Observing the orcas on-screen rather than from high up a swaying mast was, I understood, a big draw for a gaming teenager. Nevertheless I was disappointed by my son's instant switch. Frank turned his back to me, walling off my son from view entirely. *Fine by me!* my own body retorted as I ducked through the stays and shrouds and hauled myself onto the boom. I shook my hair in the wind, freeing myself. The sailor does not deal in rage.

I had not climbed the *Innisfree's* mast since I was a girl. It soared into the clouds like a beanstalk. At the very top, the radar box was a speck. I eased my toe into the first of the notches in the mast and began to climb. Even though the seas were calm, the pendulum effect grew perilous as I advanced. Heights had never bothered me; on the *Innisfree* in the past I was the one who offered to shimmy up to loosen the sail if it had caught, or take a high lookout. Perhaps heights were like tunnels – it took a disaster to create fear. The swooping motion severed me from any sense of the deck. My brain flexed inside the wind.

Back then, my muscles had endurance and my grip was powerful. But what I had now was a deep reservoir of determination. Clinging tightly, I reached the first, then the second spreader and clipped myself on. Finally I could survey an enormous area from my dizzy vantage point. All around me, the sea's surface had the crinkled quality of the ocean from a plane window, skin over a shifting blue lava. From this height I could see the orcas weaving beneath the surface. The deck was a foreshortened world: Frank's head hovered over his toes and shoulders like a figure in a video game. Sindi's thin arms extended as she hauled a mattress up through the hatch and arranged it in the sun. Every swell caused the mast to bow, taking my guts with it. And every so often (every thirteenth wave? I was sure that was the mathematics of it, but could not hold the thought steady) a bigger swell or a cross wave would come and cause the mast to orbit the sky.

But inside the instability, a riotous natural silence. I closed my eyes. This must be like the deep ocean for a whale – a silence bursting with meaning.

'Mum!' Nicholas glinted up at me like a tiny medal. Excitedly, he sent the drone flying towards the orcas. 'It's working! Watch, Mum!' Then he huddled back over the screen.

Frank stared up at me, his hand shading his eyes. 'What the hell are you doing, Helen?' he yelled. He sounded so far away. I didn't bother to reply. I turned instead to the orcas.

The chaotic gathering was slowly revealing itself as organised. The taller fins of the bulls were distributed in a wide circle, with the shorter ones of the cows and calves milling inside. What was going on? Were they protecting themselves? And if so, from what?

'Dad, what's that?' Nicholas's cry rose up to me. He pointed at the screen, then out to sea.

A shape was breaking the surface at the centre of the orcas, like an immense grey tongue flexing between one world and another. An obelisk of head with a tiny, wrinkled eye and off-centre blow hole confirmed the creature as a sperm whale. The head of a sperm whale is a third of its entire length and so I guessed the whole beast was about 60 feet long, as big as the *Innisfree*, and a deadly adversary. This area was at the edge of the circulatory migration route performed by the female sperm whales of the Atlantic, who circle the Azores, visited by the males who take a different migration route, going all the way to the Arctic alone and returning.

Never had I seen a sperm whale in all my time aboard the *Innisfree*, though they populate every ocean on earth. A bushy cloud of vapour shot forward from the whale's blowhole, glittering, and then in slow motion the whale's tail flukes ascended from beneath the surface. On and on the tail rose, impossibly slowly, until it reached a peak and trembled there, like a raft at the very edge of a waterfall. Then it fell with a tectonic crash. I could see nothing through the detonation of water, the collapsing white walls. Finally, the air cleared enough to reveal the inner circle of orcas creeping back through the mist like hyenas. At the same time, a smaller bushy spout rose inside the falling spray of the first.

A *calf*. This was a sperm whale cow and her calf. Now it was apparent that they were alone in the centre of the orcas, ambushed, I guessed, on their migration route. Dismayed, I searched the deck for the faraway bead that was my son. This was not the story I had sought when I turned the boat towards the orcas.

The drone hovered over the scene. Sindi, Frank and Nicholas were bent over the receiver.

'Let's leave them to it!' I cried. Now I wanted to get away. A visceral urge to protect Nicholas overcame me. My little boy believed that right and wrong applied everywhere; he did not understand that our human terms had no meaning here.

His drone was about to bring him close up to something he was ill-prepared for, and it was not his life I feared for but his innocence.

If they heard me, they ignored me.

The cow blew again, and curved her great wrinkled back to attempt a dive.

She was weakening, and orcas can dive faster than whales. The orcas were employing their sophisticated, if brutal, hunting method. This is to dive deep and then speed to the surface, ramming cow and calf in the soft underbelly, causing savage internal injury. In this way, they separate mother and child so as to kill the calf. I had heard of this, but never imagined I would ever see it happen.

Nicholas thrust the drone controller into his father's hands and began to scale the mast. His father yelled after him to stop, but Nicholas was climbing like a monkey. Moments before, I had wanted to turn away, but now Nicky was almost in my arms. In the corner of my eye Frank was gesturing and shouting but I pretended I didn't hear, instead extending my hand for my son to grab as soon as he could.

Although the orcas and the whales seemed fiercely engaged in their own drama, and oblivious to us, there was a real possibility that the sperm whale might escape and hit the *Innisfree*, in which case the damage would be devastating. What we should really do was get the sails up and hightail it to a safe distance and watch it all on the drone, and we would, just as soon as, just as soon as…

Nicholas arrived at my feet. 'I can't see it properly on the screen,' he said.

'It's very dangerous here,' I said. I pulled him up, clipped him on, and arranged him in front of me, wrapping my arms tight around him. The mast dipped and sprang back and a sound escaped him, just like when he was a little boy and we took him on the waltzers, a delighted and terrified *wo-wo-weeee.*

'Helen, what the hell are you doing?' Frank's voice whirled thinly through the rigging.

He could stay down there and sniff around Sindi for all I cared. My son and I were together, even if just for a little while.

'I don't think you should watch this,' I said. 'The orcas are trying to separate the mother and calf. It's horrible.'

'We have to help them!' Nicky cried.

I remembered my own rage at David Attenborough's gentle tones describing the dying moments of a gazelle in the jaws of a lion, or an abandoned elephant calf starving alone. Why did the cameraman not intervene and stop the agonising chain of events? And sometimes on the dockside, when my father's boat pulled in and released his catch, my breath had been taken away by the sheer scale of suffering that the glittering haul revealed. All that gasping of a final breath, all that pain and twitching, all that tortured ending of life. It was not a highflown wish to witness that prevented me from agreeing with Nicholas. It was the understanding that we were not powerful enough.

'They can sink us, Nicholas,' I said. 'It's down to that mother to save herself and her baby.'

The water was reddening around the calf. Orcas cannot bite a whale properly; their jaws are set too far underneath to get purchase. But they can bite the fins and flukes of their

232

prey and this was what they were doing to the calf. The calf was churning in the water trying to evade the attacks. They were like wasps relentlessly attacking a puppy.

'Let's go,' I said, but he stopped me, pointing.

The calf was ascending slowly, resting impossibly upon the bloodied surface. The softest tremble in its tail flukes betrayed that it was alive. The foam cleared enough for me to see the shape of the cow beneath her baby, like a plinth upon which the calf was lain. She was holding her calf on her back out of reach of the orcas, whilst sustaining the full force of their violent assaults upon her belly.

I held onto Nicholas, too tightly, inhaling the tiny warmth at the nape of his neck. I remembered then the crash of people upon me in the tube carriage, my arms pinned away from my belly, my only thought for the life I was carrying, not with love, nor sentiment, but blind purpose. And if I could have torn my belly open and lifted my child above my head to save her, I would have done so. If I could have clambered through the press of bodies, though I might stamp upon them, though I might consign them to death, if it would have meant a chance for her I'd have done it without hesitation. To care nothing at all for anything in this world but that tiny life was pure focus, pure freedom.

Though the cow sperm whale would likely die in this effort, I knew that her suffering was less than if she were prevented from doing it. And I remembered, briefly, before it snatched itself away, the little space in the tunnel where James and I had huddled together, the pain in my belly signalling I had failed to protect my child. James had, unwittingly, consigned me to an afterlife of suffering over that failure.

233

A cry rose up from the deck.

'They've lost the drone!' Nicholas said.

Frank was waving at me to come down, but I didn't care about him. I could not tear myself away from the sight of this mother doing everything in her power to save her calf.

Frank went to the helm and began to alter our course. He yelled at me to come down so he could unfurl the sails, but I ignored him. It wasn't over, whatever was happening here was not over.

'Can you see?' Nicholas said. 'It's weird. The bull orcas are far away and just circling, and the little ones and their mothers are the ones attacking.'

And so it was. The water around the submerged body of the cow boiled with short fins, disappearing, reappearing, turning and twisting. More red pounded into the sea as the female and juvenile orcas chewed at the cow's extremities while continuing to ram her viciously from underneath. She would not be able to withstand this for much longer, nor hold her breath. Why should it be that mothers and calves were attacking a mother and calf? The most the bulls were doing was to prevent escape and facilitate the attack. It could not be strictly about food, because the bulls could have effected the dispatch much sooner.

Orcas are known to be vastly intelligent, perhaps more socially connected and emotionally complex than humans. They work together across family groups when they hunt and appear to communicate in a highly complex way. This attack was co-ordinated across two pods, and carefully orchestrated. Were the juveniles in training? Being shown how to attack and work as a team?

The sperm whale has the biggest brain of any creature that has ever lived upon the planet, in real as well as relative terms. Their social networks are highly complex, and their care for their offspring unrivalled in its length and devotion.

So there was no getting away from it. This wasn't a simple act that we could dismiss as a natural predation event. It was an act of one complex society upon another, one family upon another. And at the heart of it all, females and young; both perpetrators and victim acting according to that bond.

The *Innisfree* swung onto a new course, chugging out of the circuit I had set and onwards south. Frank had given up trying to get me down and was observing the orcas from the rail. With the wind as it was and no sails up, our speed could be barely four knots.

When I looked back, the calf and its mother had vanished. The orcas were circling, but their movement had a chaotic anxious quality as if they were searching.

'Can you see anything?' I asked Nicholas.

He scanned the area with the binoculars. 'Maybe they've dived?' He said doubtfully.

It seemed impossible. The whales were injured and so harassed they could barely draw breath, headed off at every turn by the swifter orcas. Had they simply sunk? But if that were the case, why were the orcas seeming still to search for them?

'Er... Mum, they're coming,' Nicholas said and handed me the binoculars.

When I lifted them to my eyes, the lenses were filled with the racing dorsal fins of the orcas. It was all of them, juveniles and females first, bulls in a protective semicircle.

And they were headed straight for the *Innisfree*. Some leapt like dolphins as they cut through the water.

'Come on. We need to go down so we can get the sails up,' I said to Nicholas with extravagant calm. We unclipped and eased our way down the mast, me first in order to catch my son if he slipped.

There was no time for Frank and me to argue. We adjusted the boom and pressed the switch that unfurled the sails. It seemed to take an age for them both to extend. Next we left our course of travel, simply to get as much wind in the sails as possible. We kept the engine on to give extra thrust. The *Innisfree* heeled sharply, catching the full force of the wind in her main and foresails.

'Clip yourselves on!' I cried.

Binoculars were not needed to confirm that the orcas were gaining. This was no surprise, as they can swim at up to fifty-five kilometres an hour, and while our speed was increasing, it would never get above thirteen or fourteen knots – about twenty-five kilometres an hour.

'Faster!' I said to Frank. 'We need to go much faster!'

'Why don't we stop and keep completely still!' Nicholas said. 'Turn the engine off. I read somewhere that if they attack your boat that's what to do. So they get bored. We're supposed to note their markings and tell the coastguard.'

'Nicholas, did you see what they did to those sperm whales?' Frank said. 'That's what they will do to the boat. We must try to outrun them. If they ram us like they rammed those whales, we could sink.'

'Easy, Frank,' I said. 'There's no need to frighten everyone.'

'We are being chased by fifteen killer whales. I'm not

sacrificing my boat! We should never have stopped. Jesus, Helen, what is the matter with you?'

My heart froze as I saw the fins speeding towards us, the orcas' dark bulk leaping from the waves.

'We can do this,' I said. 'We are a team. We are going to outrun these whales and we are going to get to Cape Verde. We are not ringing the coastguard like a bunch of tourists and sacrificing this amazing boat and this amazing trip to a few psychotic overgrown fucking goldfish. Got it?'

Everyone stared at me.

'Understand? If anyone touches that VHF, getting bumped by a killer whale will seem like a holiday in comparison!'

'This is *insane*,' said Sindi, wonderingly. 'You people are off your fucking heads.'

'Okay then,' said Frank.

'If only we were closer to the coast,' Nicholas said. 'They wouldn't be able to ram us in shallow water.'

'The coast is at least a hundred miles away.' I said. 'Which rules the coastguard out anyway.'

'Maybe there's a shallow bit sticking out, nearer?' Nicholas said. 'The sperm whales maybe did that, made a run for shallow water? That's usually why they stay near the coast when they migrate.'

Frank gawped at his son. 'Where have you been hiding all this info, mate?'

Nicholas grinned proudly. 'Got a guy in my discord group who's really into whales,' he said.

'I'll go below and check out the chart and radar, see what depths we've got,' I said.

'I'll keep helming,' said Frank. 'You two' – he pointed at

Nicholas and Sindi – 'stay here and just kee; on these sails.'

'But how—' began Sindi, but Frank raised his hand.

'Sindi, just do what I tell you and everything will be fine.'

Everything was wrong with this unit, everything was wrong with Frank and me; nevertheless this *was* the unit, this was the pod, the *Innisfree* was our defence and, despite the orcas bearing down on us, I felt safer aboard her than not.

Down at the navigation desk I checked the charts. Amazingly there was indeed an area of shallower water near where we had been. A seamount? Nicholas was right, this must have been where the whale cow made a last attempt to escape. Orcas will abandon a hunt if the water gets too shallow.

To copy the sperm whales' escape, however, we would need to swing round and reverse direction completely. I didn't know how we could do this without losing speed or having the orcas head us off. Vainly I searched the chart for another area of shallow water in the vicinity, but there was none. The orcas knew this area of sea; they knew where to ambush; they knew where the deep waters were, and the shallow.

'There's no shallow water anywhere in front of us,' I called to Frank from the hatch. 'We will drop too much speed if we turn back, and they will head us off anyway.'

Frank nodded, considering the information. 'I reckon we've got less than ten minutes before they catch up.'

Back on deck, I asked, 'Do we even know why they attack boats, Nicholas? I mean, surely they know it's an inanimate object? It's hardly worth all this effort, if there's no food at the end.'

'Maybe these ones are just super angry,' said Nicholas.

'The way I see it,' Frank said, 'they can't attack us properly at speed. We will tire them out if we can just keep going. If we turn round, like you say, they can head us off. The sperm whales had surprise in their favour, but we'd be advertising what we're doing. I say we just keep going, as fast as humanly possible.' He patted the helm. 'Can you feel her, the old girl? She's on our side. She's built like a tank. They can't hurt us. And they're tired, don't forget. Let's confirm this as a bad day for the orcas. Okay?'

The *Innisfree* roared through the swells at an impossible tilt, in clear agreement with our decision. While Frank remained at the helm, making minute adjustments to keep at the best possible angle to the wind, the three of us clung to the port rail to try to keep her balanced. So violent was the heeling that Nicholas's mobile phone, which he had been using for photographs, spun out of his pocket and over the side. He flinched, bit his lip, said nothing. I had told them both often enough that phones should always remain below.

We were now sailing faster than I had ever sailed. I was awed by the sheer power we were harnessing, but behind us the orcas were whole creatures now, not just fins. Their bodies were patches of sunlight made savagely real. They were absolutely focused on us, and it would not be long until they reached us.

Barely had the thought occurred when a glossy head lifted out at the starboard side, and an orca opened its mouth, revealing the neat oval of blunt powerful teeth, like small missiles lined up in a creamy-pink silo. Then it dipped back under.

Bang!

'I thought you said they couldn't ram us if we were moving.' Sindi cried.

'It would be worse if we were still,' said Frank. 'Helen! Get the spinnaker up. We are going to outrun these bastards!' He slapped the helm with a roar. 'Come on girl!'

The spinnaker is a very fine, balloon-like sail meant for capturing as much wind as possible when there is barely any. It is not meant for windy conditions, and although it would make the *Innisfree* faster, it would render her extremely unstable.

Frank and I exchanged a look. We had never sailed in such a way before, and in all other circumstances it would be considered foolhardy. But in this wordless discussion, we both knew we had no choice.

Decision made, Nicholas and I fixed the spinnaker to its pole. The *Innisfree* was foaming at her bit, ready to race, and as the spinnaker burst into shape, she surged forward, as if we were clinging to her mane bareback at the Grand National.

Bang!

The water around the *Innisfree* now was slick with orcas. They sped underneath, and sprang, gleaming, on each side.

With this, the engine died.

'The propeller! How the hell?' Frank said.

The *Innisfree* did not slow; the engine was only ever a supplement and she had three sails full of wind.

'It's all right!' he called, more to her than to us. 'We don't need the engine. The main thing is, we're sailing!'

The banging continued, becoming fiercer. The *Innisfree* bounced and splashed, like an enormous swan running and flapping to take flight.

240

I looked over the side. A calf rose towards me with a chunk of rudder in its mouth, before flipping over like a captive performing whale. Behind it, a female arced and dived. Their places were immediately taken by two others. They were *playing*. Like cats. With a mouse. It was hard to see it any other way.

'Oh hell,' said Frank, as the helm began to spin beneath his hands. 'The rudder's fucked. Can't steer.'

When I looked back, Sindi was elbow deep in the stow. She turned round, firing a conspiratorial grin at Frank.

'It can't all rest on the *Innisfree*,' she said. 'We have to do something.'

She hopped confidently across the bucking cockpit and leaned over the side. An orca calf had surfaced, looking at us sideways, mouth open, clicking and squeaking.

In one smooth move, Sindi ignited the rocket flare she was holding and threw it into the calf's mouth. For a fraction of a second it lay there sparking upon the pink tongue, like a wand upon a princess bed, and then it blew up.

A terrible squeal erupted over the water. A fountain of pink rose beneath us. I turned away. The whale calf was floating behind us now, kicking feebly. The adults abandoned the chase to surround it. The *Innisfree*'s mast creaked under the strain of the wind; she was giving it absolutely everything, like the horse on the downhill slope, its legs a blur, foaming at the mouth. She could go no faster than her predetermined maximum, which was not to do with the wind but with her material body tied to the physics of the earth. Every plank was tensed; the sails cried and screamed. With a broken rudder, we could do nothing but give ourselves entirely to wind.

I knew straightaway which one was the mother. She had forgotten us. She had forgotten everything. She was circling her baby, she was lifting her baby; the sea was made of her anguish. And the orcas were growing smaller; we were leaving them behind, this group of killer whales around their injured infant. They were bathed in gold; their fins revolved around a dark centre; they were already in mourning.

'Yee-hah!' cried Sindi. 'We did it!'

We stared at her, amazed.

'Bloody hell, Sindi,' I said.

'Well done everyone! Well done, Sindi!' said Frank. 'Let's get that spinnaker down. What a boat. What a crew!' We scrambled to furl it and steady the boat.

'This boat is the business,' cried Sindi, her face alive. 'She needs a new name.'

'Go on then,' Frank said, 'What's her name?'

Sindi clambered onto the foredeck. She ripped off her vest and waved it into the rattling sails. 'I name you *Alpha Bitch*!' she cried. 'The meanest, fastest boat on the ocean!'

22

The wind died and silence enveloped us, as if the ocean itself was holding its breath. We were stunned, and the ocean was stunned with us. The circling dorsals faded into the waves. Sindi stood proudly a few feet away, staring out to sea, mouthing secret thoughts unselfconsciously. Was that brain matter in her hair?

She had saved the hapless family she had joined, and of course I was grateful. It was just… The squeal of the orca calf was like nothing I had ever heard before. Could I have done what she did? Could Frank? The anguish of the mother orca, as wordless as my own over Cariad, swept over me. Did Sindi know, instinctively, that killing the baby would stop the attack? Or…did she just do it anyway? I wasn't ready to hear the answer.

At any rate, something in her seemed satisfied and at peace, as if she had asserted her value to us. Her savage grin had vanished; in its place her light-filled smile once more. All around us, the ocean shifted gently. There were terrors beneath this peace, but for now it was simply water. Sunlight patterned its surface, reminding me suddenly of leaves: the vibrant palimpsests trodden into the paths in autumn near our old house. For a split second I longed viscerally for home, and then I realised I didn't know where it was any more.

'Not to break up the victory party, but while the wind's down I need to repair that rudder,' said Frank.

The sails were furled and the *Innisfree* was at a virtual standstill, her bow moving up and down in the low swell, as if she was panting.

'Hey, look at squirt,' Sindi said, tapping my shoulder.

Nicholas had pulled the spare rudder out of the stow and was examining it. 'Can we attach this, Dad?'

'Good call.' Frank said. 'The bearings haven't gone, so fingers crossed we just have to patch it.'

He armed himself with a mask and stripped down to his shorts. Climbing down to the transom, which he had installed on the stern as a diving platform, as well as for easy access to the life raft should we ever need it, he clipped a line to his belt and lowered himself into the water. It smoothed over him, erasing him. It was unnerving, the completeness of his vanishing. I found myself searching the water for him. Such a short time ago I had hated him so utterly and now the thought he might not be there made me panic.

At last he reappeared, treading water strongly and emptying his mask.

'Propeller blades are fucked. So no engine,' he called up to me. 'But the good news is that the rudder just has this bite out. So yes, not quite sure how, but your idea should work, Nicky.'

He pulled himself up, gleaming back on deck. Nicholas already had the rudder out of the plastic and was turning it over, pondering.

Shaking the water from himself like a seal, Frank said, 'We need to change course, divert to the Canaries. Get her out of the water to fix the propeller. If we patch the rudder, it should be enough to get us into port.'

Nicholas grinned sidelong at Sindi, bursting to impress her. '*Vive la compétition*,' I murmured to Frank.

'Sindi, stay at the helm, can you?' Frank said. 'Keep watch. Let us know if any more orcas are coming. Nicky, get some tools together. Helen and I are going below to get our position and check the weather.'

The kids were delighted with themselves. They each took to their tasks with a confident air, staying close together.

At the navigation deck below, I dialled up on the satellite phone and proceeded to download the GRIB file. This was a forecast for our area, usually taken once a day. We specified a size of grid, carefully balancing a useful area with the expense and relevance of the download. There was no point having a forecast for an enormous area. The GRIB file was fed into our course and we could then consider any alterations we should make.

'Small front coming from the north east,' Frank announced. 'So quite a bit of pressure on the rudder. But at least there will be wind. What do you think? Maximum 30

245

knots of wind coming our way with some rain...'

'That's also a good wind for carrying on in the other direction,' I said. 'It would be behind us pretty much.'

'To Cape Verde? Hmmm. If we turn now, we face a few days' squally sailing and then we're in port. We've got to do repairs. There's no getting away from it, Helen. Those orcas have changed everything.'

We eyed one another. Sailing was a partnership, a hard meeting of minds to solve problems of survival. Frank had been wasted as a photographic agent, which to my mind had always been a kind of skim across the surface of things. Perhaps I had been wasted as a teacher too. Here we were a brilliant team. And look what we did to anything that threatened us: we destroyed it.

He covered my hand with his. We did not need to speak about the plan further. We were agreed.

'We've got this calm for a while yet,' I said. 'Let's enjoy it.'

Back on deck, Sindi had retreated to 'watch' from the hammock with a novel, headphones on. Frank rejoined Nicholas in discussing how to attach the spare rudder, and then, together, they slipped over the side to tackle the job. I lay in the cockpit and, as the adrenaline left my body, drifted to sleep.

I woke to a lively conversation happening behind me. Frank and Nicholas had erected the fishing rod and were discussing what weight of fish it might be able to bear. Frank turned to me, smiling, and held up a wooden lure. 'Remember this?'

It was the lure from the framed photograph back at home. I stared, amazed that he could be holding it, as if we had stepped right into the photo. 'How the hell do you still have that?' I said.

'I keep important things,' he said, handing it over.

I turned it in my fingers, overwhelmed.

'Why didn't you say?' I asked.

'I didn't know I still had it. It fell out of a bag of fishing tackle I found in a cupboard when we were packing. I wanted to surprise you.'

Now, as I gave the lure back to Frank, I realised we were smiling ridiculously at each other, like the old days.

'Let's see if it still works, shall we?' Frank said.

'Nicky, there's some bait in the fridge,' I said. 'Can you get it?'

He slipped off delightedly, for the child of the fractured marriage senses any hint of reunion and gets to work believing. Frank bent over the line to attach the lure.

The first time our lure attracted a bite, the crew laughed at us. 'The fish can smell pheromones on it,' they teased. Our first catch was a golden dourada, shimmering beneath the surface. We coaxed it in together, hauling it out to *ahhs* from the crew. It gasped in my arms, impossible to hold, slithering onto the deck like a pig breaking from the line at the slaughterhouse. Frank and I pounced on it, held it down, and as one we decided it had earned its freedom. Before the astonished crew, we threw it back. It paused there, dazed, a thread of blood unspooling from its torn cheek, and then it was gone.

'Frank, do you remember?' I grabbed his hand. 'We were so…*in love.*'

He turned to me, sun gleaming on his body.

'When will you get it into your head—?'

'Years ago though. So much—'

'But it's *us*—'

Recollection was curling over itself, breaking.

'What are you saying?'

'There is nothing between Sindi and me, Helen.'

My arms reached around him, my lips found his.

'Am I? Are we?' I murmured.

'Always,' he said.

A squeal erupted beside us. Nicholas bombed into the water, clutching a frisbee.

'Nicky! Stay near the boat!' I cried.

I knotted fenders to the lifeline and threw it out. Nicholas vanished in a blast of foam, reappeared, waving the frisbee. To my delight Frank followed his son, plunging over the side, emerging beneath him. He tossed Nicholas, yelling, over his shoulder. Nicholas burst back to the surface, swam to his father and splashed water in his face. Their laughter carried over the *Innisfree* and beyond. There had been so little play so far on this trip, so little play for so long at all.

'Come on Mum!' Nicholas cried.

'Someone needs to stay on board,' I called. 'I'll watch.'

Father and son lobbed the frisbee back and forth. I thought of the endless deep below; five kilometres; more. The creatures who swam there, the legs of my son and husband waving above them.

'How do I look?' Sindi asked, appearing beside me. She was wearing my red swimsuit, from those days when I was only a few years older than she was. It had lain forgotten in a drawer until we were packing for the trip and I'd pulled it out in surprise, tested that it was still serviceable, if perhaps a little tight for me now, and thrown it into the holdall.

Before her I was speechless, able neither to protest nor compliment. The swimsuit on Sindi destroyed in a moment any notion I had of myself as continuous with the girl on the *Innisfree* back then. How could I have thought I could ever wear that costume again? The casual usurping shocked me, and yet, it was Sindi, *my* Sindi doing it. Isn't this what a daughter does? Is meant to do?

Nicholas waved the frisbee, his face rising and falling on a slow blue swell that rose from nowhere, disappearing to nowhere. How glad I was for the simplicity of that relationship. I pulled my attention away from Sindi back into a supervisory role, shouting a reminder to my son of how easy it is to move too far from the boat, how rapidly a swell can become an impassable hill. Although the wind had gone, a boat can shift quickly on a current. He waved dutifully, probably not taking it in. After all they had endured, it was impossible not to play.

Sindi clambered onto the rail and launched herself from the *Innisfree*. It was not a dive, but a leap, the first part of an arc, a breach from one element into another. I'd had no inkling of her athleticism before. She was like a flash of fire in the sky and I was reminded vividly of the orange roughy I'd seen in *National Geographic*, a new species of fish that was discovered clustered in the deep waters round tropical seamounts. It was trawled immediately to extinction, but for a brief time was an incandescent delicacy. And then, stretching her limbs, she brought to mind the marlin that had leapt in parallel beside the *Innisfree* in the old days, for miles and miles, in sheer exuberance. But as Sindi's trajectory unfolded, I saw that it was hers alone, original, the first of its kind. She reached with a lean arm and caught the frisbee, her hair working loose from its band and flying around her, and she smiled back at me like a singer who hits that top note for the first time and realises they are an artist: the widening eyes, the almost-fear that flashes across the face, awe at her own power.

Completing her arc, she cleaved the water, throwing the frisbee to Frank just before impact. My hand flew to my mouth. Oh, it was wonderful. None of this was a mistake. We were a family on a journey together, and our ultimate destination perhaps only the *Innisfree* knew.

Beside me the fishing rod began to bend. The bell jingled, signalling the presence of a fish on the line.

'Guys we've got a fish! Frank, our lure!' I began to turn the reel as my father had taught me, to tire the fish out with his own struggles. A brief serration appeared in the swell, healing instantly.

Frank hauled himself up the ladder at the stern and arrived, dripping, at my side. 'Here, I'll hold it steady, let him jump around a bit,' he said.

'Wow! It's massive!' Nicholas and Sindi clambered aboard.

The rod bent almost double, humming with the strain. Sweat beaded down Frank's cheek and neck. 'Come on lovely,' he murmured.

We could see the shape of the fish now, splinters of green flying from the water.

'What is it?' said Sindi, leaning over the rail, a towel coiled round her hair threatening to topple.

'A dourada!' I cried. 'They're delicious!'

And now its gleaming twist from the blue. The dourada's gape was the size of my open hands, the hook glinted in its cheek. We fanned out, ready to catch it as its furious eye appeared over the side. Sindi pulled the towel from her head and held it out as if catching a baby flung from a building. We were all excited now, as the handsome fish contorted against its invisible bonds. It smelled of life, and salt, and something else, a beast who would not –could not – survive, and knew.

It sprang into Sindi's arms and she clutched it writhing against her.

'Quick! Help!' she cried, and Frank pulled out the priest, a special tool for killing fish instantly. He eased between us and whacked the dourada between the eyes. Sindi dropped it slobbering onto the deck where it twitched among the folds of the towel. Was it my imagination or did its beautiful markings begin to fade, the way some wildflowers do the moment they are picked?

After photographs of us holding the fish, and a weigh-in (nearly three feet long and three-quarters of a stone) Frank erected the barbecue, and all of us, even Nicholas, had a beer. When Frank cut the fish open, eggs spilled all over his hands.

'The he's a she,' he said. The eggs sizzled in the flames, and a deep sorrowful smell rose from them.

'I've never had fresh fish in my life. It always had batter on,' said Sindi.

'Well, you will love this,' I said, passing her a heaped plate.

'Ew, look at its eye,' Sindi said between mouthfuls, pointing at the congealing ball.

I felt pity for the dead, beautiful fish, but now that the sun was setting, and the glow of the barbecue seemed to meet the flames of the sky, pity seemed no different from contentment, was simply part of love. With a grin, Nicholas picked the eye out and waved it in his palm in front of Sindi.

'Dare you to eat it,' she said.

Without hesitation he popped it in his mouth and swallowed. My son and Sindi burst into appalled giggles together.

I was leaning against my husband, drowsy with food and warmth. As the sounds of youthful laughter rose around me, and Frank's gentle replies blurred through my cheek, I realised that everyone I cared about was on this boat with me. Relaxation seeped through me, for the first time since the bomb, or even before that. Perhaps since the old days, the days when it was just about Frank and me, the future stretching ahead like the ocean. My eyes grew heavy and I fell happily asleep.

*

'Wake up darling,' said Frank. 'Here comes our front.'

I was beneath a blanket upon the foredeck, my face damp with dew. It was dawn, and the mainsail was crackling. The horizon was a blazing black line.

'How long was I out?'

'All night! I didn't want to wake you. You needed it.' He produced a mug of coffee. 'Get this in you. We need to put a couple of reefs in the main now, keep us steady.'

I gulped the coffee. 'How's the barometer?'

'Falling, but not too far,' Frank said.

The atmosphere was fizzing; I couldn't tell if it was the molecules of the air disturbed by the oncoming weather system, or the charge between Frank and me.

While Frank adjusted the sails, I went below to change into my waterproofs. Nicholas and Sindi were bracing themselves against the bunks as they dressed.

With a groan, Sindi barged past me to the toilet and threw up.

'Did you forget to take a pill, Sindi? I'll get you one. You need to grab it early.'

'Ugh,' she said, and slumped on the saloon sofa, closing her eyes. Spray foamed at the portholes; rain began to clatter on the skylights. The sky was smoky grey, except for a fracture through which brilliant light streamed. The *Innisfree* was lowering her head to the bit; she knew what had to be done. Nicholas fastened his life jacket and climbed into the cockpit, calmly like an astronaut going for a moonwalk.

Sindi swallowed the pills, and I laid my hand across her forehead. 'I'll come up in a minute,' she said.

'That's the spirit,' I said. 'Need anything? A bowl?'

She shook her head. 'Go, *Alpha Bitch*!' she murmured.

*

'Everyone needs to be clipped on,' Frank declared. It was several hours later and there was a puzzled edge to his voice. The wind was increasing minute upon minute, sending the halyards clanking, the sheets whining. The sky was darkening, and a strange twist of clouds was building in the distance.

The calm sea of yesterday was long gone, replaced with a completely different substance. The waters were angular and confused, and soon it would be too much to keep a course through them. I was very worried for the makeshift rudder. After each wave, the bow slammed down, sending us all tipping. The wind was simply too strong now to tack into. Frank and I consulted quickly: we would temporarily abandon our course to the Canaries and allow ourselves to be blown westwards. We would keep just enough sail to maintain our momentum forward.

The boat heaved into the base of a wave. 'Hold on!' Frank cried.

Sindi reeled out of the hatch, wrapped in her waterproofs, pale beneath her hood. She went straight to the rail and threw up.

'Sindi, your life jacket!'

'Sorry! Forgot!'

'Get one on, now! There, in the stow.' I swung past her to check the barometer below.

I blinked at it. Tapped it, disbelieving. It had absolutely crashed, with stunning speed, and out of all proportion to the prediction we had.

Bracing myself at the navigation table, I connected to download a GRIB file. We hadn't done this since the last one some thirty hours ago, when the weather had all seemed so clear. My mouth dried at the picture that emerged. The north west of the grid was festooned with arrows and their force indicators. Our front to the east was advancing as expected, but this new system was massive. Worse, it was about to meet our little front that we had imagined was more of a squall to be beaten through to get us to the safety of the Canaries. This was going to make a combined storm of enormous proportions.

Swaying back to the hatch, I climbed up to warn Frank. There was nothing we could do to avoid this now.

Outside the seas were heaving. The boat was rolling like a cork. I shut the hatch behind me and clipped myself on.

'Storm jib, Nicholas! Someone!' I shouted.

But they were all motionless, staring disbelieving at a massive wave coming directly for us. It was the kind of wave I remembered with my father: ugly and determined, inhaling everything in its path. I grabbed Nicholas and pinned him beneath me against the rail. As the wave loomed, Frank checked that we were both safe, and then threw himself across the cockpit to Sindi, who was fiddling with the straps of her life jacket.

'Get below!' I cried to Nicholas, opening the hatch and helping him down. 'Dad and I will take care of all this. Get dry!'

As I turned back, my son safe, the wave launched itself at us. Icy water crashed over the deck spinning Sindi and Frank from starboard to port rail. His arms were around her head, his entire body was a suit of armour around her as she careered against the corners and stows. He braced himself over her as the wave receded, gathering strength to return. His face was right up to hers and he was shouting something at her. She was shouting something back and he looked up wildly. His eyes met mine across the deck. Then, right there in front of me, Sindi kissed my husband full on his screaming mouth.

There was a long bewildered moment before he pushed her roughly away. Then, remembering himself, he grabbed her again and spun her round so that she was secured in front of him. With his other arm he held fast to the rail, checking the location of the next wave.

She struggled, utterly distressed.

'What's happening?' I cried, as if there was a conversation I was part of and I had simply missed my turn.

No one answered me. The boat plummeted once more. Sindi twisted and kicked in my husband's arms, wanting to get away from him, blind to the danger she was in.

23

THE BOAT MOMENTARILY STEADIED, my guts spiralled and I began to cry, great helpless snotty gulps that barely made it out of my mouth before being slapped back in my face. It was so dark. Somehow I dragged myself towards them and I wrenched Sindi away from my husband by the hair.

'The grid was too small, Frank!' I screamed at him. 'We've got a massive system meeting the front from the east. We are completely screwed!'

'She's not clipped on—' Frank reached out desperately.

'Did you not fucking hear me?' I kicked him in the ribs. He curled in a ball, clutching his torso.

'What's the matter with you? Yes, I hear you! There's a front coming!'

'No, Frank. It's the biggest fucking storm you've ever seen. It's going to kill us all! So maybe I should just let you both get on with it. You're dead to me anyway!'

'You've got it all wrong! I want nothing to do with her!'

'You lying shit!' Sindi strained against my grip on her hair, trying to punch and kick my husband. 'He wouldn't leave me the fuck alone, Miss!'

I yanked her face towards me. 'Give me one reason I shouldn't let you fall overboard right now!'

'I'm pregnant!' she yelled.

Frank raised his head, gasping. 'Well, it isn't mine!'

Sindi's face was a mask of hate. Her eyes drilled into him.

'That's enough!' I dragged her like a length of crumpled canvas along the deck and tossed her at the hatch. 'Get below,' I commanded. 'If I see your face up here, I will throw you over. No one will stop me and no one will care.'

She stumbled and whimpered, reaching for purchase on the deck. Behind me, Frank was pulling himself to his feet, coughing. I wanted what she had just said to spill onto the deck in a great red mass and be washed away.

The hatch opened and Nicholas extended his hand. He helped her down into the saloon and I slammed the hatch door shut. Shaking water from my eyes, I turned back to the terrifying situation now facing us.

'Helen!' cried Frank, pointing wildly.

A swell was powering towards us, furious black marble. The boat plunged so steeply into the trough it created that the deck became a wall. Frank and I slid helplessly down it, scrabbling for the rail, dangling like rock climbers who have missed a footing. The wave exploded over us and the *Innisfree* began to right herself. Frank was just a flash of neon waterproofs through sheets of freezing darkness. The mast wailed against her stays. We would capsize with the next one of these.

A wave just half the length of a boat has an eighty percent chance of capsizing it if it hits from the side. We *had to* keep moving, with the wind, so as not to swing beam on to the waves. The sails must all come down, and the storm jib, a tiny sail, must go up to stabilise us. Then there would be nothing for us to do but to go below, lash ourselves in alongside Nicky and Sindi, and wait it out.

I cowered beneath electric whips of sea, clinging to the deck. But it wasn't only the storm that was pinning me down, paralysing me. It was the shock of what I had just seen.

Every object in the world now dangled at a nightmarish angle. How could it be possible that Frank and I moved as one to the mast? Frank faced me, our faces inches apart. Valuable seconds sluiced away, as we stared into the chasm where, until minutes ago, love had existed. There is nowhere more urgent, more alive with feeling, than the space where love has quit. And yet there were tasks we must complete, right now, and together, if we were to survive.

'It's not what you think!' he cried again as the next wave descended like a lid. He grabbed me, pinning me to the mast.

The boat tipped so hard into the trough that my feet lifted off the ground, as if I were a ribbon on a maypole.

'You fucking liar! I wish you were dead!' I screamed.

'You think that's news to me? You want Saint James back!'

Both of us howled, like terrified kids, as a wall of water smashed over us. I was underwater. I could feel Frank's arm across me, and the mast bending beneath the force of the water. I did not know if I was even the right way up any more; my feet no longer touched the deck. What nonsense I had learned about the world as a child, that the elements were distinct. Sea. Sky. Land. The ocean was the only element, from which all others were flung at its whim. It mutated from one to the other and back again. Solid as a mountain, smoking with ice, its pit a glimpse of chaos.

We soared, gasping, back into air. I struggled desperately against Frank, convinced that he was trying to pull me under. 'Get off me! Get away from me!' I screamed.

'Calm down! Helen, we have to work together. When we're through this, you can hate me all you want, but right now – think of Nicholas, for Christ's sake.'

I paused, panting. He was right.

'Who knows how long we've got before the next wave,' he said. 'We have to get the jib up.'

'I loved you!' I cried. The pathetic statement evaporated into the spray.

He strained away to attach the jib. I clung to the rail and watched him, ready to catch it if it slipped from his grasp. It was as if I had been swept away and was watching him from the sea. I stared, shivering, at the man I used to know. He was a stranger now, haunted in the movements of hands and body by Frank. The stranger pointed to the halyard for me to tighten it. I did so. The haunted lips opened in the rain.

'She had a crush on me, Helen. It was one time. Maybe two.'

'Stop lying! I cried.

His face hardened in the shining darkness. He staggered over to me, pulling me away from the rail to the comparative shelter of the cockpit. He pushed me down into the well.

'You want the truth, Helen?' The stranger's face was close to mine. 'I wanted... I wished... I could pull your heart out of your chest with my own fucking hands and squeeze it and squeeze it, until James was gone. Really gone.'

'I haven't fucked someone else!'

'You loved him. You still do!'

'But Sindi is pregnant!'

Above us the boom rattled. If the stay snapped, the boom would swing with lethal force. Frank somehow reached over and cranked the winch, even as the boat rolled, almost tipping him out of the cockpit. The stay whined as it tightened.

'Pregnancies don't always work out, Helen,' Frank cried. 'You of all people should know that.'

The stranger turned his back to me.

'*Mum!*' Nicholas, poked his head out of the hatch.

I threw myself towards him. 'Get back down! Tie yourself in!'

'But Mum—'

'DO NOT COME UP AGAIN.'

In the minutes since we'd put the jib up, the wind had increased to the point where even this was too much sail.

'Forget this! We need the sea anchor.' Frank yanked the jib down.

I crawled to the stow to get the sea anchor. Water slewed across the deck, found a gap, drenched me, freezing, inside my lightweight top and trousers. There had been no time to change into my offshore waterproofs. Like fire, the sea finds the places where you are vulnerable and chews at them until they are agonising caverns.

Together we pulled the sea anchor open, and attached it to

a cleat on the deck. Frank heaved it over the stern. The boat turned her back on the waves, stabilised by the anchor filling with water like an underwater parachute.

'If we get through this,' I hissed, 'I want you gone. You and her gone.'

'Let's see what happens,' he said. He turned away and observed the sea anchor as it blossomed in the water.

Once again I felt the deluge of realities, the airlessness of paradox. It was perfectly possible to be facing terrifying danger *and* wish my husband dead *and* wish he would just touch me one more time, just one time, tenderly. I wanted it all to be over, I wanted the ocean to end it for us, the endless unravelling of my love for Frank, his for me, the complication that I now understood never ends. It is timeless and unresolvable as the ocean itself. *Till death parts us.* It was not a vow, but a statement of fact.

And as if in confirmation, a rogue wave rose beside the *Innisfree*. It rose towards Frank, who was hunched over the rail and had not yet seen it. I saw the side of his cheek, where I had kissed many times, where our son had kissed many times. I opened my mouth to scream at him to crouch down, but of course there was no time for words. And anyway, the wave actually *paused*, and turned, as if it had touched the wrong person in a crowd and now had seen the right one. Ah. *Of course*. I mean, what was there for me, really, a ridiculous coward, sick, traitorous? I didn't belong on this journey that had been set up for me. I had, of course fucked the whole thing up. I was sorry for that, I was sorry for everything. The wave blocked out the moon, like a gravestone racing towards me. Turning, I saw Nicholas was on deck, *no life jacket no line*, holding out my offshore waterproof, because his mother was utterly drenched, frozen to my bones. I understood then what the ocean had in store for me, had always had in store for me. With astounding precision, the enormous wave tipped the boat the moment before Nicholas reached me, sending Frank and me slithering on our lines and our son bouncing over the side like an empty Coca Cola can.

24

TIME IS SIMPLY A WAY of expressing change. And so, when the final change has happened – the child has vanished and does not reappear – time stops. The attempt to restart time, for the moment to be reversed, for the equal and opposite force to return, felt like a flashing guillotine inside my chest. *My son emerged from my body. I held him in my arms. We existed.* All meaning rolling away. My own eyes looking back at my hysterical body. *It's all gone too far. Yes, but what shall I do? I don't understand the intervention.* Then, the blade quickening to the speed of light, up, down, up, down, carving me into shining slices of pain. A possessed, eternal execution instead of a beating heart.

In a moment of unison so perfect it might have been choreographed, Frank and I sprang to the rail where our son had just been, screaming his name over the side, craning into the depths to catch a glimpse of him. We scurried up and down the rail, immune to the heave of the deck, the wind, the spray.

'Is that—?'

'Fuck, fuck!'

'Nicky! NICKY!'

'Can you see—?'

'Is that—?'

'Dear God. NICKY!'

Was there ever a sea so full, and so empty? Frank unclipped the life ring with agonising slowness.

'Eleven minutes,' I said.

'What?'

'That's how long we have.'

Corin had yelled this in my ear when we did a practice run for man overboard back then. He kept shouting, 'Eleven minutes, kids! Maybe a couple more if the water isn't freezing!'

Frank threw the ring over. It became a blinking fleck of orange in the heaving black.

'NICKY!'

Again, we scurried like monkeys up and down the rail. Our son was nowhere to be seen.

We faced one another.

'You stay here, pull him up when I find him,' Frank said.

'What?'

He had already unclipped and vanished into the dark. I didn't even hear him land.

No no no.

The silence was towering, exploding.

My baby. I can't just. I can't just.

I unclipped myself and jumped over.

I had on my life jacket but no waterproofs, and saw on my way down the storm jacket Nicholas had brought me, floating, arms outstretched. Of Nicholas there was no sign. *Bang*!

I bombed into the water and my life jacket inflated.

The *Innisfree* loomed above me like a fortress. I shouted for Nicholas, spinning in the freezing dark. The life ring was a few feet away, cresting a swell.

Frank appeared, yelling, signalling frantically. 'Grab the ring! I'm going to dive for him!' He pulled his life jacket off and thrust it at me. 'Stay!'

He drew breath like a boy about to test his depth limit and sank down.

Clutching the ring beneath the sheer wall of the *Innisfree*, I crawled up the slopes of water, rolling down them. I reached for the line attaching the ring to the boat to haul myself clear of the water.

'FRANK!'

The rope fell slack in my hands. I stared up at the boat's flank, then desperately dragged in the line, finding its end. It had come loose. Had he fucked up the knot?

Survival is a place beyond thought, beyond feeling. It contains only action. Keep moving to stay where you are. Stay as near to the boat as you can. Most people found in their life jackets after a sailing accident have drowned anyway. Water batters the face of the fallen, insisting on its claim. Would Sindi hear me if I screamed for her? She could throw us lines, she could operate the sling to haul us all up, when the thing that was happening unhappened. I scanned the side for a line, something to cling to, and remembered that the only other lines in the water were those for the sea anchor at the stern.

Nicholas!

Frank!

Sindi!

Useless or not, the calls flew from my body.

Sindi!

I was so cold. I slapped my face but did not feel it. Momentarily closing my burning eyes, I willed Sindi to appear at the rail of the *Innisfree*. I wished for her as hard as I ever had for James. Her name rasped from my lungs, again, again. Sindi, help! But she did not come.

My kicks grew feeble in the timeless waters. A porthole was glowing on the *Innisfree*'s flank. Nicholas's cabin? I smiled, able to imagine the inside so clearly. It was normally so messy that the shaking of the boat by the storm would have made little difference. His clothes thrown around. His pillow with the indentation from his sleeping head.

At least I was going to die.

I was going to die in the attempt.

I will not abandon you.

I will never leave you.

You are not alone, even in the dark.

I remembered when he sleepwalked to us, locked in a nightmare, his body trembling in our arms.

Here we are, baby.

Your mother. Your father.

Just a dream.

267

I thought of the babies born underwater, wriggling from their mother's body to the surface, bubbles drifting from their mouths…

'HELEN!'

A coalescing of shadows. Frank dipping out of sight, then rising above me. Pushing something.

'Here!' I waved clumsily, my voice a whisper. 'Frank! Here!'

See me.

Hear me.

Is that my baby?

I began to crawl towards the shapes, Frank's life jacket looped on my arm.

He reached for my hand.

Nicky?

'Trapped under the hull. Unconscious.'

I cradled my boy's face. It was greywhitegreyblue.

I pressed my mouth to his. I pushed a moan into my son, through the torrent of water, through the outraged howl of the dark. Frank squeezed him at the same time.

We will not abandon you.

You are not alone, not even in the dark.

Your mother. Your father.

I breathed prayers into my son.

I slapped his little face.

He coughed and time began again.

*

'What's happened to the line?' Frank cried.

'Came loose!'

I steadied Nicholas while Frank put his life jacket onto our son. Our movements were growing heavy. Nicholas coughed up more water, but his eyes did not open. Beside us, the *Innisfree* rode the waves without travelling away, steadied by the sea anchor. She yanked and thrashed, not leaving us, not helping us. The stars, the ocean, the ship, all were now simply witnesses to our desolation. The parents holding their drowning child.

*

'The transom,' Frank cried. 'We can lift him on. It's our only chance.'

With Nicholas on the ring between us, we kicked arduously alongside the *Innisfree* and rounded the stern. It rose and fell above us at an impossible height. I had no idea how we would lift Nicholas onto it, but it was the only way.

There was something wrong with the sea anchor. It had ripped and was spreading in the water, a treacherous cloud of canvas and lines.

'What the fuck?' screamed Frank, fending off the swirling obstacles, to position us behind the *Innisfree*.

The line securing the sea anchor to the deck soared too high to grab, except when the *Innisfree* ascended a wave and her stern tipped, presenting both line and transom for a fleeting moment.

'We'll hold him up,' Frank cried. 'And when she dips low enough, we push him on. Okay?'

'Okay!'

It was a hopeless plan but there was nothing else now.

Pushing the ring aside and kicking to keep myself steady in the heaving sea, I raised my son's legs as Frank raised his shoulders. How heavy he was, this little boy.

'Higher!' Frank said. 'Need to keep his head right out!'

The transom loomed towards us. Would we be sucked under? My limbs burned with the weight of my son, but stayed rigid, like freeze-charred branches.

The transom dipped, briefly.

'Now!' Frank cried.

I tensed my despicable arms that had been no use to anyone, had never even offered real comfort, and we threw our son at the platform.

The transom roared up and out of reach. Frank dived and hauled Nicky's drenched form back to the surface. Nicholas was now an object to be placed. There was no time to consider if he was alive or dead, no time to think of him as our son.

'Again!' Frank gasped. His face was white and trembling.

I took my son in my hands once more. I had no idea even what way round he was, what part of his little body I was holding above the ravaging waves.

Lights were firing in my brain. Don't leave me, I cried. Don't leave me, Nicky.

The transom swooped towards us, lines whistling.

'My fucking foot!' Frank yelled.

I could see that he was struggling to keep his head above water. Something was dragging him down.

He was spitting air, his face half underwater. But his arms were high as pillars, and Nicholas's face shone clear in the moonlight.

The transom arrived, and made its extravagant bow.

'NOW!'

We threw our boy into the air, and we both knew it was the last go.

Did the *Innisfree* brace herself? Hold the transom steady, against all the ocean's forces?

Nicholas rolled awkwardly onto the platform. The boat rose again and he shifted even further back, looked momentarily secure.

'Now you!' Frank cried. He was almost submerged, fighting for breath. With what looked like superhuman strength, he forced himself above the surface. He waved his open hand, signalling that I should step on it. His fingers grabbed my leg. And then I was rising, rising out of the water. I reached for the line, my hands slipping on its slimy surface, but with just enough purchase for me to get a knee onto the transom edge. The boat rolled me onto my back over my coughing son. I groped for the ladder attached to the stern and looked up.

Above us on deck, silhouetted in moonlight, was Sindi. She was staring down at Frank from the rail.

'Help us, Sindi! Help! Throw me a line!'

She was motionless and her voice was strange. 'Not yet,' she said.

I looked back and Frank's hands were circling in the water wildly, reaching for something, anything to pull himself free of the sea anchor that had entangled him.

'Frank!' I screamed in disbelief. Surely he would be all right?

But the stars and the ocean and the ship had returned to witnesses now after their intervention, and no help came.

25

SUNLIGHT GUSHED through the porthole. Water murmured against the hull, its reflections rippling over the cabin ceiling. Beside me, Nicholas's breathing was strong and regular. Warmth rose from his bare neck. I was alive, and so was my son. This was the kind of moment that I was made for. The moment between what had happened and what was going to happen. In that long second, happiness.

The second expanded, grew more details. I realised we were lying at a steep angle, held in place by straps and lee cloths. The *Innisfree* was tilted heavily to starboard and the windows on that side were almost submerged. I was soaking wet. The *Innisfree* creaked gently.

Running my fingertips over a cut on my brow, washed clean by the sea, I peered around me. Not a single object in the cabin was in its previous position. So much for our top-end marine drawer fastenings, built for luxury living on the high seas (Frank, holding up the catalogue, *Gotta have these!*). Doors swayed from their hinges, entire units wrenched from the wall. The *Innisfree* must have spun like a washing machine drum. A knockdown, when the boat turns right over, 360 degrees. The good news was that we didn't seem to be leaking.

But for our breathing, there was no human sound. I was scared to think of Sindi. The happy second could only expand so far, before it would crack. To think of Sindi meant to think of Frank, and I was not ready for either. I raised my hands and wiggled my fingers slowly in the sunlight. My palms were scraped raw from grabbing the lines. But my hands worked, and the sun made them glow.

Unclipping myself, I shook Nicholas awake. He rolled over and his eyes cracked open, two swollen purple carapaces. The second now evolved into another, that was no longer perfect, but was manageable, because Nicholas was conscious.

'Hey sailor,' I said, grabbing a stray bottle of water from its surprising location poking from a smashed panel in the ceiling. I helped him up and put the bottle to his lips.

'My arm...' he groaned.

'I know, but just take a sip.'

Last night, in the brief lull we had been granted before the storm surged once more, I had removed his life jacket and his wet clothes, wrapped him warmly, and somehow strapped his arm, which I could see was badly injured, to his chest with my belt. Dread now filled me as I unzipped his sleeping bag to reveal it.

A huge swelling dominated the space between elbow and

wrist, the broken bone pushing against the skin. Nicholas was studying me for my reaction, his face twitching from the pain. It took all I had not to recoil. Perhaps it was better simply to wrap it up again, accept that he would forever have a dodgy arm. After all, what did *forever* mean now, anyway? The future was not something that would simply arrive, as it used to do. Instead it would need to be salvaged piece by piece from the present. I looked down at my son's face and felt a rush of regret. Regret for my failure to protect him, regret for the news about his father that he would soon know, regret for having raised a child who, at the critical moment, just didn't do what he was fucking told and acted stupidly out of love for his mother. I remembered waking on the *Innisfree* long ago and looking down into Frank's face, in sunlight like this. What a way for it all to end.

'Nicky, we need to reset your arm,' I said, with more conviction than I felt.

Perhaps now was the best time to do this, when he was barely conscious. I'd taken a first-aid course as a trainee teacher. I did, at least in theory, know what to do. I'd need help, however. Resetting a bone was really a two-person job, one to hold the limb steady, the other to pull and manipulate. And I needed the main first-aid kit, which had a morphine shot and gauze and antibiotics. Who knew where that was now? If it was even on board.

'Sindi!' My voice echoed through the *Innisfree*. 'Sindi!'

There was no reply. I tried not to think what this might mean.

Nicholas laid his arm out, lip trembling.

'Here I am!' said Sindi. Ducking into the cabin, she tossed

274

Sailing for Dummies onto my lap. 'Clint got his leg trapped in his motorbike once. Donna made him bite on something when she pulled it out.'

I took in her torn waterproofs, her bruises and her smile. 'Well this is a shitshow, isn't it?' she went on. 'How are you doing, squirt?'

Nicholas brightened like an injured puppy at the sight of her. 'My arm,' he rasped proudly.

'Yeah, I heard that break,' she said. 'When we were lifting you up off the transom. You went bang! into the back of the boat. Snapped like a biscuit.'

'Sindi, you saved our lives. I don't think we'd have got up without you.'

'No problem, Miss. This kind of thing, *total* disaster, it's actually where I shine. I mean, wreckage is what I understand. In disaster lies opportunity. I read that somewhere.'

In a survival situation, a conviction that you will survive is the factor that makes the greatest difference to your odds. If Sindi was deluded, perhaps that was a good thing. Of course our trajectory was almost certainly down, much further down. Probably with no up at all. But this positive attitude was invigorating and very good for Nicholas.

'We will all have to work together,' I said. 'And the first thing is to look after each other, which means sorting out this arm of yours, Nicholas. Now, Sindi, could you please go and see if the first-aid kit is in the head. The stow under the basin.'

'Well the toilet's in a zillion pieces, but sure,' she said, turning away and carefully picking her way at an impossible angle. Her voice drifted back to us. 'I can't even get in. But

275

the cupboard thing is open and there's nothing there.'

'Try the saloon. It's a red box. Stuff is in the weirdest places.' I tried to keep the panic out of my voice. Clattering sounds drifted through the boat.

'Mum it really hurts,' Nicky whispered.

'I know. We're going to fix it though,' I said.

'Jesus, it's like a bomb's gone off,' Sindi called. 'Miss, there's a gin barrel! A whole gin barrel! Not broken!'

'Great!' I called. 'Bring a cup or a pan of it. Anything.'

Sindi returned holding a pan half-full with gin.

'Swallow as much of this as you can, Nicholas,' I said. 'It will help with the pain.'

Obediently, he gulped it down, and I found myself silently thanking Louis' mum for training him in efficient drinking of spirits. Then I directed Sindi to sit behind Nicholas and hold his elbow. She eyed the gin and grinned.

'Forget it, Sindi. Okay, Nicky, this will hurt. But I will be quick.'

I held the book out to him and he bit onto it. He braced himself in front of Sindi, clearly determined to endure this impressively. Then he looked at with me with such trust that I was thrust back to being a new mother, frightened by the baby's gaze, the bottomless responsibility it entailed.

'Okay, Sindi, hold tight. Here goes!' I hauled on Nicholas's wrist.

A muffled scream erupted from my son. The bones scraped together inside his flesh. It seemed impossible that the skin could contain this degree of stretching.

'Oh my God!' Sindi cried. 'It's going to split!'

Nicholas's eyes rolled back in his head. The book creaked

between his teeth. Sindi held grimly on. The bones ground agonisingly into place and Nicholas's mouth opened in a silent shriek, releasing the book. He fell back in a dead faint. The book had deep toothmarks, as if bitten by a tiny shark.

'Well done, Nicky. Over now.' I knew he couldn't hear me, but I said it anyway.

Sailing for Dummies was too big for the next job. I found a paperback wedged behind the pillow and a scrap of panelling fallen by the bunk. I sandwiched the arm between them, strapping the arrangement tightly with the belt. Placing his arm over his chest once more, I laid him safely between the lee cloths and clipped him in.

I gazed proudly at my handiwork. That was the sort of thing pre-bomb Horizon Heights Helen would have done. Perhaps she was still in me somewhere.

Nicholas's eyes flickered open. 'Dad's dead isn't he?' he whispered.

I couldn't answer. I kissed my son on his forehead instead.

'He held me up... Daddy...' He sobbed.

'Sleep now, darling. Everything is going to be all right.'

I stroked his hair as he drifted into an exhausted slumber. Sindi and I faced each other over his prone body.

'So, Sindi,' I said. 'Are you really pregnant?'

She nodded, and blushed with the innocence of a young wife in a Victorian novel.

'And is it Frank's baby?'

'Who else's would it be?'

'How far gone are you?'

She shrugged. 'Three months?'

My role, I knew, was to be the adult in this crisis, but it

277

seemed to demand of me the ability to obliterate monumental facts. *You slept with my husband. You let him die. I loved you. I'm afraid of you.* The urge to scream and punch her in the face was almost overwhelming. I was the moral authority now that we were lost on the ocean in our broken ship, but how was I meant to transform into Solomon? And yet, if I could not bring peace to the *Innisfree*, we simply had no chance.

I took a deep breath. 'Did you...love him, Sindi? Did he love you?'

'He hurt me,' she said. Then she looked at me as she had on the playing fields long ago. 'He was going to die anyway,' she said.

'You don't know that!'

'He was all tangled up, Miss,' she said. 'I could see clearly from the deck. And I just thought, it would be better for all of us if he was gone.'

'Jesus Christ, Sindi! Who are you to make a judgement like that? And watch him drown? Did you even think of me? Of Nicholas?'

'I did try to warn you, Miss.' A certain righteous tone appeared in her voice. 'I tried to explain, remember, back at the house? None of this would have happened if you played your cards better. He talked about you all the time. How sad you were.' Her eyes were wide as she galloped on with everything she wanted to say. 'He sent a dick pic to you once by mistake, and he actually said later he wasn't sorry you'd got it, that he wished your relationship was like that.'

I remembered how her cheeks glowed after the intervention, and my pride in her and what I had done for her. Who was this girl? I resented that she had the audacity to talk about my husband *at all*.

'You can throw me overboard if you like,' Sindi smiled, knowing full well that I was not capable of it.

I sighed. 'There's a baby now. It's not just about you.' The breath caught in my throat.

'I am sorry for hurting you, Miss,' she said, as if she'd broken a favourite ornament. 'I didn't mean to. But I still think it's better that he's gone. These things happen for a reason.'

'See if you're still saying that in a few days, Sindi. We need Frank.'

'Nah we don't! No way.' She burst out laughing, though nothing about this was funny.

Time to get a grip on the situation. 'Okay. This is what's going to happen now. You are going to stay with Nicky and look after him. You need to lash yourself in because I am going to right the boat and it will send everything flying. I have to trust you; I've got no choice. I have to trust that you will not hurt Nicholas.'

'What? How can you think that?' Her eyes were innocently wide. 'I love the squirt!'

I watched her settle herself next to my son. How I'd longed for her to be my daughter. Now I...

Reasons for anything held no meaning now. There was only the unrelenting present to be dealt with.

'I'll be back soon,' I said, and clambered away through the tilting saloon, manoeuvring over scattered chairs, broken glass, clinging to whatever fixed points remained. The navigation screen was smashed. There was no sound from the radio, which dangled broken on its wire. Our supplies were scattered, burst or broken everywhere. I could smell eggs beginning to rot. There were a few water bottles around, but I didn't dare count them yet, as I was sure it was bad news. The water tank was burst and empty. Taking all this in, I wrenched open the hatch.

Sun flooded over me. Momentarily blinded, I pulled myself on deck and surveyed the scene. As I had suspected, the boat was demasted, and the fallen section, still connected to the deck by the steel stays, was in the water, tilting the boat to starboard. The deck was strewn with wreckage. All manner of broken fixings, halyards, planks and smashed panels littered the *Innisfree*. One of the holds had burst open and now hung empty. The external navigation equipment was all gone, and the helm was warped and loose. To my relief, the life raft remained secure in its container. Frank had got the best one available, for six people, which would make it tolerable for four if the *Innisfree* should sink and we had to abandon ship. Once inflated we would find a few supplies inside to keep us alive for a few days. I tried not to think about this. Leaving the boat is the absolute last resort. Once inflated, the life raft cannot be deflated, and if lost or damaged there is no other way to escape.

Of the storm, there was no trace in the towering white sky. A breeze fluttered in. The ocean curved over the earth in every direction, as if the storm had delivered us to a place before time. Gentle rollers heaved the boat every few seconds as if trying to wake her from a slumber. The ocean is heartless. It destroys your boat, and smiles dazzlingly at you when you emerge. Come to me, the ocean whispered. Emptiness calling to emptiness.

The sea anchor line was still attached to the cleat at the stern, but I could not bring myself yet to look over the side where Frank was probably still entwined. Nevertheless, as I now picked my way round the deck, I was shocked at the thought that rose in my mind: *No more Frank*. I licked my lips in the heat, tasting in my imagination the chocolate he had rubbed brutally in my mouth. That would never happen again.

James. His name rose to my lips with no one to forbid it. As I assessed our situation, I began a letter, describing the damage to the mast, the plan I was making. Writing to James had been my way of surviving before. It would help me again. My tongue was swollen in my mouth, but where there should have been despair, there was now a little hope.

The *Innisfree*'s broken mast had pulled her powerfully over in the direction of its fall, and now the starboard portholes were almost underwater. Amputation was the only way to right the boat. I hopped up onto the boom, and sat astride, considering. The stays needed to be cut, releasing the boat from the broken-off part of the mast. Mastless, without engine or proper rudder, we had no means of control at all, and would simply drift with the currents. But with the boat at this angle, we would sink before too long and it had to be done quickly. *Dear James*, I prayed. Let there be some bolt cutters in the stow.

I ran my hand over the stump of the mast, soothing the boat, sorry for all she had been through. The *Innisfree* shifted under my touch, like a weary bull before the matador.

*

The stows outside were built into the structure of the boat and had weathered the capsize well. I heaved one open and found the bolt cutters, seizing on them as if they were the greatest gift I had ever received.

'Yes!'

Clambering back onto the boom, I manoeuvred the cutters slowly into position. It was a small imposition of will upon nothingness. The sound of human intervention grunted across the waters. When the first stay finally snapped, the mast shuddered, and I began on the next.

Sweat ran down my back, splinters of steel pierced my skin. How I wished I had Frank's strength. The last stay squealed as I cut, under phenomenal tension. My mind was blurry with dehydration and shock but I could not stop until the boat was free. Finally the mast was secured only by a thin strip of carbon steel. With a furious yell I severed it, and the *Innisfree* reared upright.

I had not thought the process through and was not clipped onto anything. There was no time to scream. The Innisfree righted with the force of a whale breaching, the amputated mast upending overboard. She flung me across the deck and I bounced, as my son had done, over the rail.

If not entered correctly, water can be as hard as concrete. I was dazed for a moment, bubbles soaring from my skin and my mouth. When my eyes opened into the scorching salt, my first thought was that I needed to retrieve the fallen sail from the drifting mast. It was vital to our chances of survival.

I paddled round the boat to the fallen mast. The *Innisfree* pawed the waters, disorientated. As I swam, I squinted through the water for injuries to the hull. She seemed unharmed. The mast was already bobbing slowly away, lines limp, sail billowing like a man o' war.

The idea flashed in my mind that people would one day find this mast, this stray paragraph from our story. Perhaps it would wash up on a beach somewhere and a child would play around it, until the parent called them gently away. A broken mast can only mean tragedy. Without any other clue, people would wonder what had happened. When nothing further was found, they would wonder if we had suffered, sinking, if we had shown courage. They would wonder if they themselves would show courage in those final moments. But our story was not over yet.

I pulled my knife from my ankle and slashed at the sails, taking care not to become trapped within them. I refilled my lungs at the surface then sank back down to resume my task. The sail seemed determined to obliterate me: it was like wrestling a cloud. But I fought back, slowly cutting away as much sail as I could. Any amount was better than none.

Down I went, over and over, the force of my efforts pushing me still further, until I realised I was under the *Innisfree*, caught beneath her as Nicholas had been. I bumped against the little observation window in the bottom of the hull, greened over, covered in molluscs. Tiny fish darted in alarm at my presence.

We'd never used it. There hadn't been time. Entranced, I scraped away the weed from the little window. Calm suffused my body. It seemed, at last, that there was all the time in the world to gaze inside.

The speckled green cloud dissipated. And there, at the window, real as the sunlight bending from above, was James.

He smiled.

I raised my finger to the glass – oh! – bubbles pouring from my open mouth.

Dear James. Little hammers tapping out the letters in bubbles of light. *I love you.*

An electric ache rattled my body. A visceral force was dragging me away, twisting as if on a hook. *No!* I clawed at the window, desperate to stay. Just a little longer.

Vision or hallucination, I knew what it meant. I couldn't bring him back, but I could join him.

I cried into the ocean. My mouth was full of water, my heart ached.

I thought of Nicholas and Sindi. As if from above I saw them searching the deck for me, discovering themselves alone.

And it was as if a hand reached into my chest and grasped me by the lungs, yanking me to the surface. The sky took me over, forcing air into my mouth. A line, drifting from the fallen mast, appeared in my hands. Like the reflex of a newborn grasping its parent's finger, I gripped it. I blinked up at the tall hull of the *Innisfree*, bathed in sunlight.

Dear James, Dear James, I said with each stroke. A force was supporting me in the water, giving me strength to swim when I had none left. The ragged sections of sail I had cut drifted towards me. Coughing, I pulled my knife once more from my belt, and stabbed a hole near the edge, knotting the line through. Slowly I dragged the sails with me towards the stern, unsure what I was doing, operating with sheer purpose.

The only way back on board was via the transom, as before. There was, therefore, no avoiding it.

Dreading what awaited me, I rounded the stern. Frank was floating upright just a few feet beneath the surface. He was completely tangled in lines and tendrils of fabric, the mess of which had been intensified by the *Innisfree*'s capsize.

He did not appal me as I expected. His eyes were open but there was no suffering in his expression. One arm waved in the moving water. How peaceful he was. I pulled out my knife, and I cut him free, and we rose to the surface together, my arm through his like the old couple we never became.

Surfacing multiplied my weight as if I had plummeted from space. How strong I had become, seemingly overnight. How like an ant, or a cockroach, which cannot be defeated. I tied the sails to the transom to retrieve later. Clutching Frank on a line, I slapped onto the transom. Up the ladder I went with my line, attaching it to the winch, and with the last of my strength I hauled my husband from the sea. It took a long time. The winch creaked and growled, seemingly an extension of my own blind purpose. Beneath me, in the belly of the *Innisfree*, our son drifted in a feverish sleep, and a new baby uncurled inside Sindi, drifting inexorably towards life.

26

WERE WE FINALLY DONE, Frank and I? Is this why I could haul him like a side of meat while he stared through me as though we had never been, as though I had never existed? The rope squeaked against the hull as his head and then his shoulders emerged from below. He jerked like a felled statue onto the deck, and I kept winding because it was kind of exhilarating to look at him, now.

A minute yellow fish flopped from his hair and sizzled on the teak. His face had lost the serene expression it had underwater and was mottled and fraught. His mouth was still open from where he had fought for air, cried for help.

My gaze lingered, and he had to submit to it. Shadows moved over Frank as if the *Innisfree* was hunched behind me looking down upon him too. I could do anything to Frank now. I couldn't help it, my little flame of glee at his abasement before my gaze. I am alive. You are dead. You cannot hurt me any more.

'Why didn't you leave him there?' Sindi said, appearing by my side, hand over her mouth. 'Sharks would have got him; it would have been cleaner.'

'Show some respect, Sindi!' I snapped. 'And where's Nicholas?'

'In bed. Completely out. Didn't even wake when the boat tipped back up.'

I sighed. 'Sindi, we are going to bury Frank properly, at sea. It's the right thing to do.'

Poking him experimentally with the boat hook she said, 'I watched a documentary once with Donna... All these people, hundreds of them queueing in a square to go past Chairman Mao and look at his dead body. He was in a glass case... So fucking weird.'

'Sindi, can you stop poking him please?'

Now she was lifting up his arm by the sleeve with the hook. Water gushed out.

'I'm having *that*!' She cried. Frank's sailing watch was still intact.

'Actually we need one, for navigation. Mine's long gone.' I could overlook that it was Ruth's present.

She was trying to winkle it off with the boathook. I sighed and pushed her to one side, got on my knees and unfastened the watch. There, in gratifyingly huge digits, the time, 11.12, in GMT. Greenwich! So near home! I remembered the morning sun in our London garden, the breeze lifting the edges of the patchwork tablecloth on the picnic table. Nicholas, a toddler reaching with his pudgy hand. Frank running a hand through his hair as he poured me a coffee. What was the point of such a powerful memory? I shook it away. Slipping the chronometer onto my own wrist, I silently dared Sindi to demand it. She shrugged and returned to her body search with the boathook.

The *Innisfree* shivered over an unexpected series of smaller swells. Frank's head lolled and some water trickled from his purple lips. I noticed that his eyes had filmed over and were looking in different directions. I did not feel gleeful any more. How I had loved the way Frank embraced me, enveloping me completely in warmth. It seemed the cruellest removal of his essential Frank-ness that he should be so very cold, even in this blazing sun.

Sindi observed me, puzzled. 'You realise he's dead, right?' she said. 'But it's not over for me. I want closure.'

'A burial *is* closure,' I said.

Sindi leaned against the boathook in an unnerving blend of Neptune and Bo Peep. 'That day I turned up on your doorstep, remember? The fire? Donna and Clint and the flat up in smoke?'

'Yes,' I said. 'It was Clint lighting his oxygen tank. That's what you said.'

'Well. Actually, I opened the valve and I set his oxygen on fire with his own lighter. And I did it because he was a bad person and I'd had enough. *That* was closure.' She grinned at the memory.

'But…you cried in my arms, Sindi!'

She looked affronted. 'I did not!'

'Oh for Christ's sake! Even if that story's true, it doesn't make you some kind of avenging hero. It just makes you a psychopath.'

Her behaviour on the night Frank drowned was not normal, and we both knew it. Part of me was unsurprised she had form in this area.

'Just don't make me doubt Nicholas's safety for a second,' I went on. 'I'll stick that boathook right through you and happily keelhaul you until the sharks get you.'

'Frank was a bad man!' she cried. 'Why don't you care?'

'He was my husband!' I yelled back. Even as the words left my lips, it was not lost on me that the very quality I had that Frank despised – finding excuses for terrible behaviour – was at last being used on him.

Sindi gave Frank a violent shove with the boathook, then flung the instrument over him before stomping to the other end of the boat, insofar as stomping was possible when the deck was strewn with debris and she was barefoot.

'Put some bloody shoes on!' I called after her. 'If your foot goes septic you'll die of gangrene. It's a horrible way to go.'

She had her back to me indignantly at the prow. I cleared my throat and made my announcement: 'The funeral of *my husband*, Frank Bell, will take place at…' I looked at the watch. 'Twelve noon GMT.'

I swaddled Frank in one of my rescued lengths of sail. Just his head was exposed. I dried his face with a towel, closed his eyes. Safe in a net in the cabin, I found his favourite wool beanie, red after Jacques Cousteau, and carefully put it on his head. In my gentleness was all my love for him. Frank had never seemed so human as he did now, almost ready to take his leave from those who had loved him and in the case of his unborn child, would have come to do so.

Conditions for a burial at sea were perfect. A searing sky that suggested heaven. Grand, ceremonial waters. Sindi emerged sullenly from below with Nicholas, who was cradling his arm. The gin had worn off, and his tense face showed the pain had returned, along with a hangover. He rushed to his father, fell to his knees beside him.

'It's all my fault! He died because of me!' He threw his good arm around his father, wept hysterically into his swaddled chest.

'No, sweetie, no. It was an accident.'

I glared at Sindi. *Look at what you've done. To my son!* I longed to grab her and yell it into her face, but if I did there'd be no going back. Nicholas would hate her forever, and somehow I had to keep a crew together. Instead I knelt beside Nicholas and put my arm around his shaking form.

I remembered my own father, and how his body was never wrapped like this, never reclaimed. No chance to apportion blame, declare love, say goodbye. When we were kids, an obsession with contacting spirits ran round the girls on my Fleetwood street. We clustered round the Ouija board pilfered from the tarot-reading mother of one of us, and believed the pointer into movement. We spoke to the dead, our grandfathers, grandmothers, aunties – and when all the easy dead were done, we moved onto the hard dead, the unspeakably lost, *my father*. Not him! I cried, afraid. The girl whose hand was beneath mine turned into a wicked facsimile of herself, as the letters IAMHERE rattled from the cheap plastic disc beneath her fingers, while for me *no* turned into

290

more than anything yes.

'Sorry,' I murmured to Frank, for it seemed an even greater humiliation, on top of all he had suffered already, to be a reminder of other losses, on his own burial day.

'This,' said Sindi, 'is like the worst intervention ever. And without cake.'

I said, dully, 'In the stow under my bunk you will find a box of Jaffa Cakes. It survived the capsize.'

Nicholas lifted his tearstained face. The two of them stared at me. 'You mean, you've kept a packet of biscuits back all along?' Sindi said.

'They were for an emergency. This is an emergency, wouldn't you agree?'

'Any emergency fags?'

'No.'

Sindi picked her way through the shards of broken solar panel on the deck. She glanced down wordlessly at the thin blood trail she was leaving. When she emerged with the box of Jaffa Cakes, she was wearing a pair of Frank's flip flops. She passed round the box and we each took some. I pressed one into Frank's mouth, like a wafer.

'What a waste,' muttered Sindi, through crumbs.

'This is Frank's party,' I said. 'He gets a fucking Jaffa Cake.'

I cleared my throat.

'So,' I began, uncertainly. 'Here is someone we love very much—'

'Speak for yourself,' she said.

'You shut up about him Sindi!' Nicky cried. 'My dad was a brilliant, great person. He's nothing to do with you!' He dissolved into tears once more. Sindi shrugged.

Nicholas said, 'I've got something for Dad, to take with him.' He produced from his pocket the medal he had cheated to win, that day at the swimming gala. I lifted Frank's head and he placed it round his neck. 'Love you dad,' he said.

'Well done, darling. He will like to have that,' I said. Then I continued, 'Frank Bell was a husband, and a father, and great adventurer at heart.'

A shuddering breath from Sindi broke the silence. She sank to her knees, with a wail. With her knife she began to hack at her hair. Her strange, dirty, gorgeous locks, that we all had loved, fell upon him. Then she covered her face and sobbed and sobbed. Nicholas and I stared at each other in surprise. Despite his own grief, he went to her and awkwardly placed a hand on her shoulder.

'Don't cry, Sindi,' he said.

'I'm sorry,' she moaned. She repeated it over and over, 'I'm sorry,' rocking on her knees. I didn't understand where this emotion had come from; only that we can never know, really, how we feel about a person until we are saying goodbye to them like this. Unnerved by Sindi's keening, I chewed the pearl of my engagement ring, and it slid effortlessly into my palm. How could this be? It was followed by the wedding ring. After so long of being unable to remove these talismans, there they were.

I held the rings out to Sindi. 'These belong to you,' I said. I felt no hesitation in doing this. Like the glass slipper, the rings belonged to the one whom they fit. My love for Frank did not need the rings. It was in the *Innisfree*, in Nicholas, in the memories that rose in my mind.

Sindi stopped crying. She took the rings delicately, laid

them in her own palm. 'Bet they were expensive,' she said.

'The pearl ring was his grandmother's, and he bought the wedding ring.'

I could see her weighing something up. Our chances, maybe, of ever being somewhere she could sell the rings. Or the feel of them on her fingers, perhaps. She held the wedding ring to her eye and looked at me through it and giggled. Her now short hair stuck up unevenly round her face, giving her the appearance of an urchin. She licked the pearl as I used to do, but exaggerated, like a maniacal cat.

'We would of definitely got married, you know,' she said. 'I'd be Mrs Bell. I'd have everything you had, and threw away.' She slipped the rings onto her wedding finger, held them up to look. They fitted perfectly.

'My dad would never have married you,' Nicholas said.

Sindi patted her belly triumphantly. 'Your baby brother or sister says he would.'

'What?'

I rubbed my eyes. 'Oh yes, Sindi is pregnant. It's…your dad's.'

I watched horror fighting with amazement on my son's face. He'd just wanted not to be alone so badly. He'd lost his father. But now Sindi could give him what his own mother could not.

'Do you still love him, even though he cheated on you, Mum?'

'Of course I do, Nicholas. That's all in the past. And, well, there's a new baby on the way.'

I gazed upon the body of my husband and despaired that I did not feel as Sindi did: rage, adoration, an energising avarice. I remembered then how we stood on this very deck, hands entwined, Corin performing the ceremony. *Till death parts us.*

We didn't let each other down. Not really. We really did build a life, didn't we, Frank?

Nicholas startled me from my thoughts. 'Can we manage without him, Mum?'

'Definitely,' I said.

*

As I heaved Frank over the side, a corner of the sail shroud caught on a broken rail. He swung upside down against the hull, like a chrysalis. Would there be no end to his indignities? Thankfully, the knots I had made in the shroud were strong and he did not burst out of it. It was as if the boat had reached out and caught him. The *Innisfree* did not want Frank to leave. She was clinging to every last fragment of what had been.

'Let him go,' I murmured, as I sawed with my knife at the part that was hooked. It would mean a hole in the shroud, which would mean the fish got to him a little sooner, but no matter.

'Look, Mum!' cried Nicholas, pointing excitedly over the side.

Beside the boat rose a pod of dolphins, a dozen strong, leaping from the surface and swimming right under us. The *Innisfree* was barely moving, so we were a sitting playmate. The dolphins came right up to the hull, clicking and squeaking. Sindi and Nicholas reached over the rail towards them, distracted from Frank dangling in his final ceremonial moments. Nicholas had even forgotten the pain of his broken arm.

'Look, they are all spotty!' he cried.

The creatures had dappled backs, identifying them as Atlantic spotted dolphins. Their markings made them seem more playful still, as if the sun was pouring onto children running through a leafy wood.

At last I cut through the canvas and Frank rocketed down the side. A neat splash. I had weighted him with the microwave. It would not do to have him pop up alarmingly next to the boat, as he well might once the gases really got going. And after him I threw the box of photos I had brought, cherry-picked from the albums of our days on the *Innisfree*. The box had survived the capsize, tucked in the stow with the Jaffa Cakes, as if waiting for this moment. I should have tied it shut, for of course it fluttered open, and the photographs scattered across the water. They were little splashes of light and colour.

The dolphins dived curiously down alongside Frank. The *Innisfree* rocked disconsolately.

I said, softly, 'Goodbye, my love.'

27

'SEE THAT CLOUD? It looks like a giant pizza,' Sindi said, pointing to a faint smear of white in the endless blue sky. There had been no clouds at all for days, as if the storm had licked the bowl of the sky clean. I scrutinised the smudge for signs it might thicken, join with another scrap of vapour, even produce water. I could see nothing in it that resembled food.

We were sprawled on deck in the heavy afternoon, playing blackjack for a prize so coveted that I wondered if it was a mistake to have offered it. The prospect of winning the last Jaffa Cake had set us all off on a jittery fantasy of gorging.

'What pizza will you have, Sindi, when we get on shore?' I said, gathering the cards in my shaking hands. 'I'm going for ricotta and mushrooms and pancetta...'

Talking about food in detail was something we did a lot

of now, instead of eating. It was a way of keeping us positive. Often the imaginings became banquets. Nicholas set an imaginary table. He would painstakingly describe the plates set out, the cutlery, the side dishes, a whole sensory buildup to the orgy of deprivation.

'Pepperoni,' Sindi whispered. 'With a cheese crust.'

'She's hallucinating,' said Nicholas.

'What will you have, Nicky?'

'I'm saving myself for the real thing,' he said. 'That last Jaffa Cake is mine.'

'Over your dead body,' muttered Sindi.

Exhaustion and dehydration had me in such a grip that, when I shuffled the cards, I dropped half of them all over the table. A breath of wind lifted and tipped them gracefully over, like an invisible dealer. Back in the day we used to play poker on those long still evenings. For the life of me I could no longer remember the rules. Slowly I gathered them up and attempted to shuffle again.

'Gimme that, Miss.'

Sindi took the deck from me, and expertly squared it off, divided it in two and fanned the two halves together, turning them round and performing it again.

I'd had no idea of her enthusiasm for cards, gleaned from Donna apparently, until she shook us both from our torpor on deck a few days earlier, waving this pack she'd found stuck deep in a net. Now, scratching her head feebly through her bandana, she turned her attention to her chips. These were whatever small thing could be found on the boat, to a maximum of ten each. Threads of rope, a seagull feather that must have dropped when we were near home, one of my crisp-packet dominoes, scraps of material, a fork, even coins.

Nicholas pushed his entire stake into the centre of the table.

'That Jaffa Cake had better exist, Mum,' he said. 'It's got my name on it.'

'I've stashed it in the bilge.'

Sindi moaned with longing. She, too, pushed her entire stake into the centre. Neither of them, for a moment, was thinking about water.

This was the final round. Whoever won this won the prize. I dealt the cards.

Sindi greeted her jack and a six by chewing absently on the pearl of her ring. Nicholas, his eight and a five with a bite of his lip. These were cards that required thought and concentration, which were in short supply. I dealt myself a nine face-up, and my face-down card.

'Hit me,' said Sindi.

I dealt her a nine and she stared at the cards, unable to compute what they added up to. The numbers were swimming in front of my eyes too.

'Busted!' Nicholas cried. He broke off from chewing on the end of his sling, which he had started to do in tense moments. It generated saliva, a sensation of thirst slaked, I guessed.

'No!' Sindi said, vainly counting on her fingers.

'Get in!' He punched the air feebly.

'Okay, Nicky. Your turn.'

'Hit me.'

He received a seven. His total now twenty, I expected he'd sit back ready to claim victory, but instead he frowned and said again, 'Hit me.'

I presented him with a six. 'Why did you do that, Nicky?' I said, turning over my face-down card, which was a ten, bringing me to nineteen – and victory.

'But you shouldn't have given it to me! My brain is all messed up!'

'I'm just the dealer, Nicholas.'

'Ha, loser!' Sindi cried. She didn't even care that much that she'd lost, now that Nicholas had too.

'That's so unfair,' Nicholas said. Stricken, he staggered to his feet. 'I'll go and get it I suppose. At least I can look at it.'

'Okay. It's in a bit of plastic.'

He emerged a few moments later from the hatch bearing the last Jaffa Cake. The chocolate was smeared all over the inside of the plastic. We stared at it as if it was the rarest delicacy we had ever seen.

'I wore out my brain adding up Sindi's score, Mum. I had actually won!'

Sindi protested, 'If anyone should get it, it's me. I'm eating for two.'

'Shut up. You're not a relative,' Nicholas said.

'My baby is though!' She looked round at us. 'Are you going to cheat your own baby sister or brother?'

'You didn't win, Nicholas,' I said.

Mechanically, as if he were sleepwalking, Nicholas opened the wrapper and ate the Jaffa Cake, then licked every bit of chocolate from the plastic. He gave a low moan at the tantalising rush of satisfaction it offered. His face was the empty face of an addict when they have abandoned themselves to their craving. Then he sank back down in his seat.

'Not cool, bro,' said Sindi.

Nicholas didn't even look sorry; just stunned. He said, 'I miss Dad. Why did he have to die?'

'I don't know, Nicky. Just a terrible accident, that's all.'

I looked at the grubby cards on the table, the wreckage around us, the sunburned faces of Nicholas and Sindi. If only I had simply endured after the bomb. Let the *Innisfree* stay in the playground; Sindi go into care; Nicholas disappear into the internet; Cariad rest in peace; James remain unfound and alive; and Frank follow his heart, wherever that was. What would have become of us all, then? I had forced so much, worked so hard, and tried to avoid so much suffering. And what had it achieved?

I hated the *Innisfree* then. What a fucking lie. Go back where? The dead are dead. The past is gone.

'I was going to divide the Jaffa Cake between you both,' I said. 'But I can't now. Sorry, Sindi.'

'Imagine stealing the last Jaffa Cake from your own flesh and blood,' Sindi said. Then she went back to gazing at her pizza in the sky.

*

The next morning, Frank's chronometer told me it was 04.30 GMT, and I almost ripped the thing off and threw it over the side because I was sick of knowing the time back in London, in the old dimension, which was now as unimaginable as heaven itself. The point of having GMT or UTC was for navigation, but without a sextant it was useless and therefore a major irritant. Useless things become tyrannical at sea. However, it was the only functioning navigational technology on board so I kept it, and wore it and tortured myself by consulting it.

Thirst buzzed in every cell of my body. Nevertheless, as is correct at the end of a watch, I opened the log book to note all the details of our situation. The log had materialised, battered and sodden, in a corner of the saloon, and I had dried it out on deck. Frank's last entry was the night before the storm. My first was the aftermath, written with my one remaining coloured pencil. The green loops of my entry reached out to the confident black lines of his, as if trying still to be a team.

At the back of the log I had created an evolving list of what we had and what we didn't have. Chief among what we had was gin, the life raft, a torn chart, some cans of nameless food. Chief among what we didn't have: electricity, radar, engine power, mast, rudder, much water. Means to navigate or steer. Briefly, I noted our approximate direction. Then I closed the log and looked out over the molten blue, scanning a careful 360° round the horizon. Something. Anything.

The patternlessness of the ocean can drive a sailor mad. The *Innisfree* creaked at regular, man-made intervals, as if we were living in an ancient timepiece. Without sails, she continued to move ahead, although this was only perceptible when I threw a scrap of something overboard at the bow and watched her slowly carry us past it. I timed this journey, and then could calculate that we were moving at one knot, borne on one of the currents that unfurled like a drowsy serpent beneath us.

'Hello, Mum.' Nicholas eased himself tentatively out of

the hatch. He knew he was still in disgrace.

'Hello, darling.' Resentments had to be resisted bodily on a boat, thrown over the side like mutineers. Otherwise they could easily overcome our weakened character. Hunger and thirst made children of us all.

Nicholas shyly produced something from his belt and laid it in front of me. In that moment, he reminded me of Chalmers, producing the little fawn all that time ago. I squinted through the glare and for a second my heart stopped.

'The sextant!' I cried, snatching it up and turning it over in my hands. With a sextant I could work out our position. Position was hope.

'It was down the side of one of the sofas! I was looking for something to cushion my arm.' He smiled at me hopefully. 'Can you use it?'

The sextant is a strange and complex-looking instrument, essentially unchanged, like boat desgn itself, since its invention. Its purpose is to measure the altitude of a given celestial body at its highest point from the horizon. The sun is the best one to refer to, because it is the simplest to pinpoint. We brought ours along as an afterthought because, much like the paper charts, we never anticipated needing it. All its functions have been superseded by computer navigation. It wasn't an expensive model and wasn't in a box. So it was a good omen, I felt, that it had survived the turmoil in good condition – except that all the shades had snapped off. Depending on the brightness of the body being observed, up to three shades pull out on hinges and are lined up to protect the eye and allow direct gaze upon a bright object. The hinges of ours were flimsy and had shattered. Who knew how long ago this had even happened? Even if I found the shades, there was no way to re-attach them. Like the decision of the thirsty sailor to drink salt water, the decision to use the sextant without shades is never really made. It occurs at the tipping point between surviving the moment and considering the future. To pinpoint our position and thereby improve our chances, I was going to have to look straight at the sun, repeatedly.

'Well done, Nicky! This makes all the difference in the world.'

His shoulders relaxed at my words. 'I'll do the next watch,' he said. 'You need a rest.'

'Okay then. All I can report is a tiny breeze from the north east. And…our friends are still with us.'

The dolphins were long gone, replaced by the altogether more sinister shapes of sharks. The clear waters rippled with their shadows, their fins cutting the swell so finely that I was never quite certain if I was really seeing one or it was a trick of the light. They did not play or leap, simply coasted languorously alongside. So powerful was their presence that, when they seemed to disappear for a time, I found myself searching the water for them. Worst of all, they scared away all the fish, making it impossible for us to try and catch food.

Nicholas looked over the side and frowned. 'Like vultures in the desert,' he said.

Sindi climbed on deck, yawning. 'Did you see a ship? Is it over?' she asked.

'Yes! Welcome to St Lucia!' I waved extravagantly round the boat, rolled my eyes.

'Very funny.' She shuffled over to the other side of the

cockpit beneath a shade rigged out of the heat reflector sheet. I'd strung it there to create a flicker on the ocean's vastness that might be visible, should a plane cross within range. We had enhanced it with rags scavenged from corners and bunks: sleeping bags, T-shirts and towels, all attached together during one long dawn when I worked like a demented princess spinning nettles into gold. Another storm would simply sweep it all away, leaving us with nothing, but this is what happens when you are adrift. Planning is meaningless. I was learning to glide opportunistically through moments, like a shark.

The two of them stiffened like meerkats at the sound of me pulling a bottle of water from the stow.

'So I have your attention,' I said. 'Crew meeting in progress. We'll keep it brief. Nicholas is doing this next watch. Good news is – we now have this.' I held up the sextant. 'And I am going to find out where the hell we are. And you, Sindi, your job this morning is to collect water from all the condensers.'

'Yeah, well you can't trust him to do it,' she said. 'He'd bloody drink it all and watch us die.'

'That's enough, Sindi. It's a new day. Nicholas found the sextant. He has atoned.'

'Yeah, leave me alone,' said Nicholas.

Sindi really didn't look well. All of us had cracked, burned lips and skin, but she was particularly pale and she kept quietly drifting off. I was worried about her blood pressure.

'So, time for morning rations. Here,' I said, handing the bottle to Sindi. 'You can drink to here.' I pointed with my finger a few centimetres down the bottle. 'Can I trust you?'

She nodded vigorously, then proceeded to swig like a

304

pirate and I had to pull the bottle from her swollen lips.

'What's the matter with you?'

Her tongue snaked from her mouth hunting for scraps. She dabbed a drop that had fallen on the deck.

'I'm just so thirsty,' she murmured. 'This fucking *thing* is stealing my water. It's sucking the life out of me!' She stared down wildly at her belly, her hands helpless in the air.

If I wanted to forget about the baby, which I didn't – except that the idea of it dying inside her was horrifying, so I tried not think about that – this was not possible because Sindi complained about it every single day.

I handed the bottle to Nicholas, marking the point where he should stop drinking. Embracing his new place on the moral high ground, my son drank to the mark and handed the bottle back. I took my drink, less than theirs, and stowed the bottle back in the locker. I wedged it closed with the hammer.

'How much water have we got?' Sindi asked, eyeing the stow.

'The condensers give us a bit extra. And if we catch a fish…' I looked hopefully at Nicholas.

'Fuck me – dead in a week then.' Her face was pure disdain. 'Wonder what it's like, dying of thirst.'

'You hallucinate,' said Nicholas. 'See pizzas in the sky.'

'Maybe we should kill the weakest one and drink his blood.'

'Piss off.'

'Come *on*, you two!'

Sindi slumped back. 'Can I have more water?' she whined.

'Empty the condensers and fill them up again. We will all share whatever you manage to get.'

305

We were increasingly dependent on the makeshift water condensers, constructed from sail cloth and every pan or container that we could find. The idea was that the heat of the sun would evaporate seawater and deliver it distilled into another container. In practice we got less than a litre a day in total from all of them. Still, it was a way to eke out our remaining water and to moisten our mouths. When quenching thirst is not possible, just fending off the dryness with the illusion of moisture can be enough to keep you going. Like nurses dampening the cracked lips of the dying with a cotton bud, we dabbed at ourselves, our own carers.

Sindi heaved herself out of the cockpit. Taking the bowl round each condenser, she carefully tipped the contents out, nibbling at the watery pickings. I could see it was taking all her strength not to swig the lot. It was so little and seemed to get less before our eyes. When she had emptied them all, she laid the bowl of fresh water in front of me. She then topped them all up from a bucket. Suddenly she halted in shock.

'I felt something,' she said. 'Like a sort of butterfly feeling.'

'Your baby's starting to move around.'

'Move around! But I want it to die!'

She slumped in the cockpit, her hands on her belly. The rings were digging into her fingers. How restless those rings were, never settling, marking whoever belonged to Frank.

'You don't mean that, Sindi. You're tired and dehydrated.'

Sindi twisted the rings and gazed absently out over the water.

'I know what it is!' she announced. 'That feeling. My body is rejecting the baby. You know, like an organ transplant? I mean in a situation like this, a baby is kind of a luxury? I should reabsorb it or something. It's a waste of resources.'

'Enough of that. Put your cups out,' I said, and divided the tiny quantity of water from the condensers among us. We downed it immediately.

I held up a can without its label. 'Today's mystery breakfast!'

They both groaned. 'Why did you steam off all those labels, Miss?'

'Seemed like a good idea at the time.'

I opened the can with its ring pull and grinned at them both. 'Spaghetti hoops!' Dividing the contents among us, I gave myself just a spoonful. I was neither growing nor gestating and just needed enough to keep myself turning over.

'He's got more than me,' Sindi complained.

'Okay, then. Sindi, you divide it between you, then Nicholas will choose which cup to have.'

'What?' She scrutinised the contents of both cups. 'Oh, I can't be arsed.'

Each of us had a spoon which we kept attached to our belts. The implements were in our fists, poised.

'Don't eat it too quickly,' I commanded. 'Savour it. Get every bit of nourishment out of it.'

My crew spooned the ration into their mouths, as delicately as if they were receiving the first dish of an *haute cuisine* taster menu.

*

A sextant takes a sight by means of a system of mirrors. The viewer aligns an image of the sun with an image of the horizon and from this takes a reading of the sun's altitude at solar noon, its highest point, using the sextant's engraved dial. The time in GMT is taken simultaneously. With a reading for solar noon, and the time in GMT, a position, both latitude and longitude, can be calculated. Corin, our skipper back then, had sailed long before the days of GPS and he still cross-referenced his positions using sextant and paper chart. I had a paper chart folded inside the log book, awaiting its first X to mark our own position.

In order to pinpoint solar noon, I'd need to take some ten sights in quick succession on the approach, so I wouldn't miss the sun's highest point. The human eye is no defence against the midday sun. I braced myself and raised the sextant. White knives pierced my brain as I looked at the burning bead in the sky. Patches of my vision melted, as if my retina was celluloid dropped in a flame. Tears pouring down my cheek, I strived to perform the sights quickly, without fumbling, which would mean I'd have to do them again. I used only my right eye, to keep the other unaffected.

I licked the tears as they reached my lips. When at last I had taken enough sights to be sure of solar noon, and had noted the time in GMT from the chronometer, I cut a strip from my shirt to make a patch for my eye.

Sindi stirred from an uneasy slumber beneath the shade. 'You okay, Miss?'

'Tie this, can you?'

She reached up and tied a good knot. For a second, when her fingers brushed my hair, I remembered that evening a lifetime ago when she came into the bedroom and French-plaited my hair to look like hers. Who were we then?

'Thank you,' I said, patting the bandage, blinking at the

two-dimensional world that now presented itself through one eye. Every nerve in my right eye felt raw. I hoped the damage was temporary, but I also knew that, regardless, I would have to take more sights tomorrow.

'You're a pirate!' said Nicky.

'Aye aye!' I rasped cheerfully. Then I sat down to tackle the calculations, with my pencil in the back of the log book. At last, I unfolded the chart and marked our position in a cross on the page.

'Hey, look at this, you two,' I said, pointing triumphantly.

'Middle of bloody nowhere!' said Sindi.

Nicholas picked up the chart and consulted closely.

'How long till we reach land?' he asked.

'That's kind of a how-long-is-a-piece-of-string question, Nicholas. It depends on the direction of the wind, and its strength, and the current, and what sort of sail we might be able to rig—'

'I just want this to be over!' said Sindi. 'At least if we die, then it's over!'

'Sindi, we have to stay positive. If the wind picks up a bit, we might be able to move a bit faster. These currents that are carrying us move westward. We *will* get somewhere eventually.'

*

Donald Crowhurst, the amateur sailor who rashly took part in the first round-the-world yacht race in 1968, kept two logs. One had all his fake positions, because his boat was not seaworthy and he was lying about his journey. The other was his true log, with real positions, where he reacted to the realisation that he would never see his family again, that he had failed as a sailor and as a man and suicide was his only chance of redemption. As his situation worsened, this true log became crazier and more incoherent, like a shockwave from the detonation of his decision to lie. The writing spilled into the margins; there were digressions into philosophy and poetry, words like wreckage circling a powerful gravity.

I thought of Crowhurst as I sat in the late afternoon to complete the log, with my gin by my side. (It was miraculous, and ridiculous, that our gin barrel survived everything, while the water tanks did not. I allowed myself one gin a day, at log-writing time.) Was it better to split oneself in the face of an unbearable truth? Keep two logs? Or do as I had started to do, scribble everything into the log so that it was not only a meticulous account, now with positions, but included, like a diary, my hopes and plans, lists, sketches, memories of the *Innisfree* before, in the old days. There were no rules to constrain me, now that I was skipper and the judge of what was worth recording or not. What was a proper record anyway?

My eye burned behind its patch. I sharpened my green pencil and scribbled on. What it felt like, to have a position now. What it felt like to remember Cariad, quickening inside me, and that same flutter inside me when she died. Aboard the *Innisfree* now, we could not escape our suffering and I no longer sought to. I sought to record it, to feel it, to understand its relationship to the facts. I did not know for certain, but I thought there might be wisdom there.

28

Position: 23°,05'N / 38°,15'W

WAKING ON DECK from a vivid dream of rain, I began this
day as I began every day: I spoke to the *Innisfree*. Shuffling
round her perimeter, checking her condition and the weather,
I asked aloud if there was anything I could do to make things
stronger, better, and easier on her.

It was strange that, among all the wreckage, the repurposed
objects, the chaos created by human beings trying to live
where living is not intended, I felt the past most keenly. The
dawn after a night watch on the ocean is the closest a mortal
can come to knowing that first dawn at the beginning of
time. No longer did I feel the presence of Corin, of Frank,
even the *Innisfree*'s young self. What I felt was what I had
felt sometimes then, the kindness of eternity. That was the
link between our young selves, and now. I wanted to tell

Frank then, *this is it, this is peace.*

The sun was rising in a glorious fire. I paused at the rail, overcome by the recollection of the *Innisfree* in the boatyard, just before we left, when Nicholas and I had stood in the same spot as I stood now. The dawn had swept over the deck, taking our breath away, as if she was plunging through a golden ocean, just like this. Often people who have never sailed offshore wonder why anyone would do such a thing. Here was the answer. Existence, as it really is, was being revealed to me, one curling blue scroll at a time.

And whether in my imagination or truly, the *Innisfree* murmured back to me. She would never abandon us, but she was broken and she was tired. I loved her even more. The wind was blowing us gently westwards, puffing up the simple sail we'd rigged, but even with fair winds it would be two weeks to the Caribbean. Without rain, and lots of it, we were finished.

I told the *Innisfree* that our prospects of survival were worsening. As I unburdened myself to her, the memory swam to mind of that day so long ago, stood at London Bridge Underground Station hoping to see James, when I did not think I could survive another moment. And I had come to a strange acceptance that I would never see him again. In that moment, I was reconciled to my loneliness. Putting my face into the breeze, I remembered the smell of lemons that had offered me such comfort.

'What shall I do?' I asked the *Innisfree*. 'Shall I give up?'

She did not answer.

Whether I gave up or not, she would carry on.

My patch had slipped. As I tried to adjust it, pain shot

through my head. An infection was spreading beneath my eyelids. Taking sights was close to impossible now; all I could see through my right eye was the sun, whether the eye was open or closed. But the pain proved I was alive, and was becoming an important marker in these days of boiling, broken sameness. Surely it could not be long before the infection got into my head, my blood? My dread of this showed me that something had changed. I did not want to escape reality, even though our situation was so dire. I wanted to keep my hold on it, not to disappear into hallucination, and to see whatever this was through. For Nicholas. For Sindi. For her baby. I was the skipper.

As I fiddled with the patch, Sindi emerged from below. She helped me retie it, as she did most mornings now, then she turned her sunburned face to me, opened her scabbed lips and said, 'Let's kill one of those sharks.'

'That's a great idea Sindi, but how? Their skin's so thick it's almost impossible to puncture with a knife. And they are all huge.'

'I'll think of something.'

We leant against the rail together, perhaps considering the question, perhaps not really thinking at all.

'Your old flare plan would have worked a treat,' I said.

'No flares left?'

I shook my head. But then had an idea. I pointed to the life raft. 'There's always a flare or two on there. Not the really strong ones, but it could work.'

She gave a sore, light-filled smile. 'If I have a flare, I can get us one of those bad boys.'

It was time to deploy the life raft among the sharks and

raid its meagre contents. And then that would be it. Nothing left at all.

*

I released the catches, secured the painter to the rail, and pushed the life raft over. With a magnificent hiss it began to inflate into a circular orange tent, with air-filled walls and roof. Bravo, Frank, for getting a top-of-the-range model. If the sharks ever left us alone, it might also stay afloat long enough to develop growth underneath where fish might shelter. Eagerly I observed it reach its full size.

I clambered down onto the transom, clipped myself on and pulled the raft in by its painter line. A few metres beyond, a dorsal fin broke the surface, slipped away. The sharks knew all they had to do was wait. Once I got onto the raft there would be just a thin layer of air and plastic between me and them. Securing the raft to the transom, I jumped on. Inside it smelled of new rubber, of safety, of hope. Gibbering my thanks, to Frank for his foresight, and to anonymous men and machines who had engineered this vessel, I raided the pockets. It was a life-saving treasure trove. I whimpered with excitement and hope as I found:

Forty sachets of water
Dried food
Plastic knife
Puncture repair kit
String
Flares

314

Condenser kit

Fishing kit, not that it was any use as the sharks took
  anything we caught.

Compass

Plastic grab bag

Stuffing everything into the bag, I crawled back to the
entrance. Clutching my line with one hand and the bag in
the other, I positioned myself to throw the bag onto the
transom and jump after it. Judging the distance was difficult
with just my one eye and no stability, so I was grateful to see
Sindi descending from the deck.

'Miss! Put the bag on here.' She held out the boathook.

'Okay.' I knelt on the wobbling base and held the bag out
towards her.

'Miss!' she shrieked. 'A shark!' I had not seen it approach
on my blind side. Its exploratory bump to the raft was so
violent, I tumbled back inside and the bag fell from my hand
into the water.

'No!' I screamed.

Why had I put everything in it? Why hadn't I got Nicholas
to help me?

I yelled at Sindi to try and hook it back out, but she was
already trying, dangling wildly from her line over the water,
prodding into waves. But these were seconds lost, which
might as well have been days, because the bag was already
being carried off, dragged down. I realised I was squeaking
with terror, turning my head wildly to see, even though I was
afraid to see. This was our death sentence being carried out
before my eyes. Frantically, Sindi stabbed the boathook into

the water, trying to get it under the handle of the bag, while the water around us roiled with sharks, bouncing the life raft so vigorously that I retreated further, to cling to the handles inside.

'Mum! Get out!' Nicholas cried from the deck.

At that moment, a shark rose at the entrance to the life raft. In a smooth, unthinking movement I pulled my knife from my ankle and stabbed it in its bright, dead eye. I yanked the knife out and stabbed it again. Sharks are unable to make any sound. Nevertheless, the whole ocean seemed to reverberate, and the shark twitched with such force that the raft almost flipped over, sending me sprawling against its back wall.

I could see in the chaos that Sindi had managed to skewer the shark in the gills with the boathook. She was determined we were going to rescue something from this disaster. But the shark was at least six feet of powerful muscle, thrashing for its life beside us. Its gaping jaws, with their rows of razor-sharp teeth, skimmed the raft.

'Let it go!' I cried. 'It will sink the raft!'

Sindi was clearly torn between obeying the command and the desire to finish this job. The shark gave a massive twist and yanked the boathook from her grasp, vanishing with it, as if it had been harpooned.

In the brief moment of calm which ensued, Sindi held out her arms to me. I stumbled into them from the raft, and we clung to each other, unable for a few moments to face the enormity of what we had lost. Devastated, we climbed the ladder, Nicholas helping us both onto the deck. When I looked back, the water pulsed with sharks, the raft bobbing uselessly above them.

'Where's the stuff?' Nicholas asked.

'We don't need it,' I lied. 'Not any more.'

*

Now liberated from any notion of fighting for survival, we followed, with as little energy spent as possible, our rhythms. We became crepuscular and then virtually nocturnal.

The sharks, having in some secret way got what they wanted, vanished, leaving the raft intact. Part of me wished they had taken it with them too. It rested, slightly askew, a ludicrous reminder of our failure.

Though the sharks were gone, we could not summon up the strength to try and rig a fishing line. Instead, Nicholas and I slept on the deck, waking to a brief respite of dew, while Sindi, whose failure to catch a shark seemed to have knocked the last of her strength out of her, lay curled up below.

At dawn and sunset we often saw flying fish whirring like dragonflies over the sea. One night we spread ourselves beneath the stars like flytraps and managed to intercept two of them, one on Nicholas, one on me, flopping on our chests like our own excavated hearts. We snatched at them with superhuman reflexes, cut off their heads, gulped the briny darkness that poured out, then scraping off wings and scales and gobbling flesh, blood, innards.

I dragged my lips away before mine was fully consumed, mumbled to my son, 'Sindi.'

He also stared at the fish, gripped in two hands. His

317

arm, despite everything, was healing. Carefully he took my morsel from me, added it to his and went below to give them to Sindi.

*

Sextants appear in bunks. Gin survives where water does not. Nothing is where it should be. When the end is coming, when it is certain, strange, incomprehensible miracles surround it.

Late one afternoon, taking myself below to examine the cupboards again, in case I had missed something or something new had appeared, the boat tipped gently on a swell and the round door of the washing machine tottered from a corner and arrived at my feet. By force of habit I returned the door to its rightful home. Absently I checked inside the drum in case something of use had found its way in, and my fingers closed round an object. I drew it out and gasped.

My notebook! It was damp but otherwise perfect (by 'perfect', I mean exactly as it was when I lifted it from the road). Oh. Oh. Oh. I turned it in my hands.

When I opened it, out fell James's memory stick.

The memory stick! That I picked up from the road!

I crawled into my bunk beside a slumbering Sindi, the notebook clutched to me, the memory stick in my fist. Everything would be over soon, but I had been given the gift of a little time to see my maps again in the fading light, so vivid and detailed, and beautiful and useless. As long as you demand nothing of miracles or fairytales, they come thick and fast.

A thought occurred to me. Feeling along the side of the mattress, I found the zip. There is storage everywhere in a boat: pockets here, dual-use there.

Kneeling on the floor, I opened the zip. I slipped my fingers inside and found an edge. My laptop, in its rubber case, slipped unharmed into my hands.

I opened the computer, as if it were a normal day, and simply, as it had always done, it glowed awake.

The feeble electrical gleam filled me with hope. There was very little charge and the screen flickered like an old movie. I tapped in SaveMeJames123 and plugged James's memory stick into the side, clicking the first file. I had no idea what I would find; perhaps IT paperwork, invoices, personal details about him. Instead, the stars I had gazed upon beside him in the coffee shop reeled before me. Constellations. Nebulae. I clicked through faster. It was a memory stick filled with the heavens.

Forgetting the notebook, I took the laptop and the sextant out on deck, where the sky was, likewise, a screen brimming with stars.

It would have been easier on my eyes from the start to use the sextant to take our position at night, but this had been impossible. The night sky was unreliable, often cloudy and, when clear, the stars I knew were rendered invisible by countless millions of other stars that were just as bright.

Nicholas sat beside me. 'The laptop survived!'

'Yes! I'm trying to work out the constellations,' I said. 'If I can do that, I can take sights at night using the stars. This poor old eye needs a rest…' I pointed at the patch.

'I didn't know you were into stars.'

'The stick belongs to a friend... You know, my friend from the Tube? Ah, I think... Can you see Orion on this image?'

He sat beside me and observed as I scrolled through the photographed constellations and compared them to the sky above us.

'We're looking for Polaris,' I said. 'Maybe you can spot it.' My left eye struggled painfully to pick out the detail.

'There!' he said.

'That's great! Well done,' I nodded, as though I could see it too. 'Now we need to jot that down. Can you grab the log book and my pencil?'

Nicholas went slowly below, angling himself carefully with his good arm. He was so thin now, his knees swollen, his muscles wasted. My mouth dried at the sight of his trembling movements. He returned with the book and proceeded to make a careful drawing in the log book of where Polaris appeared in relation to the other stars around it, peering at the screen and the sky. I was simply unable to help. Looking at any form of light was too painful for me now.

The screen went dark, refused to come on again.

'It's okay, I got it,' he said.

I closed the laptop, sat with it quietly for a moment. I thought to begin a letter to James, in the old way. *Dear James. Thank you for the stars.* I smiled to myself. When the sun rose tomorrow I would write to James in the log book.

'So, let's see you take a sight, then,' I said.

Together in the brilliant darkness, my son and I pinpointed our position using Polaris, which he located now with ease. I guided him through the readings, giving him the time from my watch and helping him with the calculations.

By starlight, we marked our position, another X upon the chart. And when it was done, we slept, leaning companionably together as the *Innisfree* voyaged on.

*

The next day was, according to the chronometer, Nicholas's birthday. He lay across me in the shaded cockpit all that long afternoon, playing with the lure I gave him as a present. Sindi leant against my other side.

'Hey squirt,' she murmured. 'Happy Birthday.'

She began to sing it aloud softly.

I remembered how, so long ago, her classmate Petra had said she had a beautiful singing voice, and it was true. I joined in, and Nicholas joined in, humming gently, too weak to speak.

After the last *hip hip hooray*, he said, 'When we get back I'm going to have a cake even bigger than the one for Sindi's birthday.'

'Oh yes!' I said. 'What kind?'

'Chocolate. With chocolate chips, and chocolate frosting.'

'Good choice,' murmured Sindi.

'Sindi and I will ice it for you, won't we, Sindi?'

'Might eat it all.'

'We'll have party plates,' I said. 'And balloons.'

'Louis will come,' said Nicholas.

'Bring his own vodka, though,' I said.

'And Dad will be there. He'll make a special trip from heaven.'

'He wouldn't miss it for the world.'

We looked down at the face of my son. His eyes were closed, his lips slack, his breath light. He gave a little twitch; I hoped he was dreaming of home, his mother and father with their arms about him.

Sindi said, 'You'll never guess what I used to watch with Clint and Donna. *The Waltons.* This super-old TV show about this perfect family. Just popped into my head.'

'G'night John-Boy,' I said.

'G-night Mary-Ellen,' she replied softly.

*

The sun was well past its midpoint, heavy and orange in the white sky. Nicky dozed on.

Her head against my shoulder, Sindi murmured, 'What would have happened to me? To us? You know, if we had made it?'

The question held no anxiety or rancour. She seemed genuinely curious.

I took her hand, squeezed it. 'Don't give up so easily, Sindi! The *Innisfree* hasn't. Those tiny shapes, for instance, on the horizon. Ninety-nine times out of a hundred they are tricks of the light, tiny clouds. But every so often…well, they might turn out to be a sail.'

'I can still feel the baby fluttering,' she said.

'See! You're a great mum already.'

'Who'd have known when I was lying in that casket that I'd have a little baby? Even just for a little while.'

'It's going to be all right, Sindi. I promise.'

I love you, Miss,' she said.

'I love you too.'

Later, when night fell, and the sky's sparkling cloak swept over the ocean, I gave Nicholas my chronometer and, beneath the glittering sky, he again took the sights. My patch was gone now and I didn't have the strength to find something to replace it. My right eye was blind, but I could feel in my mind all the stars I could not see. Dear James, I whispered, as I gazed upon them. Dear James. I remember you so clearly. I loved you so much.

29

WHO DECIDED THAT the flickering shape on the horizon would, this time, become a sail? Not me – my days of meddling were over. I was a sailor now, and the sailor, above all, knows that facts are there to be submitted to, not resisted. As the sun rose higher and the shape grew from tiny incision in the sky to elegant, tilted feather, I tested the evidence of my faltering eye and my burning brain against the factors that insisted that what I was seeing could not be real. I understood only too well that my irrepressible urge to live could affect our chances in unpredictable ways.

'Sindi, Nicholas. Can you see what I see?'

Nicholas sat up, shading his eyes. 'I knew this would happen, Mum! I wished and wished...' he said.

Sindi squinted across the glittering ocean. 'What am I

looking at? Oh my God! Is that a boat?'

Now that the arrival of a boat had been verified by eyes more reliable than my own, I moved unsteadily to the rail. 'Okay, girl,' I whispered to the *Innisfree*. 'Let's do this.'

The *Innisfree* nodded through the waters. I turned back to my crew. 'Nicholas, untie the shade. Let's flash it towards them. Try to get their attention.'

Sindi pulled herself up by the boom in wonder, her other hand upon her belly. The sun drenched her face in light. She was dazed in the way I had been dazed so long ago, to have everything end, and then begin again. Looking at her filled me with hope.

Nicholas and I stretched the shade between us.

'We're going to send an SOS,' I said. 'So let's flash it three times quickly…and now three times slowly, and now…three times quickly again.'

Who knew if it made sense as a communication? But everything, suddenly, was worth trying. We repeated the sequence, and Sindi pulled off her bandana and waved it. We tried to call, but our voices were shrivelled from lack of water and we gave up, coughing. Sindi slumped down, too weak to stand.

The sail grew larger still. Now I could make out what was beneath it: a slim racing vessel heeling into the waves. A flare snaked into the sky from its deck. We flapped the sheet in reply. Now I could see two figures at the prow. They were waving. We waved back. We were making a strange noise from our rigid mouths. I realised we were laughing.

It seemed to take just a moment and hours and hours for the boat to become a solid vessel breaking the emptiness of the ocean. Was it my imagination or did the *Innisfree* seem to raise her prow a little, as if she, too, was amazed to be no longer alone? The boat, a small, orange sailing boat, festooned with the insignia for the ARC race across the Atlantic, drew parallel about fifty feet away. Her name was *La Mariposa*.

Her sails furled and she drew to a rolling standstill, and the figures examined us with binoculars. The waters were too choppy for her to get any closer. I pointed to Sindi's belly, and eased Nicholas forward so they could see there was a child on board. The binoculars paused in scanning, focused on the three of us, and then were slowly lowered. The two figures, two women, identically sized, crossed their hands over their hearts. I felt embarrassed, suddenly at the squalid sight we must present. What kind of skipper was I, my boat a wreck, my crew emaciated? My hand went to my filthy, shrunken T-shirt. I pulled it uselessly down and pushed my hair away from my eyes. Of course, my infected eye must be horrific.

While one raised the binoculars again, the other tried to communicate something with her gestures. At first I could not see where she was pointing, and then I realised she was indicating the Innisfree's stern, and the life raft which was still tethered there. Of course. If we could get ourselves onto it, we could be pulled across to them.

'We need to get on the life raft, you two,' I said.

Wrapping Sindi in the reflective sheet, I led them both to the steps down to the transom, grabbing on my way the log book, the notebook and the memory stick. I tied them round my waist in a shirt. We were a babbling Lazarus family now, brought back to life by hope.

'Is this really happening Mum?' Nicholas asked. 'Are they

going to save us?'

'They are,' I said. 'You first, Sindi.'

She nodded and turned slowly to descend to the transom, trembling with the strain of managing her own bodyweight. Once on the platform, she crawled into the wobbling opening of the raft, disappearing from view. I signalled to our rescuers that one of our party was in the raft. They waved in acknowledgement and turned back to organising something on deck.

'Okay Nicky,' I said. 'Your turn.'

As he swung down, he looked round the *Innisfree*'s deck and said, 'Goodbye boat! I am never, ever going to step on you again.'

He scrambled into the raft. Now it was my turn. Only having one good eye made it hard to judge distances, so I had to concentrate minutely. As I wriggled between Sindi and Nicholas, I could see that one of the women was aiming a life ring at us. To it would be attached a line. If we could just grab the ring, they would pull us to *La Mariposa* and our rescue would be complete.

My hands were poised to untie us, and push us free. The life raft bobbed expectantly and Sindi and Nicholas fidgeted to get their balance. But a real sailor never leaves her boat, not unless it is actually sinking. The *Innisfree* was swaying gently before us, as if she was absorbing the sea's motion to make our exit easier.

A boat adrift is a hazard to other vessels. Nor could we tow her – she dwarfed the vessel we were being rescued by.

I could not leave Frank to the sharks and I could not abandon the *Innisfree*.

'Mum?' Nicholas asked, impatient to get going.

'Nicholas, I need you to go back on and open the seacock valves,' I said.

'What? I'm not going back on! What for?'

'We're sinking the boat.'

'Can't we just leave her?' Sindi piped up.

'I know that's your go-to for every difficult situation, Sindi, but no, we can't. She's a hazard. More than that, it's not right. Nicholas, it will just take a moment. Open the valves in the bilge and come straight back.'

He rolled his eyes and reluctantly dragged himself back onto the transom, the raft squeaking against his legs.

'I don't understand you, Miss,' said Sindi. 'You spend so much time on stuff that doesn't matter.'

'You don't need to understand,' I snapped. To Nicholas I called, 'In the bilge, remember. Both of them. Open them right up!'

Faintly, I heard him crawling in the belly of the *Innisfree*. She swayed just like she did on those long beautiful evenings in harbour, back when Frank and I were young, and we'd loved her without understanding any of the lessons she had to teach us. She had not minded. She had forgiven everything.

Nicholas reappeared down the steps and I held out my hand to haul him onto the raft. There was a worried frown on his thin face.

'I mean what if this whole thing doesn't work? What if they sail off without us? We have nowhere to go back to.'

'What?' said Sindi.

'Calm down everyone. It's all going to be fine,' I said.

Stay with me. Did I hear her whisper it? The air froze in

my lungs. How right it would be – the skipper with her log upon the deck, a friend to the boat to the end. To drift down to where the other skipper lay? It would be so quick, the *Innisfree* tipping slowly and then galloping, crests flying, a rush of white and stars and an endless night.

My child was safe. Sindi, with her child, was safe. I could make my own choices now.

'Do you want me to stay?' I whispered across the water. My hand hesitated at the entrance.

The *Innisfree* bucked a little, yanking the rope that held us to the transom and tipping us back in the life raft.

'Let's go, Miss,' Sindi whispered. 'Please, I'm scared.'

No answer is an answer. I sighed, and, balancing upon the slippery rubber, untied the raft from the transom. Water was echoing in the belly of my beautiful boat. Pulling out my notebook, I used it as a paddle to push us away and start moving towards *La Mariposa*. At that moment, there was a shout and then a splash, and the life ring landed in the water about twenty feet away.

'Come on Nicky,' I cried, and the two of us found depths of strength we didn't know we had to paddle towards the ring, me with the book and him with his hands.

The waves, though small, had the head-down determination of goats and we had to fight for every inch. But at last I reached out madly, desperately, and made contact with the ring. I pulled it to us and swiftly tied our line around it.

We slumped back in the raft as our rescuers winched us to their side. It took less than ten minutes before two concerned faces smiled down at us from the gunnels, one in sunglasses, one in a baseball cap.

'Hello, friends! Are you okay?' the one in sunglasses called.

'Yes! My name is Helen. We have one pregnant girl, and an eleven – no, twelve-year-old boy. I am so glad to see you!'

They set about expertly lowering a sling made of sailcloth, and carefully, Nicholas and I helped Sindi into it, strapping her carefully in. Sindi was barely conscious now, but her fingers instinctively gripped the rope, and her other hand rested on her belly. Her exhausted eyes fixed on me as she was winched up.

A few minutes later, the sling reappeared. When Nicholas was safely in, he pointed at the *Innisfree*. The water was creeping higher up the hull. We were so low in relation to her that she still seemed tall. It didn't seem that she was sinking, not really. I watched as Nicholas jerked up the side of *La Mariposa*. Hands extended to him and his thin little body was hauled onto the deck.

Making sure the log and memory stick were secured around my waist, I tossed the notebook into the water. It was the past. It flapped soggily towards the *Innisfree*. I wrestled myself into the sling, clipped myself in, and now I too swayed and bumped against the hull. At last, hands reached for me and gently lifted me over the rail. I wondered if something had happened to my eye as I seemed to be seeing two of the same smiling face.

'Hello, Helen,' said one. 'Anything broken?'

'No,' I said. 'Thank you. Thank you…'

'Have some water,' said the other. She eased me into a sitting position. A water bottle appeared at my lips. 'Not too much at once.'

'Sindi is the the girl. Nicholas is my son.'

'They are fine. Here, can you walk?'

With an arm each around my waist they lifted me. I had lost so much weight that my legs wheeled without touching the ground for a moment. 'Are you…twins?' I asked.

'Yes,' they chorused.

The one on my right, with the sunglasses, said, 'From Spain. And we were winning our class before you showed up.'

'Oh no, I'm sorry.'

The other sister said, 'We can do it next year. Don't worry. How long have you been drifting?'

'Nearly a month. There was a storm.'

Suddenly lights in my head were sparking. Words were hard to form. I was uncertain then if I was alive or not. I searched the deck for Sindi and Nicholas, for verification that this wasn't a dream, a moment of hypoxia.

Sindi was propped up on deck under a shade, sipping water. She lifted her head drowsily. 'The baby's moving,' she said.

'My name is Ava,' said the twin in sunglasses.

'And mine is Lisa,' said the other. Her baseball cap had a big butterfly on the front. 'I am very worried about your eye, Helen. Does it hurt?'

'I… I can't see through it…' I mumbled, and I felt upset about my eye, my poor eye. My hand went feebly to it.

I heard Ava on the radio putting out a mayday. Lisa appeared with a tube of cream which she smeared gently upon my eye. Its coolness was blissful. Then she set about unfurling the sails. 'We've abandoned the race,' she said. 'We're going to head towards wherever is the nearest ship.'

'Wait…please…' I said, grabbing her arm. 'I need to watch her go.'

'The *Innisfree*?' Lisa said. 'Oh yes, I get it. I don't know your story, but she's served you well I think. Time for her to rest.'

Lisa sat beside me; offered me the binoculars. I shook my head. There was no need for them.

'We're watching the *Innisfree* go down,' said Lisa to Ava as she emerged from below. Silence fell over us all.

The *Innisfree*'s prow rose a little as water gushed into the stern. Her name glittered in the sun. Bubbles were rushing from her portholes and I thought of the cabin where Frank and I had carved our initials. I thought of all our belongings lifting from their places in the water, like an explosion in slow motion. Then something happened in the balance of the water inside, sending her crashing forward, as if she were a whale breaching.

I was sorry I had not been more for her, I was sorry to have brought her back to life only to fail her, but, as her prow sank below the water and *La Mariposa* shook with the force of her dive, I felt her forgiveness. She had done her work, as I had done mine.

The waves boiled and foamed around her as she plunged into a world we would never know. The sun gilded her swirling wake, lighting her way as far it could, until at last the ocean closed over her and she was gone.

ACKNOWLEDGEMENTS

THANKS ARE DUE to many who have been part of *Ocean*'s odyssey into the world:

Simon Edge of Eye Books, my astute and brilliant editor who has brought such insight and polish to this novel. Publisher Dan Hiscocks who radiates the kind of quiet passion for books that keeps authors going. Ifan Bates for the stunning cover. Julia Eisele of German publisher Eisele and Simone Caltabellota of Atlantide in Italy who have championed this book so strongly. I am blessed in my publishing team, and so is *Ocean*.

Jane Harris, for your friendship, guidance and shining example of standing by your principles. Graham Linehan, the joy of your company will stay with me always and this book owes much to our friendship. Amanda Craig, Gerard Woodward, Clare Pollard and Jane Campbell for generously reading the book in manuscript and giving quotes.

My fellow boat-dwellers and friends at South Dock Marina, especially Miryam and Patricia Brizuela and Simon Mustafa for all you have made possible in my real life and in this book.

Dan and Emily Bower of *Skyelark II*, the elegant yacht that inspired the *Innisfree*. Sorry for being the worst crew member you ever had, but this book would not be what it is without you. A toast to the Biscay Bandits: Peter Holroyd, Tim Halford, James Byng, Rike Krumbeigel, Seb Oster and Søren Oster: the greatest band of rogues I ever had the honour to be part of.

My subscribers to *Monday Night Reads* where I first released *Ocean* as a podcast. Your responses and enthusiasm refined this book and kept me going. You are friends of *Ocean* indeed. (www.pollyclark.substack.com)

Creative Scotland who generously supported me at a critical juncture with an Open Fund Award, and the Society of Authors who awarded me emergency funds during the pandemic.

Julian Forrester, your love and encouragement continue to sustain me. Lesley Serpell for understanding beyond measure. Emma Pearse, advisor, Scrabble adversary extraordinaire and dear friend.

Jenny Brown, who has believed in this book since I set down the first words, and is so much a part of the finished creation. Thank you for never giving up, even during the most tempestuous of times.

Finally, the one who left before the end of the story, but who is woven into it nonetheless. Thank you, and we'll always have Andrew Edmunds.

Also from Lightning

The Darlings
Angela Jackson

**The daring new novel from the award-winning author
of *The Emergence of Judy Taylor***

At fifteen, Mark Darling is the golden boy, captain of the school football team, admired by all who know him. Then he kills his best friend in a freak accident.

He spends the next decade drifting between the therapy couch and dead-end pursuits until he marries Sadie. A mender by nature, she tries her best to fix him, and has enough energy to carry them both through the next few years.

One evening, Mark bumps into an old schoolfriend, Ruby. She saw the accident first-hand. He is pulled towards her by a force stronger than logic: the universal need to reconcile one's childhood wounds. This is his chance to, once again, feel the enveloping warmth of unconditional love.

But can he leave behind the woman who rescued him from the pit of despair, the wife he loves? His unborn child?

Exactly the kind of humane, life-affirming, humorous read I needed
Catherine Simpson

Angela is a true writer and an extremely powerful voice
Bidisha

Eccentric…compelling…subtle… A dark, humorous novel, led by domestic scenes and keen observations, in which a troubled man's crises have clear consequences
Foreword Reviews

If you have enjoyed *Ocean*, do please help us spread the word – by putting a review online; by posting something on social media; or in the old-fashioned way by simply telling your friends or family about it.

Book publishing is a very competitive business these days, in a saturated market, and small independent publishers such as ourselves are often crowded out by the big houses. Support from readers like you can make all the difference to a book's success.

Many thanks.
Dan Hiscocks
Publisher, Eye Books